The Pilgrim Soul

Anne Miller Downes

With new illustrations
by Gloria J. Laurie

The Durand Press
Etna, New Hampshire

The Pilgrim Soul
This edition published by:
   The Durand Press, 374 Dogford Road, Etna, New Hampshire 03750

Copyright 1952 by Anne Miller Downes
Illustrations Copyright 1997 by Gloria J. Laurie

Printing history:
J. B. Lippincott Company, first edition published 1952
   (Library of Congress Catalog Card number 52-9539)
The Peoples Book Club edition published 1952
   (Library of Congress Catalog Card number 52-9539)
The Durand Press edition published May 1997

Cover and text design by: Nomad Communications, Norwich, VT 05055
The text of this book is set in Adobe Garamond.
Printed in the United States of America by BookCrafters.

Cover photographs by The Durand Press.
Front cover: Forest Road near the Dolly Copp Campground.
Back cover: Entrance to the Dolly Copp Campground,
   The White Mountain National Forest.

"When You Are Old," by William Butler Yeats.
Reprinted with the permission of Simon & Shuster
from *The Collected Works of W. B. Yeats, Volume 1: The Poems*,
Revised and edited by Richard J. Finnernan (New York: Macmillan, 1989).

ISBN   0-9633560-9-7

Imprint is last number shown: 9 8 7 6 5 4 3 2 1

Author's Acknowledgment

The author wishes to thank Mrs. Mildred Peterson McKay, Librarian of the State of New Hampshire, for her invaluable help in authenticating the historical facts concerning the life of Hayes and Dolly Copp and giving the author access to letters of contemporary value and such old books as

    Willey's: *White Mountain History*
    King's: *The White Hills*
    Weygand's: *New Hampshire Neighbors*
    Crawford's: *History of the White Mountains*
    Dr. George N. Cross' most carefully documented:
      Dolly Copp and Pioneers of the Glen.

For Eleanor and Jonathan

When you are old and grey and full of sleep,
And nodding by the fire, take down this book,
And slowly read, and dream of the soft look
Your eyes had once, and of their shadows deep;

How many loved your moments of glad grace,
And loved your beauty with love false or true;
But one man loved the pilgrim soul in you,
And loved the sorrows of your changing face;

And bending down beside the glowing bars,
Murmur, a little sadly, how Love fled
And paced upon the mountains overhead
And hid his face amid a crowd of stars.

— William Butler Yeats

The Pilgrim Soul

CHAPTER I

ON A SPRING DAY in the year 1827 on the lower slopes of Mount Madison in New Hampshire, two native Americans viewed each other with curiosity and keen interest.

Above, the American eagle left his brood in the niche of a rocky cliff and soared out into the blue, circling for a moment as he looked down at the other American standing on a boulder below.

What did the eagle see? A strange little creature somewhat like the Redskins yet different, for though standing like them on only two legs, this body was concealed by leather and homespun, this face was bare and pale, the head covered with a curling shock of yellow hair, and a large bundle formed a hump on his back; while in his hands were carried an axe with shining blade and a long-barralled flintlock gun.

Soaring high in long straight lines across the sky, in search of food in lake or stream, the eagle could see valleys, hills, the silver ribbons of streams containing the fish he coveted, the dense forests, the far horizons.

The little two-legged creature on the rock, a half smile in his blue-gray eyes, watched the bird so majestic whether in flight or at rest. The man knew the mis-named bald head was beautiful with white feathers, knew those eagle eyes could discern objects with ease, one, two or three miles away, knew the spread of wing was often six or seven feet, knew his habits of building a nest either in the tops of ninety foot pines or on mountain crags, knew how he came with the same mate to repair that

nest each spring, knew how hard he worked to feed his gluttonous young. He also knew the falseness of the stories told about the eagle who, quite like man, was about equal parts good and bad and, on this spring day, the man felt a curious affinity to him and an envy of him. If he could only soar up there for a few minutes and view this valley and mountain side!

For he, Hayes Dadavah Copp, had come to conquer it! This wilderness. He possessed neither the size and brute strength of the huge bears roaming through this forest, nor the ferocity of the wolf, the craftiness of the fox nor the cunning of the numberless small creatures that filled trees, soil and stream.

The smile left his eyes as he thought of that which to his fellowman would surely disqualify him from participating in such an adventure. He knew he was possessed of no worldly goods—in fact he was penniless; and yet he was starting on a long journey for the purpose of buying this great tract of wilderness. He was going to clear that stretch of land lying in the valley and there, not far from the stream, would someday be his farm, his home.

What did he possess? In all the chronicles handed down through the years one comment was always made about his grandfathers, his father and even now of himself— "they were men of prodigious strength." He wanted to pit that prodigious strength against wild beast, almost impenetrable forest, hostile Indian, and even the violence of nature itself.

He was young, only twenty-four years of age and he might have chosen differently. He bore names already honored in the history of the new land. There was William Copp immortalized in the name, Copp's Hill, in Boston. That William Copp had come over from England on the "Blessing" in 1635, had cleared, in the north end of growing Boston town, a half-acre of land, the site of the Old North Church where signal lanterns were hung to inform Paul Revere of the march of the British troops to Lexington and Concord in 1775. There was the site of the Copp's Hill Burial Ground, one of the oldest in Boston.

His grandfather, Samuel Copp, had been again the *first* to clear a farm, back in 1767, in the west end of Lebanon, Maine, a man of consequence and Lebanon's first representative to the General Court, a selectman, an elder in the church, a lieutenant in the Army. His fine old houses might some day disappear but the name would be immortalized for the bridge over the Salmon Falls River would always be called, Copp's Bridge.

It was this Samuel Copp's wife, Hannah Hayes, for whom the boy had been named Hayes Copp. She was a woman honored and remembered in her community, giving to her sons the blood of the valiant Scot, Benjamin Hayes, one of the Covenanters, self-exiled after the Battle of Bothwell Bridge, coming from Scotland in 1680. A proud ancestry, for in the bodies filled with prodigious strength were hearts filled with grit and pluck and the courage to make a reality of the dreams of freedom that could never be wholly eradicated from the minds of men.

In neither face, body or habiliments did this blond boy look the part of a hero, for his shoulders were already a little bent with toil, the expression of his face was earnest, even unduly grave for his years and, in the many lonely hours when he had followed the plow or planted and reaped on his father's farm, his eyes had come to hold a steady inward look. Work—always work. When scarcely big enough to wear the coarse homespun pants that his mother spun and wove and sewed, he had had his many duties, chores graduating in quality and quantity as the small boy grew in strength and stature. In the widely scattered homes in the north country, families numbering ten, twelve or more were the rule rather than the exception and there was little patrimony to be divided; each son faced a choice of staying on his father's land as a meagerly paid hireling or striking out for himself, facing the wilderness as his forebears had done.

Choosing any of the ways of gaining a livelihood already presented to the sons of pioneers—years in schoolrooms, careers as politicians, the law, store-keeping, any life sitting behind a desk—made no appeal to Hayes. He belonged to the land and as much as any Redskin he breathed freely only in the out-of-doors.

So Hayes Copp stood on the boulder that spring morning neither feeling nor looking heroic. He was of only medium height, already worn, serious, but in his eyes there was a piercing directness, an unwavering manner of peering into the shadows of the great forest as he made his way unerringly over the snowy ground toward the stream, finding the blazed Indian trail that led south.

Once over his head, far up, the male eagle soared, giving its high clear call, *cac-cac-cac*. It was spring, the mating season.

Hayes Copp walked alone.

CHAPTER II

KNOWING THAT with the twistings and turnings, the climbs and descents, he must travel near one hundred miles if he were to reach Concord, the capital of his state, he pushed on steadily, sometimes walking fourteen to eighteen miles a day.

What did he eat? Where did he sleep? Neither question would ever be of less moment to an American traveler of future generations than it was to Hayes Copp on that long trek. Food? The streams were teeming with trout, the forests overrun with every form of game and he had only to choose, load his musket, kill his game, build his fire and cook his meal. Often under the far off twinkling of the stars or in the safety of deep crevasses of the rocks, or with friendly Indians, sometimes under the sheltering roof of a white man's home, he took his needed rest. He hacked his way through tangling underbrush, through hollows where the deep winter snow had not yet been melted, at first following old Indian trails, then further south finding rough roads but, by the end of the day, given only a chance to lie down, he slept soundly.

With ease he made his way up the Peabody River, leaving behind the great mountain peak, Madison, whose feet rested on the low slopes bordering the land he wished to buy.

He passed through a wider plane, south of the trackless solitude of wilderness, closely following the stream while he searched the sky line for his first sight of the mighty peak, Washington, or as the Indians named it, "Apriochooke"— "Mountain of the snowy forehead and Home of the Great Spirit." Farther north he knew the Indians called it "Waumbick"—again meaning "Snowy Forehead" or "White Hills," the last name generally adopted by the usurping white man.

Hayes had heard tales of the fame of this mountain having reached into distant places; tales of foolhardy attempts to climb often ending in the tragedy of frozen limbs and broken necks; recently he had heard of more and more travelers making the ascent on horses trained to keep their feet from slipping between the logs laid crosswise on rough roads, and now as he emerged from the forest into the plain he saw a gathering that caused him to slow his steps.

Before the little roadhouse some fifteen or twenty Indians were taking a rest on a journey north in their canoes. There were men lying on the ground smoking, squaws moving about with their babies slung in baskets over their backs, others offering brooms and other articles for sale, all sharply contrasted with a group of travelers assembled for the purpose of ascending the mountain.

Hayes circled around behind the group wondering, as did many another pioneer, at the perplexing thoughts that must dwell in those Indian minds. Here they lay now humbled and growing more and more dependent on the whites, they, the original owners of this rich and lovely valley. Always they had worshipped this mountain as the abode of the Great Spirit and no Indian had ever climbed to its peak, for long ago out of the cloud that rested on its top, had come a voice saying, "Here, the Great Spirit will dwell and watch over his children. He covers steps above the green leaves with the darkness of the fire tempest. *No footsteps are ever seen returning from his Home in the Clouds.*"

Lazily lying on the ground, the glittering eyes of the Indians watched the profaning white man prepare to ascend into this sacred place. Again and again the footsteps of these bold, adventurous, impious people had returned from the clouds lying on the "White Forehead" to vie with each other in describing views and panoramas but with no words concerning the Great Spirit.

As Hayes turned from the Indians he found a guide standing near, a tough weathered fellow who boasted that his horses had made that ascent sixty-seven times. Hayes looked toward the travelers now getting ready to mount. What horses! They were shabby looking animals and the travelers cut sorry enough figures seated on steeds whose long tails, long manes, uncurried and shaggy coats matched the creaky saddles and bridle-reins which more often than not were composed of old straps fastened together by knots.

Now all heads were turned as two young travelers rode out from the stables to join the climbers. They, young, gay, richly dressed honeymooners, were mounted on their own handsome horses. The guide murmured, "Down easterners. G'wan lead—show us how! That hoss haint been up sixty-seven times." He spoke laconically, "W'ant be leading long. Fine clothes w'ant look so pretty when he gets up thar crawling on all fours."

The guide turned away to swing up into his own creaky saddle and Hayes watched until the little cavalcade started, hoping that the footsteps of the gay young couple would return from the home of the "Great Spirit."

It was early in the day and he soon reached the Ellis River, finding the trail widening into a rough road and less frequently did he meet Indians and far more frequently did he encounter white men.

He was approaching a small fairly new settlement called Jackson. Here was familiar ground for the place was first settled by one Benjamin Copp and a young, vigorous wife. It was only some sixty odd years ago that Governor Wentworth had granted 23,000 acres to the settlers here in the east. With packs on their backs Benjamin Copp and his wife had come up from the south as the hostile Indians moved or were driven further north into their own country.

Here were enacted some bloody scenes. One famous redskin was caught after murdering two white men. The settlers tied him with ropes to a wild stallion who dashed through the forest leaving blood on the barks of the trees as the Indian was reduced to pulp.

To Hayes as he thought of the facts he knew concerning these small settlements, stories were always those of individual encounters. Up through these valleys came no great migrations. No Copps came in covered wagons. They were merely hardy individuals considered rich if they owned one horse or a cow or pig. They were merely daring men with their wives, children; with household goods, more often than not wholly on their backs, braving the wilderness with faith in God and in their own strength.

Because of his own purpose of going into an almost impenetrable wilderness and building a home, what he knew might have brought indecision or timidity into the heart of a weaker man; instead, as he thought of Benjamin Copp Hayes only quickened his long strides over the rough path.

Benjamin Copp had existed for twelve years alone with his family before one other neighbor had come to settle here. In the time left from fighting off wild animals, hostile Indians and the fury of the elements, he scratched out a living from some cleared soil. There was always trout—sometimes dried, sometimes eaten fresh, other food, too often eaten entirely without salt. This Benjamin Copp thought little of carrying for ten miles a bushel of corn in a bag slung over his shoulder, never lowering the burden until he dumped it on the mill floor, having left his wife and children barred and locked in their cabin until his return. Benjamin Copp's footsteps did not lag in that journey.

As the sun was still high in the heaven Hayes Copp planned to pass through the town, follow the valley to the southern point and get on his way to Conway before he slept again.

Long before he came abreast of it, he realized that something unusual was going on in the vicinity of the long, low-roofed log building that was both general store and inn. He had no money to spend at such places and usually avoided them, wanting merely to pass; but here his road was blocked and, with the countryman's sharp curiosity, he must see what was going on to draw together what to him appeared like more people than lived in the whole countryside.

As he circled around the fringe of the onlookers who had formed themselves into a semi-circle, there was a sudden blast of horns, then as they ceased their raucous din, a villainous looking old man scratched out a jig on a fiddle. As Hayes looked over the shoulders he saw the reason for the gathering. In the center of a cleared space were peddlers with two pack horses loaded high.

All knew that most of the settlers who came to these woods arrived fairly well provided with plows, tools, pots and kettles, traps for hunting and thus needed nothing much from the outside world until they could afford to buy cattle. Their women folks were warned against these lying, cheating, good-for-nothing traders who bartered baubles and worthless stuff for good board and lodging, or for knitted goods, farm produce, rags, or, if they chanced on the most gullible, brass and copper.

Many years later Hayes was to hear tales of one Jim Fisk, a future partner of Jay Gould. He was to hear of his coming up the Connecticut, stopping at each town where he sent ahead a man to pick the prettiest lady in the village and present her with a paisley shawl. After the lady had flaunted it in the faces of all the other women until they were sick with envy, Jim Fisk drove in with a load and in spite of infuriated husbands, sold paisley shawls until his pack was empty. Hayes often wondered why folks called it an original trick for here, on this spring morning, before his eyes was enacted a play with much the same plot.

Only a few feet from him a crafty looking youngish man swung from his back a tin trunk. The man with the horn gave a few blasts, then in a wheedling voice asked that the prettiest girl of the valley step forward.

At once there was such a laughing, twittering, shoving and giggling among the women as brought guffaws from even the most suspicious of the men. The fellow was unloading his wares—some woven baskets, a brass lamp, Bibles, small glass and tin ware, needles, scissors, perfume and then women in their calico dresses and heavy shoes and plain bonnets craned their necks to see him open a box of jewelry. Experience had taught them that the peddlers' clocks and watches never kept time, that the gold was a cheap wash, that the stones were colored glass but now they sighed as they looked for surely the trinkets were pretty.

He was calling, "Buttons—buttons" as he opened another box. There were some useful buttons, then from out of a little bag he drew a string and held it dangling. Buttons the size of half a dollar, designed with spidery openwork, each glittering with tiny red stones which he called rubies. Carefully he detached one and held it up as a gift for the prettiest female. Of course when she owned one button she would buy the string to match it; then her envious friends would hasten to outdo her in purchasing gaudier ones.

Hayes was not now looking at the peddler's wares for his attention had been drawn to a group of five girls near him. Laughingly they twined their arms about each other as they watched the unloading. In their center was one girl from whom he hardly removed his gaze. Never had he seen such eyes. They were the deep blue of the sky—the intense blue he had so often seen reflected in a lake on a perfect summer day. It was not only their color but their flashing brightness that fairly charmed him.

She was smaller than her companions-dainty for a country girl, her hair as yellow as his own, her lips red, and as she watched the peddler she chatted and laughed, her slender body swaying this way and that in her excitement.

Sometimes, leaning against her companions, she swung a tiny foot in and out like a pendulum. He noticed the foot, saw the fine high-topped shoe. Perhaps she wanted folks to notice because she sometimes made a little-tapping sound before swinging out the foot. Vain of the little feet, was she?

He had been so engrossed watching the swaying body, the swinging foot and the flashing eyes that he had missed some of the peddler's talk, but now he saw him approach the group and with an obsequious bow and smirk present the "ruby" button to the girl with the sparkling eyes.

She drew back and Hayes hoped she would not take the button but he would not have known why he did not want her to touch it. He was unconscious of his wide grin as he watched her shake her head. Then with a proud toss of the blond hair she freed one hand and raising it to her neck, pointedly began fingering a string of beautiful gold beads which had been hidden by the collar of her calico dress.

The peddler turned and found another group as the men near the horses began unloading spinning wheels, small organs, chairs, woven baskets of various sizes, brooms, pewter ware and even beds.

In spite of admonitions the women crowded about them examining their wares. The men stood back for they knew the character and habits of these men too well; knew that many of them were the sons of the old fur-traders, knew their fear of being caught in the forest where they were terrified of Indians. Often they begged lodgings at farm houses, entertaining the farmer, and his family and friends with recitations of old ballads, or singing to the accompaniment of melodeons or Jew's harps or violin.

There were some more trusted who brought glassware from Sandwich, splendid specimens of wroughtiron, beautiful hand made chairs, but the majority were hard drinking, swindling traders and the cautious husbands warned against the lot. So now the men stood by ready to intervene if their wives appeared to be willing victims of some chicanery.

Hayes lingered until the sun was low in the west and the people were drifting away and the peddlers were repacking. Down at one end of a plank bench he sat watching the dispersing crowd. There were folks—some whom he knew and some who knew him—going into the store where, along with boxes of produce, barrels of flour and sugar, shelves holding tea, spices and medicines, a little of this and a little of that, over in a corner was the postoffice.

Now with frontier friendliness men approached him, questions were asked and cautiously answered and he found himself in a group still discussing the peddlers.

The girl was near him, her flashing eyes looking into his. He could not know how conscious she had been of his ardent gaze throughout the afternoon. He found himself talking to her or at least listening as she talked to him but what was said or how he managed to answer he never would remember. After all he had only to listen and smile for she was glibness itself; the words spilling out of her pretty mouth with a fluency he had never before encountered.

They stood looking into each other's eyes with awareness and when she went away she turned and flashed back a smile that left him dumb, awkward, his mouth slightly open, an expression of childlike wonder in his eyes, a tightness in his throat and something in his heart that no length of years would ever remove.

In the large hall, logs were burning in the stone fireplace for the night had turned chilly; travelers were regaling themselves with dinner washed down with plenty of rum but Hayes went off into the shadows, circled about the house where he found a shelter in a shed near the stables. He wrapped his blanket about him and laid down to sleep. He had even learned her name. A name so pretty, it was fairly singing in his heart— Dolly Emery.

CHAPTER III

BEFORE THE FIRST COCK opened a beady eye to the faint light coming from the eastern sky, Hayes rose, made a hasty toilet at the stableyard pump, passed the still-darkened windows in the village houses and struck out rapidly into open country, definite purpose adding speed to his long stride.

John Emery. That was the name he had been groping for. The memory was singularly clear. Not long ago one John Emery had stopped overnight at his father's farm and, gathered around the kitchen fireplace, the men and women had retold the stirring events in England and Scotland which had led to their forebears emigrating to the new land. To a frontiersman the leaving the old country, arriving in the new land, settling and building towns was not history; it was simple reality. A boy could feel and remember the comradeship engendered when the two men found that the first William Copp came over on the "Blessing" in 1635 while Anthony Emery came on the ship "James" in the same year.

Anthony Emery had been a man of great physical strength and boundless energy, also—something not too common—a capable businessman who had amassed wealth. He had built and maintained a home in Maine, reared a family and had become a man of considerable importance in his community. Then had come a serious dispute in his Town and he had openly, brazenly questioned the authority of the court. He had asked, "What is a court?" maintaining it was only a group of men like the citizens who had placed them in authority and liable to errors in judgment as was any man. He went further and maintained the citizens had a right to debate and question any acts performed by their government. He was promptly brought before the "Town," reprimanded and fined five pounds for his "mutinous courage."

And that was not the end. Only four years later he was again fined for entertaining Quakers in his home. Angrily he told them the Lord would put human kindness, charity toward the hunted and oppressed above the petty restrictions of secular church rules. Then the church joined the Town in ostracizing him and, furious, he sold all his land and houses and journeyed into the deep wilderness of New Hampshire to gain greater freedom. Before leaving he made a speech long remembered and often repeated. The sum of it, as Hayes remembered, was that he was "Jealous of his rights and would gladly suffer for his conscience' sake."

Hayes saw no absurdity in attributing to the girl with the flashing blue eyes the attributes that had distinguished old Anthony Emery. That she was one of his many descendants he had no doubt and that she would suffer for her conscience' sake; that she would be independent; even more that she would be capable and energetic he did not question. Dolly Emery. From the sun rising higher in the east, sending its slanting rays across wide meadows, from the sound of bird song in the trees, from the tumbling water in every little brook there was a music he had never heard before: or was it only something in himself that sang over and over the pretty name—Dolly Emery.

Never would it occur to him to deviate from his route and find the farm of John Emery where he would have received a warm welcome. He was no visitor, was possessed of no small talk and in his own humble opinion there was nothing about either his past, his present errand or in himself that would be of the slightest interest to anyone. He left the country where both the Copp and Emery families had been first settlers and with feet as directly pointed as his eyes went on toward the south.

Nevertheless as he traveled, something of his awkwardness and shyness left him for, day by day, he met more people who, often engulfed in loneliness, were eager to entertain a traveler whether friend or stranger, glad to pour out their own news or knowledge, eager to hear anecdotes or enter into discussion.

As he saw more and more of both farms and towns he began to look with new eyes at the women he met. Naturally he was expected to marry, for no man in a pioneer country contemplated a home without wife and family, the latter always visualized as consisting of many sons and some daughters, both of inestimable value.

Now, as he journeyed through the country he looked sharply at these women, the mothers of stalwart sons. How much of a kind they were! Women with broad backs, straight backs, ample waists, some handsome, some homely but nevertheless capable, keen, knowing how to spin, weave, sew, cook, harvest and preserve fruits and vegetables, tend the sick, attend Town meetings, arguing and understanding issues as clearly as their men, attend church, definitely sure of their beliefs. That was what a man needed—women with great broad backs, plain in calico or perhaps "stuff" for meeting, feet used to heavy shoes that were guaranteed to wear. Yes, after that brief stop in Jackson he was beginning to look at women with new eyes.

On one late afternoon he came into a clearing where beyond the patches of moist ground newly turned by the crude plows, he saw a small weather-beaten log house and on the "rock" that formed the doorstep a curious creature sitting in the sun puffing on a clay pipe.

As he approached the little woman who looked like a tiny dried-up mummy, she did not move a muscle. Sparse white hair was drawn into a knot at the neck, tied with a piece of tape, the end hanging down her back. The nose and chin nearly met over a sunken mouth, the weathered and wrinkled cheeks were sunk into deep hollows beneath high bones but the eyes were bright and the voice amazingly strong as she greeted him.

"Whare you from?"

He explained, mentioning the part of the country from which he had come and she moved over quite courteously making room for him on the "rock."

For some minutes they sat in silence, he feeling her eyes studying him.

At last she spoke. "I've heered it's daunting terrible up thar, full o' rocky hills and clothed with infinite thick woods."

Hayes laughed and told her it "wan't so skeery." He found few words to describe it to her but soon they were meeting on a common ground and she evidently hugely enjoyed telling him all about herself. At last she stopped to indulge in a cackling laugh.

"You're fair confounded?"

He was confounded for she proved to be eighty-eight years old, the mother of ten children, forty-eight grandchildren and eighty-two great grandchildren. More than that—as surely as she had created such a considerable population for the country just so her husband had created the Town nearby; started it, taught it, nurtured it, guided it and before Hayes left he was sure that same parson had blessed it and damned it.

He sat thinking of all those children, pondering, then asked why with so many children was she here?

Now it was she who looked confounded. "Where would I be?"

Soon the answer became clear. She was where she belonged, living with a son, Tom, the only one of the ten who was a bit "tetched"—not harmful, took a good living out of the piece of earth and was "fended" against the Town. Hayes understood and together they awaited Tom who had gone up "yonder wood for game."

When she invited him into the two-room cabin she proudly showed him the entry in her Bible—born in 1738, married in 1754. The Revolution was a distant memory of her early pioneer life though she spoke of two brothers killed while "battling under Stark." More poignant and fresh in her mind was the death of her husband. He had been the first minister "in these parts" but mostly without a church building, preaching in the Town meeting house, quarreling for twenty years with the Baptists on the hill, fighting for his salary which was never "rightly paid" but was eked out in food and clothes. She and her girls were allowed two dresses each— a good calico for Sunday and a plain calico for every day.

When Tom returned and the simple meal was cooked they sat at the plank table eating. The grizzly Tom, a man nearly sixty years of age, stared at his mother with a vacant smile while she told how her husband opened the first school right in this cabin, then fought the Town until they furnished a "place"; how he organized the Town Meeting, chastised the sinners, disciplined the frivolous, baptized, buried the dead, prayed and—swore at times. She laughed at the memory. He was "powerful with words," a fighter but he always "fought for the Lord."

Their guest must rest overnight then, in the morning, he must see that church edifice in their Town—all painted now and with a bell-tower and a bell which rang out calling to every meeting whether for worship, or for district, state or nation.

They had hardly finished their meal when the "tetched" Tom, removing only his shoes, climbed up into a bunk under the rafters. Soon Hayes wrapped his blanket around him and stretched out on the floor in front of the dying embers but when or where the old lady slept or if she ever laid down her pipe or ever left her chair he was never to know, for when at the break of day he opened his eyes, she was stirring the fire, preparing the gruel for their breakfast.

As she stood over the pot, Hayes turned his head, finding his eyes close to her feet. One was thrust forward, protruding from beneath the rusty black of her skirt, a small foot, seeming to him more suitable for a doll than for a human being. For a moment he lay smiling into the kindling logs. Where were the wide back, the broad hips, the heavy feet in manlike shoes?

He lay thinking of her words, "whare would I be?" Not with one of her sons and daughters, cozy in the corner of a warmed room of the farmhouse, her chair near the fireplace but here in the weather-beaten cabin, still the mother, taking care of the only one of her ten children who was "tetched," shielding him from the taunts and ridicule of the Town.

He accepted the hot gruel, thanked her and before the sun was visible about the eastern mountains was on his way.

He turned to look back at the edge of the clearing and saw her standing in the doorway gazing after him, her tiny shrunken figure insignificant and grotesque but with the memories spanning most of a century, her sharp humor, her hospitality she was to remain mighty in his heart and he was never to forget her.

CHAPTER IV

ON THE ROADS leading out from the little city of Concord, farmers were going about their morning chores; in the houses lining the few streets women were preparing breakfasts but Hayes Copp stood empty and hungry in front of a large barn looking across the deep ruts of a muddy road at a building whose majesty and beauty seemed to him to fulfill the wildest dreams of the pioneers of New Hampshire.

For two days he had wandered into every corner of the city gleaning all kinds of information, using his eyes and ears to good purpose. Sitting beside one loquacious old fellow on the Post Office steps he had been given a shrewd countryman's version of the story of this building.

The old man chuckled, "Looked for awhile—between 1782 and 1808—as though our legislature would have to be 'put on wheels'. By gorry, they met in eight different cities, Portsmouth, Exeter, Dover, Charleston, Amherst, Hanover, Hopkinton and Concord. Not 'till about twenty years ago did they come home here to stay."

Now as Hayes stood in the early morning light he felt a personal pride in the fact that the Capitol Building was completed only eight years ago. Somehow it seemed closely contemporary with himself. He did not have to be told that it was built of New Hampshire granite but he had learned that the stone had been hewn at the State prison. He had also learned that the cost had been $82,000 and—more astonishing—they had spent $875 for furniture alone. To him the great rooms and corridors heated by wood stoves seemed to promise complete comfort. That men and women visiting from all parts of the country agreed that the Senate chamber was the most beautiful one in the nation did not surprise or particularly impress him but this morning as he stood gazing at that great dome there was a strange mixture of awe and practical curiosity in his mind. That anything so beautiful could be conceived and executed by the mind and hands of men! They had told him the dome had been modeled from one on a building in Paris and the eagle raised into its position in 1818 while the brass bands played, thirteen toasts were drunk and speeches were made.

That eagle with its wings partially expanded was six and one half feet in height standing on an inverted acorn rising nine feet. He had learned the figures and his eyes measured it all in feet and inches but there was no known measurement in existence of that pride that filled his chest and tightened his throat as he stared at the eagle now the emblem of his country. The sun's rays caught the gold of the ball at the acorn's top and he could hardly tear his eyes away to turn to a man who was coming from the barn door, greeting him, identifying himself as the head stableman and preening himself more than a little as the custodian not only of the legislators' horses but of inside information on any and all matters concerning the government.

Hayes was at a great disadvantage for never before had he found himself so far out of his own element. He was empty and hungry for he had scarcely eaten in two days. There was no game in city streets, no fish in the puddles of the roads and no money in his pockets for use in grocery stores. It was for only a second that he hesitated when the stableman started to move away remarking his breakfast was waiting. Then he turned back, "You've ete?"

A moment of struggle, then gnawing hunger conquered and he accepted the cordial invitation and soon was inside one of the small white frame houses.

Here in the little city as it was in country districts, the kitchen was the heart of the house and when Hayes was seated at the long board amidst many people—grandfather, grandmother, tall sons, helpful daughters and little ones whose chubby hands were steering milk into hungry mouths—his own appetite went unnoticed and he ate heartily.

Not since his descent of the mountain far up north had he spoken to any person of his ambition or hinted at his purpose. To friendly questioning, his answers were smiling but evasive but as he returned to the barn with the stableman, whose loquacity was as amazing as his fund of information, Hayes, devoutly in his heart thanking the Providence that had led him, gleaned the exact information he needed and before the sun had reached the high point that would tell him it was noon, he stood alone on one side of an oaken desk stating his purpose to three men who watched him closely. He was slow of speech, rough, uncouth, his brows knitted in an anxious frown, but his eyes were intense and his mouth was set in determined lines.

Out on the desk they spread a crude map. Fingers traced the turnpikes, the rough forest roads north and farther north and then the fingers stopped at a vast unchartered area.

"You came from here?"

He corrected the location, accurately indicating the exact spot.

They smiled and asked more questions. The Indians still infested that country? There were no inhabitants? Not one settlement? Only Indian trails? Why did he want so much land? How did he plan to clear it? *Alone? With his two hands?*

His age? His past occupation? And all the time they were measuring, not only the land but the man. Already those legislators in some of their flowery oratorical speeches were proclaiming that Maine produced potatoes, Virginia produced tobacco, on through the list of states always ending, "But New Hampshire produces men."

Here before them was another of those Copps and they gave consideration to his request and roughly drew a line about the section of wilderness. Then came the crucial moment and they could not have dreamed of the hard beating of the young man's heart, the tensing of the muscles of back and shoulders and jaw for when they, after due discussion, stated the price he answered quietly.

"It is a fair price."

"You have the money with you?"

"I will pay it in wheat, barley and oats."

There was not a copper in his pockets but he had answered with pride.

"When?"

"When I harvest them."

They looked at each other. They looked at him and with no hesitation promised him the deed.

❧

The sun was slowly starting its downward dip toward the western horizon when Hayes stood for another quarter hour gazing with quiet, smiling eyes at the great dome of that granite capitol, taking his last look at the eagle with its half-spread wings. As direct as its flight across the blue skies of his mountain wilderness, he saw his line back from here to his land. He turned and walked rapidly through the narrow streets out past the farms and struck into the forest for home.

CHAPTER V

ON ONE EARLY summer day the wild pigeons roosting in the trees of the Glen at the foot of Mount Madison were frightened by strange sounds which caused a flurry of flapping wings and a scurrying in every direction. An axe had been laid to that hitherto unmolested home with which Nature had provided them. Blow after blow echoed through the deep forest alarming the deer drinking at the river's edge, alerting the grouse who stopped drumming on fallen logs, causing the brown bear to stand immobile listening. Soon, following the sound of the axe, there was a crash and one tree lay prostrate on the ground. Hour after hour the axe was swung and the sunlight filtering down into the opening, shone on the polished blade as Hayes Copp struck unerringly.

When the sun had reached its meridian, the axe was hitting lightly but sharply, stripping off the branches, leaving the poles ready for building a small lean-to, something for immediate shelter while he worked on his log cabin. With an energy that seemed inexhaustible he labored that day and the next, placing the uprights, laying the cross-logs, then covering all with a blanket of hemlock branches.

He had carefully located this, his first shelter, before large flat stones on which he could cook his food. Along one side of the interior he constructed a large bin and in it he placed his precious seeds and the few necessary tools he had purchased in Jackson on his way back—again on mere promises of future payment. Also in that bin he placed his Bible, the book that constituted his entire library.

A home? Nothing to brag about? When the first pale light began to spread over the eastern sky, Hayes would open his eyes and gaze at the roof and three sides of his lean-to and no Roman conqueror after adding to his kingdom the wealth of vast foreign conquests, no eastern Mogul contemplating his immense store of gold and jewels, ever felt richer.

On the morning after the government men had finished surveying and marking his purchase, he shouldered his musket and went down to the river's edge where was his inexhaustible supply of water, clear, pure as Nature provided before the polluting habits of man should bring contamination.

Making his way through the dense forest, he found one by one the marks on the great trees that indicated the extent of his land. Following through the plain then leaving the river bank, he approached the mountain and there on its lower slopes, not far from the boulder on which he had stood many weeks before, he examined the last mark. It was cut deep into a giant pine and he knew that, barring hurricane or lightning, that tree would stand throughout the years of his life.

From this vantage point he assured himself that he had chosen the site of his home with vision for the land formed a beautiful intervale with here and there small areas of grass. Under all he knew how rich and black was the soil for as yet the greed of man had not diminished the humus stored by Nature through countless centuries of falling leaf. He knew that deep snow would cover the surface of the Glen from November until May but he thought of it as beneficent, protecting the ground against freezing and keeping it saturated with moisture.

He saw in his vision the good oats, potatoes, wheat, rye, peas, perhaps, if the summer were dry and hot enough, some corn besides the usual turnips, pumpkins and squash. Also he saw—although it seemed a far distant dream, cattle grazing and a horse in the stable.

His land. As he rapidly descended the slope a great pride filled his heart—and something, else. He never would have dreamed of either thinking or speaking of his love for the land. Translating feeling into words was foreign to his nature but the swiftness of his movements, the light in his eyes, the sureness of his aim as he killed his game, the strength of his stroke as he swung his axe, all expressed that something that was part of every heartbeat of Hayes Copp.

As day followed day, the sound of his axe reverberated through the forest and he pondered the miracle of his possession for although he was the first occupant of this virgin forest, he had not been the first owner.

Long ago, in the days of the French and Indian wars, King George the Third, who owned "everything," rewarded one Thomas Martin for "services to the Crown" with a great tract of unexplored wilderness which was known as Martin's Location and so it was still called. However, no Martin and few white men had had the temerity to follow the Indian trails that led into the almost impenetrable forest.

Now alone, with two bare hands, his axe and a few tools, Hayes worked from sun-up to sun-down, felling trees, digging out roots, burning worthless stumps and branches, piling up logs for winter fuel. In small patches he planted a few vegetables, tried for a little wheat. Before the leaves began to fall, among the sheltering trees stood his log cabin. Out of the stone chimney smoke rose in spiraling clouds and, as the days and nights grew colder when the little animals sought their burrows and tunnels, the larger animals crouched in their dens, the two legged creature came to his home, barred the door, cooked his meal and slept.

He journeyed into Jackson and returned with a bag slung over his shoulder containing some salt, some meal, pork, and seeds for the next summer's early planting.

The days grew shorter but still the steady strokes of the axe could be heard and one by one the trees came down, yard by yard the clearing grew.

When the leaves were dry and thick on the ground, one night he heard a slight crackling sound and he knew some

redskin was prowling about his cabin. As he swung his axe during the following day, he watched. Again and again something like only a darker shadow moved stealthily from tree to tree in the deep dark pockets of the forest.

In no way did he change his habits but he was wary; then one day when he brought back some game to cook for his noon meal, a pathetic looking figure emerged from behind a tree and timidly approached his door.

There was little extra flesh on the frame of Hayes Copp, for the arduous labor, the long walks, the sparse food, the lack of fats had left him gaunt. He knew well the story of some of the Emery family who had first come into the wilderness farther south. The men had worn stiff belts and as the food grew scarcer they tightened those belts, watching with foreboding when the last holes would be reached—the holes that spelled total starvation. With leather thongs Hayes had been tightening his own belt but he had never felt the slightest diminishing of his prodigious strength.

Looking at the Indian standing before him he saw a creature as near starvation as a human being might come and still walk and talk. He motioned to the Indian to sit on one of the tree stumps which he used in lieu of chairs, while he cooked not only game but, going into his closet, brought out some meal and pork and a taste of precious salt. Then with meager words and strange but illuminating sign language they talked.

Had the white man coming to this continent not believed—and nothing ever shook this faith—that God had ordained the extinction of the Redskin, that God had ordained that white civilization should spread over this rich and beautiful land—he, the white man—sometimes illiterate but often highly cultured—would have recognized that few tragedies portrayed in his classic literature depicted greater suffering or deeper humiliation than that endured by both the conquering whites and the vanishing native Redskin. Perhaps nowhere in the length and breadth of the continent was there greater cruelty than in this land lying under the shadow of the White Forehead.

These were not undersized, indolent Indians of the enervating southern climes, these were strong men inured to the rigors of as bleak and trying a climate and terrain as any on the continent.

The Indians inhabiting these White Hills were the Sokokies or Pequawkets and the Anasagunticooks, all tribes of the Abehakis. In favorable spots in the rich valleys they built their villages and encampments and in some places strong log forts. They were tall men of enormous strength and equally enormous hatred of the white intruder. There were a few of the great chiefs whose physical strength, courage, and even cunning was so great as to claim the admiration as well as the most bitter hatred, of the settlers. Their curious legends were learned and wondered at. Their story of the Great Flood was not unlike that of Noah. They believed that as the waters increased there was left only the peak of Mount Washington and on that the Great Spirit took up his abode, sending his children down into the fertile valleys as the water subsided, admonishing them, as every Indian admonished his children, never to ascend into that holy place. Always the mountain tops were sacred places.

Every white child heard of Squando, who mixed Christianity with his own religion into an unholy brew that caused him neither to drink nor smoke but murder white men to please the Great Spirit.

There was Assacumbuit of the Sokokies, the greatest of them all, who still awaits an epic poet to depict his fabulous story. His brutal courage and unparalleled ferocity inspired fear and hatred even in his own Indian followers.

This Assacumbuit carried a huge club with notches indicating the number of white men he had killed and won such great renown with the French as their ally that Vaudruil sent him to France. At Versailles, Louis XIV presented him with a gold sword as the Chief told the monarch that the hand receiving the sword had murdered one hundred and forty of his Majesty's white enemies.

Both red man and white feared and hated him and eventually he fled to Canada.

Not least among the great names was Chocorua. One day he was pursued by a white man up and farther up the great mountain until he stood on the summit. Near him the rocks formed an almost perpendicular drop of over one hundred feet.

The white man aimed. Chocorua pled for his life, reminding the hunter of all his friendship for the white settlers and the need his harmless, scattered people had for his leadership but the hunter was thinking only of the gold that would be his if he brought back the scalp of Chocorua. As he raised his musket to fire, the great Chief lifted his arms to heaven, called on the Great Spirit to curse these people and leaped over the precipice. White men named the great mountain peak Chocorua, thus honoring the courage they would have annihilated.

As familiar as the story of Valley Forge to a son of the Revolution were the histories of massacres, ambushes, personal tragedies and breath-taking bravery told to Hayes and his brothers by father, uncles and friends. They knew that many of the New Hampshire Indians lived in strongly fortified villages, built for themselves good houses that were well furnished, that their churches were richly adorned with plate. Until the white man came the only foe they feared was the mighty Iroquois living far to the west over the mountains.

It was only sixty odd years ago that a great war-dance was held in one such village. As brave young warriors and fair Indian maidens danced, they swung in the air twenty scalps taken from pale faces. Three white captives listened to their wild incantations and no Indian guessed that one of them was the great Robert Rogers and that his intrepid Rangers would soon attack and wipe out their entire village, taking as plunder from their church two hundred guineas, a silver image weighing eight pounds and a quantity of rich wampum.

Up and down the valleys and hills the remnants pursued each other until neither Indian nor white remained. Many of the relics of these Rangers were still being found—the remains of military dress, rusty buttons, gun-barrels with rotten stock, copper kettles and hunting knives.

Often Hayes pondered these histories, living alone in his wilderness. "An eye for an eye, a tooth for a tooth." Could it have been otherwise?

There were chiefs who lived on after their early exploits, some in poverty, some blind, at last making peace; but none, either cruel or kind, escaped an enemy more heartless and devastating than anything the white man could invent—the frightful pestilence that wiped out villages, encampments and forest dwellers until only a sad weakened remnant of the great Sokokies remained. Those that could travel at all gathered together their squaws and children and, mile by mile, many dying by the way side, made their weary way to Canada.

Before Hayes Copp on that late fall afternoon sat one of the pitiful remnants of the once great Sokokies. The dark skin of his face was stretched over sharp bony structure, the small eyes were devoid of fire, the braided black hair was matted, the clothes ragged and the hand he stretched out for food was a mere trembling claw.

Slowly, through meager words and sign language, Hayes learned his story.

The pestilence had attacked his little settlement and one by one men, women and children had died while the few survivors had fled in terror. He had been left for dead but miraculously he had lived. He had been one of the strongest. Weak and emaciated he had been alone, hardly able to survive. His strength was returning and he heard the sound of the axe. He watched Hayes build his cabin, watched him fell the trees, crept close at night hoping to find scraps of food from the meals he smelled. Fear of the white man and his gun had kept him from approaching.

He devoured the chunks of venison that Hayes handed him but like precious jewels he looked at the salt shaken into his hand, then bit by bit lapped it up with his tongue and almost as slowly savored the meal. Pathetically, he tried to tell

Hayes that he believed in the white man's God. He was a Christian—a good Indian.

What did he want—besides survival? With his few halting words he explained. It was a curious interchange. On the floor at his feet he indicated the little Peabody River, then the Androscoggin, then there were little circles and Hayes knew they were a string of lakes far up north—lakes he had never seen but of which he had heard. Then the Indian stretched his arms wide and with much reiteration he indicated the great plains where a mighty city stood.

Hayes asked, "Quebec?"

The Indian repeated the word. There he would find his people. There he wished to go.

That he was too weak for such a journey was evident. That the white man would shelter him, share his precious food with him was also evident; however, when the shadows began to fall, Hayes gave the poor creature a blanket, locked his closet and laid down to rest with his musket close at hand ready to spring to action at any sign of treachery.

It was something far different that wakened him. He had slept deeply but jumped into a sitting position as some strange sound assaulted his ears—a sound that caused instant terror to grip him. No Indian form lay stretched where he had left it. He was out of his door, peering about hastily, for again there was the crackling. He was right about the frightening sound—fire. He ran toward the blaze some distance nearer the low slope of the mountain but long before he reached it he slowed his steps, then crept up stealthily to gaze at a strange sight. On a wide flat stone the Indian had built a fire and into it he was throwing pieces of the game he had secreted in his tattered garments. Now silhouetted against the flame, the weak emaciated heathen was dancing. It was as fantastic a sight as Hayes Copp's eyes would ever witness. The Indian was offering sacrifice to his gods, propitiating the evil spirits, praying for the help of the Great Spirit who dwelt up there in the mountain top; perhaps thanking that Great Spirit for the kindness of the white man.

Hayes slowly retreated but when he reached his cabin he watched until the strange ritual was ended, until the fire had burnt out and the poor fellow, weak, panting, exhausted, had stealthily crept back to his place.

For some weeks Hayes fed him and then one night after a repetition of the same dance, he bowed his head almost to the ground, smiled, held the white man's hand, then turned away to disappear into the forest and often in that long winter Hayes wondered where he might be. He would never know if he again saw his own people on the great plains before Quebec or whether his bones were whitening in some hollow of the wilderness.

CHAPTER VI

WHEN THE LEAVES had fallen, after the black frosts had come and light snow covered the ground, in the chill of November nights he lay in his bunk listening to perhaps the most mournful sound in all Nature—the wailing of the screech owl the long *loo-loo-ooo-ooo*, the tremulous call seeming to express all the sadness inevitable in existence, all the mystery and despair found in the human heart, the most melancholy music ever uttered. He was not depressed with superstitious dread; instead he smiled knowing the little bird was not much bigger than a robin, a friendly little furry-feathered, gentle, amiable looking creature with brown and white feathers as soft as a kitten's. Hayes knew that if one frightened him or came too near his nest he would swoop down and strike with his sharp beak but otherwise he was a menace only to the little mice, grasshoppers and beetles which he needed for his supper.

Hayes was never alone. When he saw the leaves move and a creature approach with a heavy waddling movement he stepped aside politely to let the skunk pass; and not far away might be an old coon plodding along through the underbrush. Scampering on every side of him were the tiny striped chipmunks emerging into adulthood after their infancy in dark burrows. How quickly they learned acorn-lore, how much like human hands were the front paws, how much like children they tumbled and played and squealed and chattered. He knew the mole, the newts, the gray squirrel and, like any man who turns the soil, knows that he spends most of his hours of labor in the company of a congested population of meadow mice. No man could count them—thousands upon thousands, of chunky, fuzzy little fellows with wild eyes, alert, trotting about, constructing marvellous subways and labyrinths under the grass or under the snow in winter; living snugly unseen by the average human eye but not hidden from the curious eye of a boy.

When the settlers in towns spoke of "Up thar in that *howling* wilderness," they shuddered at the thought of cold winter nights when the little animals found shelter and safety in tunnels and burrows, leaving the fox, the wildcat, the wolf, the bear, to roam through the forest seeking for food. Half famished, gnawing hunger infuriating them, they became killers. They howled. They would, like man, attack any prey that would save them from starvation.

As he lived day by day in that forest surrounded by living, breathing creatures large and small, he came to think of himself as not so different from them, for were not their fundamental wants the same? They, like him, must have food; also a home of a kind that is suitable for more than mere shelter for it must be a place to breed and raise young in safety. In common with every animal that lived in the forest he knew that he must constantly ward against death.

However, he also realized that his eyes were myopic compared with that eagle's who saw a fish three miles distant and swooped from the blue in a straight line to obtain it; knew any dog might hear a sound perhaps a mile away; knew a wheeling flock of pigeons possessed a beautiful expertness in forming precise angles in their flight and ability to land on a narrow ledge of his roof that left him gaping with astonishment; knew his strong arms were babyish compared with the strangling hug of a huge brown bear.

Then, one mid-winter day with the temperature well below zero, he walked through a section of his forest that constituted a clean pine grove. On the crisp clear air there was the scent of resin and, patterned after the bare branches above, blue sky was laying softer blue shadows on the snow. Suddenly Hayes stopped. He looked up at the wonder of the burning blue above, unaware of the glow in his eyes. Not in words but in deep feeling he felt himself the one creature who, not through blind instinct, could devise, invent, plan, work and dream and wonder about God and creation and destiny.

He knew at first hand the cleverness of both large and tiny animals, each working in its set and determined way, but man was different.

He had felled trees until there was a path of sorts over which a sled or wagon could make its way from one end of his land to the other. It was the beginning of a road. He, alone of all the creatures living on that land, could dream that some day that narrow passage might grow to be a highway connecting the southern villages with the small prosperous towns developing up north.

He had made a beginning and some day he would have something to offer a partner. There would be something a girl might be willing to share. Twice he had seen her within the year on his trips to Jackson or Bartlett. She was a friend of some of his kin and often visited at the farm of his cousin, one John Copp. Only once had they again spoken to each other but he felt there was some awareness in her shy smile and in the brightness of her blue eyes.

He also knew, in his sober moments, that he was building that dream on nothing—absolutely nothing at all. He knew he was stupid and tongue-tied in her presence; knew that no man with sense would expect those dainty little feet to walk beside his clumsy, muddy boots over this rough land. Still he worked and dreamed.

There are days, outwardly adventureless, that are destined to remain sharp and clear in a man's memory. Could it be that there can occur an adventure of the mind and soul, unrecognized?

He was returning to his cabin, his axe slung over his shoulder. The sun was setting in one of those dramatic exhibitions of color when even the snow is overcast with a ruby glow. Back of the bare branches of trees great bars of crimson changed and reformed. Then a hunger such as he had never experienced before gnawed into his heart, a loneliness, a wanting that he could not satisfy. He was lonely; not for the company of chattering people but for someone to share his deep feeling for his home, for his forest, his rich land, and even for the creatures with whom he lived.

From the great beast down to the tiniest insect, each found his mate. Male and female; God had created them. He opened his cabin door and went in to prepare his supper alone, to eat alone, to sleep alone.

When he had finished eating and thrown the refuse into his fire, he added heavy logs, then going to his closet he brought his Bible and laid it on the cleared boards that constituted his table. When it became too dark to see the print he lit one of the precious candles he had purchased on his last visit to Jackson.

Through the four long winters and five springs that he lived alone in the wilderness it was said of him that he read his Bible from beginning to end. Hayes would have laughed at that. He was not given to stunts.

Up and down through the valleys, in log cabin and frame house the entire library sometimes consisted of that one book—the Bible. Often it was read until the covers were replaced with pieces of hide, until the leaves grew old, yellow, mended. Out of the reading and belief in that one Book, had come the knowledge, the inspiration, the unshakable beliefs that had formed the moral fiber of Hayes' forebears for hundreds of years. Some became intolerant of the views, beliefs and habits of their neighbors. In this frontier country some became hard, fanatical in their religion—"an eye for an eye, a tooth for a tooth"; others read and re-read the New Testament and absorbed its teachings of love and charity. "Love your enemy"—"do good to them that hate you"—Hayes called that a hard doctrine; "Do unto others as you would that they should do unto you"—too hard for mere man? Men might believe in that, strain for it, but never accomplish it. And still throughout the new land as in the old, men read, prayed and pondered and sinned and repented; but always in the minds of these men was the knowledge of some Truth and in their souls was some vision of what they believed God had ordained.

When Hayes had a problem to solve, contriving some mechanical gadget, mending a needed tool, devising a plan, he habitually sat down resting his elbows on his knees, his proposition lying before him. He would sit for a long time, his brows knitted into a hard frown, his eyes intent, then, when he saw the solution, with terrific energy he rose and went to work.

Now by the flickering light of his candle he pondered over the teachings of this Book without the aid or hindrance of preacher or accepted belief, forming his own opinions and accepting truth as he could see and understand it, finding it the food that assuaged the hunger in his heart and life. A slow, amused smile in his deepset eyes would have been the only answer he would have made to the labels manufactured by man.

There was that story about Adam and Eve. He brushed it aside thinking all things—even like his gun—could be used for good or for evil purpose. To him, the love of man for woman seemed a glorious part of the love for God—to lie with a woman, bring children into the world was as much God's plan as causing the sun to rise and shine and warm the earth. To know you are naked? Did the moose know he was naked? The baby came without clothes and lived to be thankful for the garments that either warmed him or delighted his senses.

That anyone living close to Nature could doubt the existence of God would have seemed to him impossible. Just as firm was his belief in prayer. Not in studied words, but in fullness of the heart, some strange straining and yearning toward the Power that was the Source of all good, he could pray believing, "Ask and ye shall receive."

And he had much to ask. To be protected from death, to grow stronger and stronger, to clear his land, to harvest his crops, to barter cunningly, to possess a home that would be strong and safe from enemies both human and animal. To bring "Home" that girl... If that were religion, then Hayes was religious.

CHAPTER VII

AFTER A TERRIFIC STORM, one May morning the skies cleared and Hayes stepped out of his door to look up at the breaking clouds and see the small patches of blue appearing. Then his eyes lowered to watch two birds mating.

Spring. Yes, spring again and for how many springs had he, in his aloneness, watched the mating of the birds? To him on this May morning it mattered not for the winters, falls, springs and summers had merged into his mind as mere natural changes in his days of gruelling work. However, on this May morning there was something different in his countenance, some unusual light in his eyes, something less grim about the set of his mouth.

He smiled broadly at his thoughts. He had seen the male bird come alone from his winter home back to the same place he had known the summer before; seen him fly from tree to tree as he selected the site for his new nest. The bird was staking a claim even as he, the man, some summers since, had staked a claim. The bird was singing loudly, announcing to the world that his title to the home spot was secured, his mate had been chosen. When she started to make the nest he would bring bits of twigs and wisps of this and that and stand ready to fight to the death any creature that would dare to molest either her or their young.

The pattern of all Nature? The little male bird seemed to realize the universal greatness of his destiny and the wonder that was spring so he sat on a low branch of the tree, carolling loudly as his feathered throat quivered and throbbed.

All through the forest the tree buds were swelling, small green things were pushing their way up through the ground, everything was changing color and one with ears attuned could hear the murmur of life.

Hayes Copp's throat would not throb with song but his heart was beating more rapidly, for he, too, was starting out on a journey and in a crude way he had burnished up his plumage. He had, in the clear water of the river, cleaned not only his body but his clothes. Rough and worn and old, they were clean of all that he could scrub off. His locks were shorn and the yellow curls lay close about his shapely head. Out of his "bundle" he had taken the good wool shirt that his mother had woven and sewed for him as a parting gift when he had left home.

He locked his barn door securely, stood a moment looking off over his cleared field where the earth lay dark and rich, ready to produce the wealth on which he calculated so closely. For the two last summers that wealth had increased beyond his dreaming, for he had already paid off much of his debt, not only in Jackson but some measures of wheat and oats had gone to the government men. With what was left he would barter artfully and skillfully for livestock and some furniture.

Today, he left his axe at home but, with his musket over his shoulder, he set out on his long walk with rapid easy strides.

Here, surely, was no "young Lochinvar out of the west." Here was a youngish man with shoulders too far bent, brows too often frowning above deepset intense eyes, mouth wide, straight and too often wearing an expression of grim determination but, fortunately, of all this lack of ease and polish he was unaware. The clear surface of pond or river had been his only mirror and he had had little need for thoughts concerning his appearance. What was in his heart was to him all that mattered. If it was a lonely heart, hungry for love and companionship, it was also, on this May morning, filled to overflowing with something in perfect harmony with the beauty of the universe.

Never before had he put the long miles behind him so quickly. When he reached Jackson he passed through without stopping, turning off at a rough dirt road, now muddy and filled with small pools of the water left from the recent storm.

His cousin's farm lay on this dirt road which reached the town of Bartlett some miles beyond. Already the farms he was passing had an old, well established look about them. Most of the houses were well painted, their whiteness in pleasant contrast to the green of grass and tree. Even the unpainted places appeared well cared for and homelike, their smallpaned windows reflecting the low afternoon sun. The contrast to his own wilderness country was sharp and caused him some uneasiness. A group of women was emerging from the door of a farmhouse and even above the sound of horses' hoofs and the creaking of a farm wagon he heard the shrill voices as they called to each other. Their shawls were dropped to their shoulders as they bared their heads to the spring warmth. Over their arms his sharp eyes saw the bags made of calico or homespun cotton and he guessed it had been the meeting of a "sewing bee." Some few climbed into farm wagons but others in groups of two or three, still calling to each other in high-pitched voices, went to the road starting their long walks to their homes. A mile, two miles or three? What was distance to them compared to the pleasure of meeting, gossiping, uniting in some endeavor and feeling the sweet companionship with others of their kind?

Seeing them enhanced his uneasiness. The great highway, connecting the seaports with what was becoming the great commercial artery of the Connecticut River was teeming with life. Each home was a community in itself where fathers, mothers, grandparents, children and often many helpers gathered about tables; where there was no hour of the day without human intercourse, without the sound of human voices. On Sundays they crowded into the meetinghouses; on week days their children filled the small school rooms; at week ends there were dances in country barns or what they proudly called balls at the Inns. They worked, they played, they planned, dreamed and loved and married always in the association of other human beings.

Here in this lively community Dolly Emery had been born and raised. The expression of grimness deepened in his face. With startling vividness an incident of his boyhood came to his mind. His own father, traversing a lonely hill road, had stopped at an old farmhouse where lived people he had known for many years. Getting no response to his knocking and sensing a curious atmosphere of decay about the place, he searched for the two old people and found the body of the woman in the well and the old man hanging from one of the rafters in the barn.

Hayes remembered his father's saying, "There are those who cannot endure loneliness. She was illfitted for her life. She came from Boston."

❦

Once an uncle of his, expecting to represent Coos County, had been denied a seat in the legislature because of the lack of communication in all the land cut off by the mighty towering ranges of the White Mountains. Some twenty odd years ago when he was a mere child, a company had been formed called—and he remembered his feeling of respect in hearing his father name it—The Tenth New Hampshire Turnpike Corporation. It was designed and developed into the means of bringing the north country into communication with the seaports and the Connecticut River. He remembered the sense of tragedy recalling even into his child's mind when a neighbor taking his valuable load of furs down the river in winter—the only time in which such journeys could be made—broke through the ice, losing his life as well as his wealth.

Every boy in the countryside knew that sixty years before some man named Timothy Nash was out hunting when, trailing a moose up through one of the ravines he came on an old

Indian trail that led through a notch. Other men sought out the trail because it was hard to believe that human eyes had seen what Timothy had described. Then a seasoned traveler had returned, saying that the scenic grandeur had few equals in the world.

Hayes had been about fourteen years old, already a strong, self-reliant hunter when he first followed that trail south. He had felt a reverential awe standing on the narrow path at the bottom of that gigantic cleft in the mountains. The peaks towering thousands of feet overhead were enveloped in clouds and he had been unable to form any idea of their height.

A frightful place for a mere boy to be for the Indians habitually drove their captives through that notch to torture them in the wild country north. When he returned home he was severely punished and his tales of the adventure were received with scepticism. Only his father, looking at him thoughtfully, realized there was something in the boy on which he had not reckoned.

Hayes knew there was a real hotel in that mountain district today and all along the route from Bartlett there were small inns and over the road, rough but everywhere usable, in winter, could be seen, long lines of teams, sometimes half a mile of them, coming down from Coos. Now, drawn by tough Canadian horses the sleds were loaded with butter, cheese, pork, lard, pot or pearl ash and valuable pelts. When the teams returned they brought the merchandise needed for the homes, and in this new traffic he knew Dolly's father was active.

He passed many farms and he thought soberly of the bustling, often gay life along the Turnpike and in the fast-growing towns—all completely cut off from his wilderness by the mighty ranges of mountains. His mouth was set more grimly as he looked at the pleasant farms.

At last he stopped before a prosperous looking place where the large barn was connected by several sheds to a low-roofed substantial house.

He glanced at the seldom used front door but made his

way through the yards to the kitchen. The door opened to his knock and he smiled widely at the surprise and pleasure on the face of his cousin's wife, Eurania. Soon the entire family joined her in hearty welcome and seated at their supper table his plate was filled and refilled.

His "bundle" had been taken to their "company room," his musket was placed against the wall in a corner of the hall.

After the hearty meal when his cousin, John Copp went out to his barn to attend to some last chores, Hayes followed him and, as would be expected, lent a hand.

They had finished their work and were walking toward the house when Hayes stopped on the path and spoke.

"Cousin, I would speak with you."

"What concerns you, Hayes?"

The eyes were direct, the tone solemn. "I wish that, in the morning you would fetch Dolly Emery here."

"Here?"

Hayes nodded. The two men stood silent, then a broad grin spread across John Copp's face.

"I'll gladly drive you to her home, Hayes."

"Here." Hayes spoke with decision.

"I hardly need ask your purpose, Hayes, but why not in her home?"

"There are too many there."

There was a hearty laugh, then John pondered. "This is no time to show a faint heart, Hayes. To see her father, sooner or later, could not be avoided."

Hayes nodded, "I have no faint heart. I wish first to see Dolly alone."

"To offer marriage?"

"That is my purpose."

John promised and they walked back to the farmhouse, sitting a while about the open fire discussing weather, crops, news of relatives, news of state and nation. As the men rose, John's wife smiled up at Hayes. "You are much talked about, Cousin, in all the countryside. Is it not time for you to marry?

Many a young woman would like to be asked to share that great land you now own. It was told about that you sought that mountain side in hopes of finding gold but I believe you are finding the gold in your rich harvests. What do you say, Cousin?"

Hayes smiled. "I will heed your words, Eurania."

Was it the unwonted softness of the bed, the closeness of human beings that so disturbed his rest? Long before any of the family was stirring, he rose, dressed and went out to walk about the fields until others should rise and smoke from the chimneys tell him that breakfast was cooking. The younger children were sent off to school with books under their arms. The hired men were out in the fields and John long since had disappeared down the winding road toward the Emery farm.

Hayes had never before experienced such agitation. While washing her breakfast dishes his cousin saw his nervousness. She placed a chair near the open fire.

"Won't you take some rest, Cousin?"

"Thank 'ee kindly." However he still paced up and down, his heavy boots thumping on the wooden floor.

With her back turned toward him she waited until she could control her desire to laugh aloud, then, with a sly upward glance she spoke soothingly as to a child. "John has told me of your purpose, Hayes. It is worthy and I wish you well."

There was no answer and she continued, "We have known the girl from babyhood, Hayes. As your cousin who would do you a service, I should tell you, she is not like the farm girls you have known. Our Dolly is a high-spirited wench. There are those who would say an untamed one. She may not take readily to the harness—unless it is her choice. But if it chanced to be the desire of her heart, she would pull more than half the load, for no woman, wife or mother or grandmother of any age, matches her skill. None here can equal her in the fineness and firmness of the thread she spins; none can hope to equal her in the weaving."

She waited, looking at him. He had stopped his pacing

46

and now stood as though riveted to one spot drinking in her words, but although she waited, he did not speak.

She continued with a sly twinkle in her eyes, "You know that John has gone to fetch her here. Long ago she promised to bring me a pattern for a quilt and help me in the cutting. It is a very unusual one made of large stars which will be like the sun shining among little moons. It is one of her own devising but she has promised me the pattern." Now uncontrolled, the sly smiling gave way to laughter "How surprised she will be to find you here!"

She had finished her task and now she stood near him by the cleared breakfast table. She must find some way to help him, to dispel this dread that gripped him and left him tongue-tied. On the table she spread out a piece of brown paper and handed him a stubby pencil.

"It would please me, Hayes, if you would indicate here what you have been doing. Here"—and the clever woman drew a circle — "is Jackson. Through many miles going north you follow the Indian trail, then here is your land. Where does the river lie? What shape does it take? Where have you built your cabin, by the river or near the mountain? John says you've started to clear a road?"

He took the stubby pencil and clumsily began to indicate the shape and extent of his land, the river, the rich intervale, the cabin and the cleared spots where he raised his crops.

Both were bending over the table when there was the sound of horses' hoofs outside the door, the gay light chatter of a high pitched voice against John's heavier tones, then the sound of light footsteps and the door opened.

Dolly Emery. The cheerful, airy salutation to her friend died on her lips; the bright blue eyes opened wide and stared in surprise at the man, then quickly her face flushed a rosy red and for a moment taken off her guard, she found no words. But before anyone else could speak she recovered, tossed her head airily and with a glibness of tongue that seemed more astonishing than her beauty to the man gazing at her with a half-idiotic grin transfiguring his face, she mocked, "So it's you, not your cousin, who wants the pattern for the sun and moon quilt!"

He was clutching the pencil, still half bent over the table when he turned to see why his cousin did not answer. The reason was simple. She had disappeared. He stood alone facing the girl.

Her blond hair was parted in the middle, and combed smoothly into a knot at the neck. She wore a dark brown dress of cotton homespun material. The basque was plain with only a row of dull brown buttons closely placed and reaching to the straight collar. Beneath the full skirt her little foot now swung out and she too leaned over the table.

"The farmer pretends to be an artist?" She mocked with light laughter but her sharp eyes saw the lines, the inquisitive mind sought the explanation. Now the clever cousin's merciful device paid dividends. Haltingly but with increasing ease he pointed out the meaning of the lines.

Close to him, her shoulder almost touched his rough coat. She laid her hand on the paper as she leaned over listening.

Without warning, in his blunt, direct way, he turned looking into the blue eyes. "It is my wish to share it all with you."

She drew back, again momentarily speechless with surprise.

He was doing the talking now, pressing, as his heart thumped painfully against his ribs. His breath came unevenly but his eyes never wavered as he looked into hers. "It may seem to you too hard a life. I plan to build a house for you but it would be better for you to plan it. It may be many harvests before my debt is all paid. I lack cattle and have not yet cleared grazing ground sufficient for many. I own no horses. The mountain land is wild but the Glen is rich, the yield so great, I wonder. The cabin is without furnishing. I would wish that to be your choice." He stopped, then with great dignity he ended, "It is my wish to share it all with you."

The silence was painful, then suddenly the room rang with the gayest, most mocking laugh he had ever heard. The little foot swung out as she leaned back against the table, steadying herself with her two hands. "The Town is overfull of young men, Hayes Copp, who coax a girl into the woods with talk of love."

She stopped with head bent, glancing up out of the corner of her eyes, a mocking smile about her lips. "You speak only of cows and roads and your need of someone to cook your meals and to spin and weave you a shirt."

A crimson tide started at his throat and burned up through his face until it reached the blond curls above his forehead, but it was a feeble tide compared to the burning ardor in his eyes.

"My heart is given to you, Dolly. My eyes are blind to all others. I have long prayed that you would say the same to me."

She turned her head away, lowering it until he could not see the bright eyes which filled with tears even as she bit her lips to help regain her calm. Her voice was low, almost a whisper, as she finally turned to him. "Many a man has asked me, Hayes Copp. I have kept myself for you."

He reached out to touch the hand but withdrew his own, as heavy—purposely heavy—footsteps sounded without the door which was opened and John walked in. One glance told him the outcome of their strategy and his smile was wide and expansive as he called his wife and soon there were no tongues tied into silence.

The sun was riding high and Hayes prepared to leave. When could she come? His question set the woman thinking. Within the month, he asked timidly? Firmly he was put in his place, engulfed in masculine ignorance. The girl must prepare. To go into a rude cabin where there was not to be found a sheet or proper chair or bed or cooking utensils? Dolly needed time to spin and weave and with what all her kin and friends and her father would give or spare, prepare properly. There must be a wedding. Firmly, seconded by John's wife, Hayes was taught that he knew nothing of women's ways but his education should begin at once.

When she was ready, word would be sent him and he

would come for her.

There was no hope for it. He must leave it all to Dolly. Not again did he speak to her alone. When he picked up his musket and started toward the road, they all gathered to watch him depart. John laid a kindly hand on his shoulder but spoke as admonished by his wife, "When it comes time for the wedding, I shall help you choose a new coat, Hayes. It would be becoming of you."

It would be dark long before he reached the Glen but the path was so familiar he felt his feet would find it were he blind-folded. Perhaps he was not far from sightless, for his head was in a whirl, and all he saw was the girl and all he heard were the words, "I have kept myself for you."

CHAPTER VIII

IN MUD CAKED BOOTS Hayes sowed and planted and cultivated and weeded. In any hour in which he could take time from his fields and garden his axe could be heard ringing as more trees crashed to the ground and his clearing grew. Tall piles of evenly sized logs rose behind his cabin, ready for the winter's cold.

Then came the hot summer days—long days in which he could almost double his hours of labor. Occasionally some man, hardy and curious, made his way up through the old trails to stop and see what was happening on Martin's Location, for the courtship of Hayes Copp and Dolly Emery had become a subject of interest and, over cracker barrels in the general store or over their rum in the taverns as over tea cups or roast beef dinners, the matter was discussed. It was said that bets were laid that pretty Dolly Emery would never leave her gay, bustling life on the great turnpike to bury herself in any northern wilderness

When some such a traveler came to his door, Hayes received him with becoming hospitality, fed and housed his horse, cooked his evening meal, gave him bed in which to rest, then, in the early morning after a hearty breakfast, returned to his gruelling work; while, through all the hours of the visit, the host had spoken little and no prying loosened his tongue. Courteously but definitely the visitor was dismissed.

Perhaps it was no wonder that fanciful tales spread through the towns. It was said that Hayes had slyly bought the land from the government pretending to make a farm while all the time he was digging for gold in the mountain. One man said he saw shining nuggets in that closet when Hayes went to it for some meal. Why else did he keep the closet locked, carrying the key in his pocket? Perhaps Dolly was in the secret and knew of the gold.

Oblivious of all the talk, Hayes was, on one hot August day, felling a tree to widen a narrow passage in his rough road when, between his axe strokes he heard the muffled sound of a horse's hoofs. He paused to listen.

The sound became more distinct; louder and louder and nearer and nearer it came until he saw the horse's head emerge from the forest, then the powerfully built animal and on its back he saw a man whom he knew, a face at sight of which his heart seemed to jump in his chest, then throb until his throat tightened with amazement and foreboding.

He stood half bent over the axe resting at his feet until he felt some return to his normal self control. He advanced slowly as the man halted and prepared to dismount.

Only the intensity of his eyes showed his perturbation as he approached and bowed with dignity, "I bid you good day, Mr. Emery."

Curtly but pleasantly the man bent his sandy-gray head and replied, "The same to you, Mr. Copp."

Acknowledging the courteous invitation, Mr. Emery removed the two bundles tied to his saddle, followed Hayes to the barn where the horse was tethered, then into the cabin.

Without impudence but nevertheless openly and frankly, Mr. Emery stood looking from ceiling to floor, from wall to wall, from sleeping bunks to closet. His eyes rested on the few stumps that served as chairs, at the plank that served as table. He walked to the door, speaking authoritatively, "Before the dark, for I have only a few hours to spend and must be on my way home early in the morning, I would like to see your land."

The man's heavy boots followed close on his as Hayes led him on that rough tramp; first to his garden, then to his cleared fields, on to the river, through denser underbrush circling through the forest to the foot of great Mount Madison, he pointed out the marks cut in the great trees.

As they stood on a rise of ground, soaring out into the blue a male eagle gave his loud, clear call directly over their heads. Mr. Emery looked up and a slight smile containing some of the mockery of Dolly's smile curved his lips. "One of your neighbors? I suppose the others are bears, wolves, wildcats?"

Hayes answered soberly, "There are many."

The man pursued, "Indians?"

"A few small encampments in that north forest. They are not powerful. Those who have come near have been friendly."

"Only a few unfriendly ones could wipe you out. One of them could murder a defenseless woman left alone in that cabin."

Hayes was silent. It was too true and his heart felt heavy and altogether sick with ominous presage of trouble.

They returned to the clearing. Mr. Emery looked up at the mountains. "By gorry! You are in a nest of giants here. Will you name those peaks? I am not sure of them from this angle."

Hayes pointed and named each.

"All but Washington to be seen from your front door." He added, "A noble prospect." Then, shaking his head, "For eagles."

Now Hayes followed Mr. Emery, who walked to the garden, bending down, picking up some soil in his hand, kicking at the ground with the toe of his boot.

He turned abruptly. "I would like to eat. I'm half famished."

He sat on one of the stumps as Hayes, awkward, and somehow losing his customary dexterity, opened his closet, took from it his few cooking utensils and began preparing the meal. There were no cloth for the table, no refinements, scarcely necessary implements but, with a show of good nature, Mr. Emery offered to turn the spit at the fire as the game cooked.

When the food was ready he opened one of the bags that had been attached to his saddle and set a fair sized cask of rum before them. Both the good food and the drink had their effect and by the time the meal was finished, he leaned back, lit his pipe and with a curious but not unfriendly expression, watched the young man clean up. Not deviating from his usual custom, Hayes scrubbed the board, burned his refuse, locked his closet, laid fresh logs on the fire, then, at last, took the seat at the end of the fireplace opposite his guest.

He was not unduly disturbed when the questioning began. He had expected it, for this man had a right to ask and he had a duty to think carefully and answer honestly.

First Mr. Emery would like the story of the purchase of the land. Following, came requests for the exact amount promised in payment, the yield per acre of oats, wheat, the amount paid off. Had Hayes realized the value of pelts from the animals roving about him?

Mr. Emery leaned over, a quizzical smile in his eyes. "You came into this wilderness, alone, empty handed?"

"I had my musket and axe and soon added tools."

Mr. Emery tilted back his head and for some time seemed to be reëxamining the ceiling. "When do you start building a decent house?"

Hayes swallowed twice, then spoke bluntly and firmly, "When Mistress Dolly gets here. It is for her, I will build it." Then before the man could answer he added, "I will wait for her to furnish it as it may please her."

"By gorry, Hayes Copp, you may lack more than I like to overlook but you do not lack courage." He rose, stretched, and standing with his back to the fire looked down at the bowed head of the young man. "If it is possible to sleep on those boards, I would thank you to let me try, I am weary, for I have ridden hard."

Hayes moved to rise, but was held by a firm hand on his shoulder. "I'm failing in my purpose in coming here. I will be truthful and tell you the state of things. Through the summer days, Dolly's mother has washed out her eyes weeping. I have lamed my tongue arguing, scolding and offering every bribe my poor brain could devise and all to no avail. The best we got so far has been her promise to wait—then we begged her again to wait, hoping some sense might enter into the girl's mind. I'll warn you now, Hayes, no one on earth can manage that girl." He stopped to laugh. "Her mother sent me here for what I now see for a fool's errand. She thought I might persuade you to see the fearful injustice to my daughter it would be to bring her into this wilderness. If you would withdraw your offer of marriage it would solve the problem."

Hayes moved out from under the hard pressed hand. He stood for a moment with head bent, then his brows met frowning, his eyes bored into the eyes watching him. "I thank 'ee, Sir, for saying that which I wished most to hear. I entreat you most earnestly to convey to her my message. It is this. *I shall come for her on the day and hour she wills.*"

Mr. Emery's laugh echoed through the small cabin "By gorry, let's sleep."

It was scarcely light enough to see in the cabin when Hayes arose and prepared the breakfast. After the man mounted his horse he sat a moment, turning over and over the reins in his hands. He looked down at the head covered with the blond curls. "I intended to depart with part of my message undelivered, Hayes, but as you have compelled me to fail in my mission—"

Hayes waited, looking up, his eyes unsmiling.

The man stopped to laugh again, then he finished, "She won't break her promise to me to wait until the first snow falls. It is easier traveling then. She ran after me half a mile to overtake me and begged me to deliver her message. She says to come in the first days of November."

There was a suggestion of sadness added to the gruffness of his voice as he added, "Some day I'll manage to send up here a few chairs and comforts for my daughter."

Hayes replied respectfully, "I thank 'ee, Sir."

CHAPTER IX

A LIGHT SNOW was falling on the already white ground one early November day as, over the roads, heavy farm wagons made their way; men and boys and women on the backs of horses passed those trudging on foot, all aiming to reach the little Meeting House in Jackson.

It had been told that Hayes Copp had been these two days in the home of his cousin, John Copp, being made fit by the town's barber and tailor. The details were common knowledge. John, thinking of his own huge bulk and forgetting how gaunt and thin his cousin had become since living up in that wilderness, had ordered far too large a coat. It was said that there had been argument concerning the other portions of his costume, Hayes needing to be persuaded to remove his great boots and wear shoes, to discard the heavy wool shirt and even allow himself to be half strangled in a necktie.

However, the result of Eurania's efforts pleased the women folk who admired his curling yellow hair which the barber had washed and left glossed and close cut enough to show his fine head. His strength, his earnest, modest expression pleased them also; but after one satisfying look, their eyes, as were those of every pair of masculine eyes that day, were fastened on the bride.

That she had sent to Portland, Maine, to have her shoes made they all knew and every neck was craned to get a glimpse of the tiny feet. The women sighed as they looked. If their hearts were filled with envy as they studied her gown, one could not blame them. Here was no display of riches, for the Emerys were, like them all, hard working farmers with the good and bad luck of harvests and with many mouths to feed. Here was something else. They asked themselves how Dolly achieved that beautiful color. What secrets did she possess in dyeing her fine yarn such a heavenly blue? That she had woven the cloth, as soft and fine as challis, fashioned and sewed the gown, they all knew. About her neck, close to the little collar which was fastened by a gold pin, she wore those beautiful gold beads. That was expected, for it was said that she even slept with them on. For her head she had fashioned a small cap, white and fine as lace, though crocheted of thread-like cotton. Buttons covered with the same material, closed her tight basque.

Beneath the many folds of the skirt the little feet walked firmly by her father. When she joined in the responses, repeating the parson's words, her voice was clear and strong, her head was held high and there was an expression of excitement—some thought a mischievous gleam—in her bright blue eyes.

Later, speaking of Hayes, she heard, "Poor lamb, he looked dazed. How he swallowed and choked." It was even said that at the rather hurried breakfast at the Inn which followed the ceremony, he again seemed to choke when swallowing the food that Cousin John prodded him to notice on his plate.

There was much of practical concern on the young man's mind. He had expected to arrive at Cousin John's, get his good new coat, hurry on to the Emery's, hear a few authoritative words spoken by the parson, then, still in his heavy boots, begin the journey back. He had planned a great surprise for Dolly. Long since, he had bargained with a farmer far north for a fine cow. This man was to deliver the creature and Hayes had no way of knowing on what day he might appear at the cabin with the animal.

It was with consternation that he heard the plans, from Cousin Eurania. Much more time was to be consumed than he had expected. It seemed that on the day before the wedding there was to be a family party at the Emery home with all the kin and friends for a fine dinner. There would follow on the next morning the early ceremony at the Meeting House in Jackson, a quick breakfast at the Inn with Mr. Emery as host, and the start of the long journey before the day was too well advanced.

After all, they universally concurred, a wedding was for the bride and, no one could doubt that this bride was enjoying her last days with all the bustling gaiety contributed by relatives and friends and family. She enjoyed the expression of astonishment and pleasure in Hayes' face when he saw some of the gifts bestowed upon her. There were utensils for cooking; some fine pewter spoons and mugs, some goose-feather pillows encased in hand-woven cotton cases, small articles for her personal use, but, most amazing of all—her mother had given her a beautiful silver teapot, pitcher and sugarbowl, one of the precious heirlooms brought long ago from England. Her father's gift was a fine strong work horse.

As he looked, Hayes' expression turned from surprise to apprehension. How was all this to be transported? He puzzled long over this and his solution would become countryside talk for many a day.

After the noonday dinner at the Emerys, he rode the horse when they returned to Cousin John's home. Hurrying into the "company room" he stripped off his fine habiliments, donned his old boots and trousers and went to the barn. First, in the nearby woods he cut birch saplings and trimmed and smoothed two, coming back with slender but strong poles. In the barn he fastened these to the sides of the harness, leaving the ends to drag on the snowy ground like runners on a sled. To the poles he fastened crossbars and on these he bound tightly the leather trunk containing Dolly's trousseau, the sacks packed with kitchen utensils, the precious package containing the silver set and dishes, the Indian basket containing the food contributed by Cousin Eurania for the journey, then,

later, after the ceremony when they had quickly changed from wedding garments into traveling gear, there also was hung his own "bundle" and a bag containing Dolly's fine shoes.

When they were ready to start, she wore a dark wool dress of homespun, a long dark coat, a cleverly contrived woolen hood with ends tied under her chin.

Now, with kin and friends and half the countryside crowding about them, Dolly mounted the horse while Hayes in his tough boots walked by her side. He little knew that he had fashioned an equipage that was to become famous—Dolly Copp's "Bridal-car." They would never know who had given it the name but the appellation stuck.

While her mother clung, weeping, to her, her father kissed her, the children shouted, the friends cheered, men lounging at the Inn door removed their caps, the "bridal-car" moved out of the Inn yard into the road. Again and again she turned and waved but Hayes did not look back. Close to her side he walked, hardly conscious that his feet touched the ground.

Would they never get out of the town? Now again active, there was a change in his countenance and often he joined in her high-spirited laughter as she chatted and exclaimed, "Do turn your head and look, Hayes. How they gawk! I think you should apply at once for a government patent on this car. Do you think another head could have conceived it or other hands executed such a contrivance? How the women envy me this ride. I have heard of English coaches in which ladies in delicate garments of silk and velvet ride about the cities. I believe their very backbones might be jolted apart had they passed over these frozen ruts in such a manner."

He joined in her laughter not knowing whether she mocked or praised, knowing only the sound of her voice was such music in his ears that he cared not what her words might mean.

The snow had ceased falling and now a bright sun shone on the pure whiteness. However, Hayes knew too well the shortness of a November afternoon; knew also that many of those miles must be put behind them before they should reach the shelter he had in mind for their night's rest. The horse was fresh and well used to rough roads and he urged him on, sometimes walking rapidly, sometimes half running beside him; often, over rough places, he led him.

Deeper and deeper into forest land they rode and now the sun was low, the shadows black and Dolly's chatter less. It was fairly night-darkness when he stopped, tied the horse to a tree and helped Dolly down to the snowy ground. First the horse must be fed and cared for, then he untied their blankets and with the basket of food in hand he led and she followed close until they came to an enormous overhanging rock. Into the opening he guided her. Here, where he had often slept, he had fashioned a bridal couch of broken branches, and, completely sheltered from storm, he made their bed.

They ate but enough to dull the edge of their hunger, then, while she did not even untie the strings of her hood, he wrapped her in the heavy blanket and laid down beside her, his musket close at hand.

There was tenderness in his voice. "You can sleep in safety, Dolly."

She laughed. "I have no fear at all. I'm sure your ears are sharp; you would hear the step of bear or wildcat?"

He answered honestly. "My nose is not so keen to smell; but nothing will molest us."

Throughout that night Hayes slept but little and, thankful when he saw the first gray light diminishing the blackness of the sky, he, without disturbing her, crept away, attending to the natural needs of both man and horse and, when she opened her eyes, there was a fire, a bowl of gruel, a cup of hot tea and slices of the home cooked bread from the basket.

He looked down at her. "It is a fair day."

She jumped up. Through the bare branches of the trees she saw the blue sky, saw the sun shining on the crust of snow. Like the spontaneous carolling of a bird, she called out, "You're right, it is a fair day."

When she chattered and seemed to daudle over her breakfast, he chided, "There are many long miles ahead."

In a moment she was up and soon mounted on her horse and again he led to the old trail. Fresh and rested, the early hours were filled again with talk, the food ready in the basket saved much time but as the miles seemed to lengthen, the trail grew narrower and more difficult. As the sun started on its downward path, they grew more silent, merely pressing on and on. Twice the braces of the "bridle-car" loosened and he must stop to secure them, but only once she asked for rest. "I feel my own backbone is too much jolted."

The "fair day" was proving false to its promise for clouds, dark and menacing, were gathering overhead and snow was again beginning to fall. So thick and white it came that Hayes led the horse, while Dolly pulled down the hood to shield her eyes from the blinding whirl of white.

"Are there many more miles, Hayes?"

"Less than three but the trail grows harder."

"My desire is to press on to home, Hayes."

They pressed on and at last Hayes turned to smile at her. "Bear up for in another hour we will be in the clearing."

It was so dark he could not see the expression in Dolly's eyes as he led the horse along his own cleared road, over the open space to the cabin door. The outlines of the cabin were scarcely discernible through the blinding snow storm. The horse stood; Hayes, opened the door, went in and lit a tallow dip and the kindlings under the logs in the fireplace and returned to bring her and unload the "car"

He was working at the packages when she stepped alone over the sill and stood in the one-room cabin. In the dim light, she peered about and for a moment her lips were pressed hard together.

She was still standing, staring from empty wall to empty wall when he returned. Suddenly she untied her hood, threw it aside; then removed her long coat and the room echoed with her shrill, merry laugh. "First, I would have the goose pillows and my blankets. You'll soon build me another closet in that corner to hold my china? Now we'll leave it packed. The trunk we will open because it holds my work dress and apron."

"First I will take the horse to the barn."

She spoke lightly, "There *is* a barn?"

When he had brought in all the various packages, set her trunk by the wall, taken the horse to the barn and returned, he found her standing before the fire looking at the flames spiraling up from the burning logs. Her face looked pinched and the drooping head and shoulders showed fatigue.

He stood awkwardly looking at her. There was tenderness in the tone of his voice. "It is small and mean in your eyes, Dolly. It is but a beginning and cleared fields and food were my first need; but you shall have a house to your liking."

Her smile was tremulous and she bit her lips. "It is warm and safe, Hayes. I make no complaint."

They satisfied their hunger. She went to the wide bunk and spread her blankets and laid her pillows. She undressed in the warmth from the glowing logs, put on her long flannel night gown and crept into the bunk. When he lay beside her, she turned to him, wound her arms about his neck and spoke softly, "I'm not yet your equal in endurance, Hayes. I am far spent."

He held her close until her regular breathing told him she slept. Long he lay staring into the semi-darkness of the room, thinking of the silver teapot, the fine china, the dainty boots and the heart beating against his. He knew his shoulder was wet with her tears.

During the night the storm had subsided, the skies had cleared. He had long since attended to his horse and brought in logs while Dolly, in her work dress, was cooking their breakfast. He was returning with a bucket of water when she ran out into the clearing. Looking up at the giant peaks, looking off at the cleared fields, at the dense woodland beyond, she stood without cloak or bonnet and as he approached her she called in her clear high voice, "It's beyond anything I dreamed, Hayes. It is ours? All ours? Up and down the Glen?"

Lamely as though unable to think of words of his own he merely repeated, "Up and down the Glen."

"You have felled all these trees? You have cleared all this land alone? All *alone*, Hayes?"

He stood, awkward, gazing at her. He was filled to choking with a happiness, a rapture which his wildest dreams had not anticipated.

Then she came to him, wound her arms about his neck and spoke tenderly, "I was over-tired last night, Hayes. Now I truly say to you, I would not be anywhere else in the whole world."

CHAPTER X

THOUGH THE LITTLE CABIN may have seemed "small and mean" to her eyes, throughout that day and in the weeks that followed she was filled with excitement, telling him she was now what she had long wanted to be—a partner in his great adventure. There was nothing small or mean in the grandeur of that great out-of-doors as she followed him over the snow, asking questions about his harvests, his life, until she knew the history of his days from the hour when he had arrived and built his lean-to.

Sometimes she teased him with gay, mocking laughter. "When the door could be locked in the snug cabin, why didn't you come for me?"

He stared at her in astonishment. "It would not have been fitting. There was so little to offer."

"Oh—there's so much more to offer now?"

His confusion and perplexity brought red to his face. "You would have come?"

Her laughter echoed through the woods. "I always knew, Hayes. It was written plain in your eyes and face." Then she surprised him again. "I knew of all your journeys, of your buying and selling, through your cousin John. You don't know how the tongues have wagged concerning you and your wilderness. It was great fun to see their shocked faces when my plans became known. No one believed that I would defy my parents and come with you."

That she was as his Cousin Eurania had said "an untamed

one" he began to realize, but no cousin's words could have prepared him for her high spirits, her excitement, her love for the adventure or for her warmth and her sweet manifestations of affection.

Sometimes when working alone in the forest he found his mind disturbed by strange thoughts. Not until she came to the Glen, did he wonder so continuously how Dolly Emery came to love so simple, so modest a man. Had he been one of those many farmers living along the Highway and had he offered his hand, would she have chosen him? Was it the adventure that enticed her? Would the excitement wear off? When such fears entered his mind he hurried back to the cabin only to be met by a happy, surprised face, shining eyes and a kiss so sweet as to be an intoxication to his senses.

Harassed and often angered, not with the crudeness of their living quarters but with the lack of all she needed in order to function as the capable cook and housekeeper that she knew herself to be, she said she must find new ways of being a worthy partner.

Like a refrain she repeated, "I am yet unequal to you in endurance, Hayes." The fish, the game, the gruel, the wheat cakes, she learned quickly to cook over the burning logs. "Without pans or proper kettles or butter I can't cook you the food I know how to prepare. I must learn to count sugar and salt by the grain—it seems to be so precious."

Again in desperation she would sigh, "Without my spinning wheel and loom, I pass many idle hours."

But in high spirits she learned to fill those idle hours as she followed him to the forest. When the great trees lay on the ground, she swung a hatchet and learned to strip off the branches; learned how to trim and smooth; and, with shining eyes she would turn to him and say, "My strength increases. Soon I shall equal you in endurance."

Warning her that the day would come when the river should be frozen and fish could only be gotten by breaking into the deep pools where the trout would hide, he taught her to save his time for heavy work with the axe while she did the fishing.

Without a thought of danger she went often to the river and soon became an expert fisherman, proudly bringing back the fresh trout and cooking them for their supper.

Down in the cities and villages folks were looking forward with excitement and anticipated pleasure to the celebration of Thanksgiving. Through Hayes' clearing, the snow lay even and white on the ground but still he and Dolly rejoiced because the weather remained pleasant, no frightful fall hurricanes had visited them.

In the early hours of one morning, long before there was a suggestion of light in the eastern sky, Hayes wakened and stealthily dressed, his ears keen to a sound without. He was picking up his gun when Dolly opened her eyes, whispering, "What do you hear, Hayes?"

"A moose. Yesterday, I saw his tracks."

"Don't go far."

He was quietly opening the door. "The day is mild. The current runs free in the river but the ice is deceitful. If you go for a string of trout, watch where you step." He turned smiling. "You may eat marrow-bone and fresh trout for your supper. A moose skin would make you a jacket, for the long coat is cumbersome."

The door closed. Impetuous, she thought to dress and follow him but knowing how she might frighten the wild creature and how this would anger Hayes, she lay until the light grew strong, then went about her household tasks.

In the days following she would hear the tale of his hunt that had lasted so many hours. Clambering over trees, up steep ledges, through mountain streams, lying prone, scarcely breathing as the huge animal came into view, then raising his musket, firing. After trying in vain to shoulder the animal, he made a birch halter and mile by mile dragged him home but as he approached the clearing a sight met his eyes that in one single moment filled his heart with a fear such as he had never before experienced in his entire life. An Indian was coming out of his door.

Far oftener than the tale of any moose hunt would Dolly relate the story of that day and the weeks that followed.

Wearing a tattered jacket of Hayes' she went to the river. The day was one of such beauty that she exulted in breathing deep of the crisp air, looking up at the mountains, now truly "White Hills" for the snow lay deep on their sides.

She had tested the ice along the banks, safely and cautiously found her trout and was preparing to return to the cabin when, almost silently, around the bend of the river there came into sight a canoe, seeming to her startled eyes filled with Indians.

She was standing in an open space, knowing it was too late to hide and fearful of showing cowardice by running. She waited, trembling in every limb. For a moment the paddles were poised, then with deft strokes the canoe shot nearly to the icy bank.

Desperately in her heart she prayed that she might hear Hayes' feet behind her, but she knew that hope was futile. The thought came to her, giving her a strange courage—she must act as he had taught her. She must be unafraid. She must show friendship.

Silently she stood and waited. The canoe came closer to the bank and with guttural speech an Indian spoke to her. Not one word could she interpret and not one glimmer of understanding entered her mind through his violent attempt to talk through sign language.

Then it was her eyes that brought comprehension to her mind. Cooler and more collected now, she saw there were two men, a squaw with a bound infant, a young boy and, lying on the bottom of the boat, was a young child, a girl whose eyes were closed.

Now she realized the man was begging for help. Again and again he pointed to the girl, then up through the clearing toward their cabin. She thought quickly, "He knows the place. He may be a friend of Hayes. The girl is sick and they want shelter and warmth at the cabin."

She nodded her head and the Indian turned to the others seemingly assuring them and giving them orders, for immediately the other man stepped out of the canoe into the river and waded ashore. The Indian who did the talking followed. They pulled the canoe part way out of the water, while the squaw, clasping the infant, stepped over onto the ice. The weight was too much; the ice gave way and with a splash squaw and baby were in the icy stream. There were hoarse cries, a fearful hubbub, pulling and hauling, and soon the squaw stood on the bank, both she and the baby shivering as the icy water dripped off them. The other man raised the sick girl in his arms and the wretched company made its way through woods and cleared space to the cabin.

Logs were placed on the embers in the fireplace; they laid the girl on the floor before it while the squaw stood shivering at one side; then with only her instinct to guide her, Dolly took one of her own wool dresses from the hook, stripped off the poor bindings on the infant, rubbed her dry and wrapping her in the wool, laid her in the bunk. She gave her fine long coat to the now partly undressed mother as the two men talked and gesticulated and watched her swift movements.

Then she turned to the child. Had she taken into her house one dying of the awful pestilence? Again she remembered Hayes' comforting words when he told her that white men slept in the huts of the Indians when all around them there was death from this pestilence but the white men never seemed to contract the disease. Whether this was always true or not, could not matter now. She knelt by the child whose dark skin looked blotched, whose clothes were filthy.

Feeling the pulse, listening to the breathing, she felt sure there was a high fever. Oh, if but for a few minutes she could go to the shelves on which her mother stored all their good home remedies! That wish was a waste of her time. At least she knew the first principle of all healing—cleanliness. Standing slim and young, her yellow hair neatly gathered into the knot at her neck, her eyes bright and blue now seemed to snap with decision and she, by quickly learned sign language, told them she would do something necessary for the child but they should go out of doors.

Meekly and obediently the men obeyed and the small boy followed, while the mother crouched at the end of the fire place. Dolly warmed water, stripped the child, bathed her and fed her spoonfuls of thin, hot gruel. Her face was grave for the next step required real sacrifice. She went to her closet and took out a clean white sheet and wrapping the child in it, carried her to the bunk and covered her with a blanket.

Then she did something that amazed the squaw, whose clothes were drying before the fire to which she had crept nearer. Dolly knelt down before the bunk, bowed her head, closed her eyes and prayed as she had never prayed before— for the return to health of the child, for the sleeping infant, for Hayes' safe return and for her own safety.

The squaw was again wearing her own tawdry apparel when Hayes entered the clearing, dragging his great moose. The Indians saw him and ran toward him, lifting the animal from where he had dropped it as he fairly sprang to the cabin door. When he saw Dolly standing, flushed, but with intense eyes watching the sick girl, his head fell forward and moisture dimmed his eyes.

Explanations were quickly made and they stood looking at each other. Then the reaction came. She again found her limbs trembling and she could hardly control her longing to be clasped in his arms and be allowed to cry as a woman could.

He spoke gently, "Have no fear, Dolly."

Darkness was closing in fast. Great hunks of moose flesh were cooking over the fire, trout was ready and sitting on the floor, the strange company ate. With his expertness in understanding them, Hayes learned their destination. They were inhabitants of one of the few small encampments left in the forest many miles north of them, but they could not get far with the sick girl.

When the food had been eaten and their refuse burnt, Hayes planned. The two Indians and the boy should sleep in the little barn beside the horse. The squaw with her tiny infant should lie on the floor by the fire. Near her he laid the girl wrapped in the clean white sheet, hoping the bunk was not already contaminated.

Wakeful, Dolly often crept close into his arms that night for wolves, smelling the fresh meat, howled about the cabin. Again and again he reassured her, "There is nothing to fear." That there was much to endure he might acknowledge.

Once or twice she slipped out to look at the child, finding her sleeping while the squaw's bright eyes watched suspiciously.

In the morning the strange men brought water from the river and then, surprising Hayes, they told him something that would always seem more than payment for the kindness they had received. They led him to a slight rise in ground in easy distance of his cabin and pointing to the earth they indicated a place. There he should dig a well, close by for the white woman.

Should they dig for him? The ground was not deep frozen. He nodded and they went to work. Down, down, farther down they dug until the water was found. Around the opening they built a low circular dry wall of stone, while Hayes stood smiling with satisfaction. Yes, it was a fine well. Also it meant another night in the barn and more meals about the fire, more and more of his store of food to disappear.

On the second day Hayes spoke again to them, not without trepidation. His wife would care for the child. Already her fever was less, her heart beating normally. They should go home and when the child was better—in another moon— come for her. The small wasted girl would surely die if they moved her now.

The squaw was not consulted. The father made the decision and soon all were loaded in the canoe, the paddles dipping in the still open stream and Hayes watched them depart, thanking God for the mild days that had stayed the ice forming.

Now he made of branches carefully woven together a small bed for the child. Day by day and week by week Dolly fed her and cleaned her, at last seeing life and health return. The skin was clear, hunger assured returning health. One day, although the child cried in fear, she washed the black hair, patiently combed and smoothly braided it. She grew very fond of the little girl, although the child at first had sullen moods. Her small black eyes looked wonderingly about the cabin and Dolly knew she missed her parents and brother. Before the new moon, she smiled and played and Dolly would remark thoughtfully, "There seems no difference in Indian children and white children."

The winter closed in; the river was icebound; often at night their sleep was disturbed by the howling of wolves or the screeching of wildcat or the snapping of fox. Then in the second moon two Indians came down the river with sleds. When they entered the cabin a healthy little Indian girl stood shyly smiling and it was with sadness in her heart that Dolly gave her up. Before they ate, after being sure the child was safe, they brought from their sled two skins—one a wildcat fur measuring full six feet across, the other a handsome moose skin. They laid them on the floor at Dolly's feet. They added two woven baskets and a blanket.

Before they took the child and went away, the father bowed to the ground and murmured as he rose some Indian words. Hayes could but guess the words, though he understood the two last ones. The sentence had ended, "Dolly Copp." They had learned her name.

Alone that night, Dolly sat on the cat fur, handling the beautiful baskets but Hayes told her she was not counting the greatest gift. No Indian in their wilderness would now molest her. To them all, Dolly Copp was a friend.

CHAPTER XI

ON A DECEMBER DAY Hayes stood near the cabin door equipped for traveling. He was going to Jackson and beyond to the Emery farm for needed food supplies and to obtain Dolly's spinning wheel, loom and yarn, together with many small articles that she needed.

Fearfully she tried to dissuade him from making the trip. "Your ears have not been affronted with one complaint, Hayes. On the fair days we may still be able to clear that field so we may sow in the spring for grazing. With all that venison and salted fish, using the meal sparingly we can live through the short winter months until the good weather comes again."

He turned his anxious eyes and looked long at her. "The winter months are not short, Dolly. They are long. Your need is great. The snow crust is hard and I can travel over it with speed. It may well be my last chance to make the trip."

"What if a violent storm overtake you?"

"There are shelters where I have often sought refuge. If I am delayed you should have no fear."

"Couldn't you with more ease pack the load upon the horse?"

"His feet would break through the crust and tangle in the underbrush, perhaps with a lost shoe or a broken leg."

"Wouldn't a sled on the river ease the carrying?"

"The risk would be great. The ice is still thin. A break through the crust and all would be damaged or lost."

She walked restlessly up and down in great agitation. "If

you would let me go with you."

He frowned. "We waste words. There is more wood than for a week's burning, more food inside the cabin than for a week's need. The horse is safe and can endure. You will bar the door and wait in patience." He embraced her tenderly, removing her clinging hands and stepping out onto the hard crust of snow, bending far over before the freezing wind, soon was lost to sight.

He had said truly; her need was great. She turned slowly toward the fire. Long she stood staring down at the burning logs, then she sat down on her cat-rug, clasped her knees with her small hands and was lost in thought.

Grievously she missed the little Indian girl. For many days no amount of coaxing could persuade the child to speak her name and when she finally did cautiously murmur a word of many syllables, learning it was beyond Dolly's ability. However, when Hayes listened and the little girl pointed to a long scar on her face, he, smiling at the child, said, "It means Scarred Cheek?" She nodded. But Dolly would have none of it. That was no suitable name for a little girl.

"I will call her Cheeka. Somehow that sounds pretty."

Now Dolly sat thinking of her. Little Cheeka. How she had come to love taking care of the little body, washing, dressing, feeding, seeing the strength and activity return. How empty the days were without the child.

Although there was no complaining, Hayes knew. He always seemed to understand and feel her need. Then some days ago she had said to him, "Hayes, I have reason to think we may have a child. I shall note the crescent of the moon and count. My mother taught me that it is in the third moon I shall take care. If it is God's will, He shall reward our care of Cheeka by sending a little girl of our own."

For only a day he went about his work while a hard frown knitted his brows. She must have her loom and spinning wheel. Angrily he thought of the farmer who had broken his promise about delivering the cow. In the spring he would fetch it for her, not one but several. Also sheep. Even goats and hens. He thought, "Her need is great," and he prepared for the journey.

Alone in the wilderness! Could she not have made him understand that fear was greater than any "want?" In the bitter cold and darkness of the night she wakened, "My endurance does not yet equal Hayes'," she thought as she lay trying to differentiate the strange sounds without. What was that crackling noise? Was it ice in the tree branches or wood shrinking in the cold? Was this very cold greater than any she had before known? There was one lone cry fairly rending the night air as though some animal were suffering in anguish. Was that a ferocious hungry wolf? She pictured him standing alone lifting his head toward heaven and howling to the stars as his hunger maddened him. Now he was joined by a chorus of lesser voices. Would he lead his pack to find some poor victim? She saw them, jaws dripping with blood, as they tore and devoured.

There was the sound of many feet running outside the cabin and she shivered as her heart seemed to grow small and fearful. Something of great weight struck hard against the cabin wall. Could the bars of the door withstand a huge brown bear if he smelled the heat and food within?

The wilderness stretched so far in every direction. She was a small and timid and fearful creature, lying alone in this vast forest.

How dark it had grown. Then she realized there were no embers lying thick and warm in the fireplace. She had even lacked his skill in laying the logs for the night. She saw the stones were dark and cold. The fire had burned out.

"I am not worthy," she thought and a sense of shame filled her. Would that she could feel strong arms about her and his voice saying, "There is nothing to fear, Dolly. Nothing will hurt you."

If the day would only come again. Often in the bright sunshine, working with her hatchet beside Hayes she had said, "Never could I be lonesome with those mountain peaks about me. They're so grand. They're like mighty friends guarding us." When this dark night passed and the day should come she would see and feel them again.

She slept for how long she did not know, then wakened. She could see the cabin walls. She drew her knees up tight against her chest. The cold was reaching icy fingers even beneath the blanket and bear skin in which she was wrapped.

She watched the light increase, thinking with shame, "I shall never speak of my cowardice. He shan't hear that the night lasted a hundred years. He must never know."

She rose, kindled the fire, laid on the logs and sat close until the warmth and cheer filled both her and the room. Now she felt the desire to work. There would be, she reckoned, two or three more nights and long days between. They would be as nothing to her. Should she sit, as he had bade her, quiet, useless by the fire, waiting his return? Would he have heeded such an order?

She laughed and ate heartily of the good food. She need not spare the meal for he was bringing more. The dried and salted fish she ate greedily. She made tea and used water lavishly. The well was near and she should go bravely for all she required.

It was the second day. A feeling of comfort came to her as she thought of the horse in the barn—the other living, breathing, friendly member of their household. Why should he miss the opening of the barn door, the usual administrations for his well being and comfort?

She pulled on her boots and lifting her skirts high she went to the barn, tugged at the bars until they were opened, always laughing and chattering in her high-pitched voice. She wound her arms about the horse and laid her face against the neck of the animal. He should be fed, watered, combed and curried and made to feel cared for. Although the task was new to her, she performed it merrily and competently. She returned to the cabin, feeling a glow of satisfaction.

At noon she cooked and ate. She had been a spendthrift

in using the water so she would go to the well and replenish her store. Again in the heavy boots, holding her skirts high with one hand, she went out, closing the cabin door behind her against the bitter cold.

She lowered the bucket, drew it up dripping with the clear sparkling liquid. How heavy it was. She stopped a moment to look up at the mighty peaks that were once again friendly and protecting. She had taken but one step through the snow when she heard a sound that made her stop and listen. From whence it came she could not tell. It seemed to her ears to sound like the low growl of a dog, mingled with a soft but distinct padding sound. She listened and it was repeated. Now she was sure it came from beyond the cabin.

Rather hurriedly she started toward the house but the bucket was heavy and her feet sank in the deep snow. She must not slip on the path made of stones which the Indians had built along the rise approaching the well.

She had taken several steps when the growl, now menacing and nearer, caused her to look up. Then it was that her heart seemed to stop beating and her limbs shook. With dilated eyes she saw the brown bear directly in front of her door. His huge jaws were open, dripping, his small beady eyes were fastened on her.

Terror gave her wisdom. She dropped the bucket and plunged with a fleetness magnified a hundred fold by terror, toward the back of the cabin She heard the great padded feet following her. With such a shriek of horror as must have echoed through the forest she plunged through the snow around to the other side. Did she imagine she felt the hot breath on her neck or was it only the heavy breathing of the animal as somehow, half blind now, in such terror that gave her unwonted strength, she reached the front of the cabin, fell against the door, and somehow closed and barred it?

She had sunk to the floor a weeping, shaking creature. Scarcely breathing, she heard the heavy thuds as the animal pawed and growled. All through the hours of that day her

limbs quivered—even at times she wept at the thought of the horrible fate that she had somehow narrowly avoided.

The darkness of night was closing in. She had no wish for food. She had no wish to light her tallow-dip. Her ears seemed numb with listening for the muffled steps without. Half tremblingly, she carefully arranged her logs, and without undressing, wrapped her blanket about her and laid down in the bunk. A great sickness seemed to pervade her whole being and it was not now only for herself she feared. What if Hayes returned, loaded with his heavy pack, unaware of the great beast?

She could not sleep and the long hours dragged on. In some way she must warn him! The way she chose took courage. With her ear pressed against the door she listened for a long time. Nothing but silence. Surely the beast had roamed off into the forest in search of other prey. Cautiously, slowly, inch by inch, she opened the door, looked about, then against the heavy log that formed their doorstep she set his axe and hatchet. Quickly closing and barring the door, she crept back to bed.

❦

At the door of the Emery farmhouse the father spoke, "Boy, your back will break under such a load."

"It has borne greater."

"There is a gift I wish to make you and Dolly. Without asking, I see how you like these two young hunters. It is no common dog. You shall choose which of the two shall go home with you."

The glow of pleasure in his eyes and face expressed his delight before his, "I thank 'ee, Sir. That is the kind of dog I have long wanted," was spoken.

Two of the farm hands were to drive him through Jackson, and along the rough narrow road as far as was passable for the heavy farm wagon to go. Even to the last Dolly's mother was adding packages and entrusting Hayes with messages, for he had delivered the information concerning the expected child.

Laden with goods and news, he set out. The heavy wagon creaked and rattled as they passed over the deep ruts, never stopping until the road became undefined. From here, Hayes must start alone up the Indian trail. By then the short day was ending. Astonished, the men could only repeatedly ask, "You can travel that near three miles in the dark?"

He could not tell them what it was that so lightened the heavy pack on his back or what seemed to give such strength and cunning to feet and limbs. With only a smile and "I thank 'ee kindly," he was gone and soon out of sight in the deep woods.

It was after midnight, the moon shining clear on the whiteness of the earth when he, leading his dog, emerged from the forest into the beloved clearing and saw the cabin. How beautiful was the night! Above twinkled myriads of stars and the moon hanging out of the deep night-blue sky shed a flood of light on the dark logs of the house.

He was approaching the door when the moonlight, glistening on the axe, turned it to something like a highly polished piece of silver. He stopped, seeing the hatchet and then his sharp eyes saw the trampled snow. All about the house. He followed to the corner, noting the steps from the well and the bucket lying on the snow, its copper bands gleaming.

He was easing the pack from his shoulders to the ground as he called, "Dolly, open."

She wakened, lying still, wondering if she dreamed, then, as he repeated the call, she ran stumbling in her haste and unbolted the door.

He had set the great pack against the house, for there must be unloading before the loom and spinning wheel could be eased through the door. After removing his snow shoes, he entered.

It was he who tied the dog, lighted the tallow-dip, who stirred the fire, placing fresh logs for now she was laughing, crying, patting the dog, exclaiming about him, chattering and strangely trembling so that she sank upon the bunk to conceal her weakness.

To neither of them could come any desire for sleep until many questions were asked and answered. First, he must have explanation of the axe and hatchet and trampled snow. She began haltingly, then in a torrent of words she told all—her frightful cowardice in that long night, her joy in feeling herself brave and calm on the following morning, her trips to the barn, then her escape from the bear.

Through it all he had worked as he listened, removing the ropes from the bundles, carrying in the food, the many packages, then the precious spinning wheel a little harmed but nothing he could not mend. The loom filled the room and soon they could hardly find space for stepping but the talk went on.

There was no word of chiding but she saw the dark frown and the angry light in his eyes. When she said meekly, imploringly, "The lesson you tried to teach me I have learned through fearful suffering, Hayes."

He spoke gravely, "That you are safe is all we will speak of now."

At last, lying in the bunk she spoke of the axe and hatchet. "It was my fear that you should be taken unaware that caused me the deepest anguish, Hayes."

He understood and kissed her tenderly.

Anxiously she added, "He was still here early in the night. I do not think my fears caused me to imagine I heard the beast."

"I do not doubt. It will be necessary to kill him before he does harm."

"You speak as though he was a fly."

He laughed. Then, because there seemed no need of sleep he told her news so exciting that she could scarcely find words enough to express her astonishment. There was talk—not only talk but sound plans—for building a road through the Glen. Far north, some six miles through the forest, there was the place until now called Durand. Its name was changed to Randolph. The government had given title to one man, named Daniel Pinkham, of a tract of land lying on either side of the river south of them in a place that was, much later, to be called for him, Pinkham's Notch. This man would be empowered to build a road connecting Jackson with the town called Randolph. Excitement was deep in Hayes when he explained that the road would cross the river below them and follow his cleared path.

A road to pass their door! When? It would be years and gruelling hard work before it should be accomplished but at such a time their house should face a highway and there would be people and vehicles passing and no longer would they be alone in the vast wilderness.

Then he added, "Two men will be spared by your father. When the ice is thick on the river, sleds will bring the planks and all the planed wood ready for building. In the spring when the ground is so softened that a cellar can be dug, they will come here and we will begin the building of your house."

At last they slept and when she wakened she found Hayes cooking breakfast for his hunger was great. For all the hours of that day, she laughed and talked and exclaimed as she opened the precious packages and together they placed the loom and he mended the spinning wheel and they found the small space of the cabin floor so full that they would always have to move about with care.

So intent and happy was she with her treasures that she scarcely heeded the long hours when he left the cabin without explanation of his activities. One late afternoon, he came across the clearing, the young dog at his heels and with a bag of meat slung over his back while across his shoulders was hung an enormous bearskin. Never had she seen his face so lined, his stooped shoulders so proclaiming his fatigue. She saw he was far spent. There was blood to be cleaned from his clothes but he was curiously silent when she plied him with anxious questions. Only once he smiled, "I do not doubt it is one of the largest skins to be found on any door in this countryside. The beast fought well. We can rest knowing he will trouble us no more."

CHAPTER XII

THROUGH THE BITTER DAYS of storm and such penetrating cold as seemed to reach through the heavy logs, challenging their right to live with only the help of one small fire, they fought through their first winter together.

Hayes was training his fine dog to hunt. Sternly he commanded him to wait for orders, to return from the scent when called, when to hold captive and when to kill, the man exulting in the companionship of the animal he had long wanted against the time when there would be need of protecting livestock.

Deep in the forest he set the new traps he had bought and one day he returned with the skins of twelve sables, telling Dolly, "They should make a pretty collar for your coat." This pleased her as did the fisher which she was already wrapping about her neck.

In the cabin there was a sound that was as music to their ears—the steady hum of the spinning wheel as Dolly's little foot worked the treadle. Steadily and tirelessly the small foot moved. Beautiful were the lengths of yarn, twisted so smoothly and made ready for knitting or weaving. There was besides the wool her mother had sent, a sack of cotton, and flax as well and her bright eyes glowed as she filled every moment of the day with the task at which she was so expert. The loom was but a home-made, crude one and it was with something like awe that Hayes saw her deft fingers manage the warp and woof, finally laying before him cloth so smooth and strong that he could only smile and try to find words for praising.

There were nights when the little cabin seemed to shake and tremble, when the wind rushing through the ravines on the mountain side or across the great forests seemed like some living monster bent on destroying all that was in its path. They heard giant trees crashing to the earth and Dolly wakened but there was no fear.

One day she asked, "Your great eagles have gone from their rocky crags?"

"When there is no fish they must seek it farther south."

"Isn't it strange, Hayes, that you could endure where that great creature cannot?"

"That is but a matter of food. His home will stand. He will return to find it safe and strong in the spring."

"With the same mate throughout his life? Then another brood of eaglets will wait for his hunting to bring them food?"

"That is his way."

'I'd like to see that great nest. My father says that he is the very sign and symbol of our country. Why is he called bald when his head is covered with thick white beautiful feathers?"

"Do you not name a horse splashed with white a pie-bald horse? The word means white. We should have named him White Eagle."

"I've seen one close by after a cruel hunter had brought him down. I was a child but I remember my fear and sorrow at seeing so great a creature dead. His beak was yellow like our corn. My father said he could not exult in seeing one of God's most impressive creatures murdered to please the vanity of one man. He spoke in great anger. Do you feel like that?"

"Your father was right."

"I want to see him. Could we climb to that point next summer?"

"It is too high above the ground for your eyes."

She plied him with questions and found he had seen the nest. "I have heard that once one was weighed and came to near two tons. The tree must be strong to hold such a nest."

He smiled at her. "Each year he adds to it like a man, and, like our own children, the eaglets grow slowly. There is one thing very strange and it can be said of no other bird. When the eaglets leave the nest on the first flight, he soars straight, then circles about and often has gone a full mile before he returns to his home. He is a mighty creature."

She smiled. "It's good to live with him. He is like the great peaks."

He said dryly, "Also like the great storms." He added, "The ice is hard and thick. I hope daily for the sleds and lumber."

But she returned to the matter filling her mind. "When the ice in the river breaks, I shall watch for him. Some fine day I shall hear him call and see his great wings outstretched and wish he could hear me call back to him. I shall say, 'Welcome home, neighbor.'"

He laughed, for he liked her fancy.

Then, one day, the first sled with its load of lumber arrived at their river bank. There was an enormous commotion, men hallooing, a running here and there. Load after load was drawn upon the frozen stream and soon piles of planks were stacked beside their cabin.

Dolly was often lost in wonder. How could Hayes find the days long enough to hunt for their meat and small game, bring in their needed fresh fish, plow their cleared land, plant his crops, start the more extensive garden of her wanting, dig a cellar and build a house. She wondered.

In the last months of winter, on days without blinding snow storms he had felled more trees on the path leading to the spot where the new road was planned to cross the river. He had cleared out the underbrush and now workmen had erected a narrow bridge.

When that was finished, he had worked near the barn constructing a long shed joined on one side to the abode of his horse. This was to be a cabin for the workmen. There were three bunks, a large flat stone on which to build their fire and

a hole in the roof to allow the smoke to escape. It was strong and snug; sleeping in it no man wrapped in blankets would suffer from cold. In their cabin they again arranged the loom and all their cooking utensils so that Dolly would have freedom of movement in preparing food and still leave space for all to be fed before the fireplace.

It was exciting and Dolly chattered and laughed as they prepared for the building of this house.

There came a time when her eyes opened wide in that wonder and she exclaimed, "The lumber grows to many times the size of our cabin. Is it to be so large a house?"

"I plan to build a good house."

She must wait and watch. As the days grew long and the sun's welcome rays melted the snow, the blood seemed to flow again warm and quick in their bodies. No more the poulticing of hands after work in the bitter zero weather. The good days of "sugaring off" came and Hayes carried in the buckets of sap and she "boiled it down" in her large iron kettle. Now the heavy coats, the fur caps were thrown off and the men sweated as they worked. Their big pickaxes were heard breaking into the cellar area and soon, within the oblong marked off by stakes, a great hole appeared. Now the shovels lifted and flung the soil aside. Now stone was laid on stone until the firm wall appeared. Now great kettles of porridge steamed over the fire, larger hunks of bear flesh or venison or game brought odors that made hungry men's mouths water in anticipation. They brought her flour and they marveled at her dumplings and puddings and wheat cakes.

One laughed boisterously as he told her, "Your fame is spreading through the countryside. Many would gladly brave the trip to eat the food they hear of."

Gaily she answered, "You only flatter that you may see more wheat cakes on your plate."

As the strong beams were placed and the outside boards were ascending foot by foot, Hayes often left them to turn his crude plow in the moist earth. One night when the others slept he sat with frowning brows.

"What bothers you, Hayes?"

The frown disappeared and he smiled, "Only the small-ness of the fields. With one bushel of oats, I can reap sixty bushels in harvest. The need is great for more cleared land. Another year should see the paying of the last bushel due the government. For all that which we owe Mr. Emery, several years will be needed for we must have sufficient for ourselves."

She looked astonished. "Surely we aren't in debt to my father. Isn't it his right to give to his daughter?"

The muscles of his face set hard. "Of that I will judge. The land is rich and to no man could I be beholden."

"But to my father?"

"The debt will be paid."

"As you will. But I would like to say something."

He waited. She looked down toward her dress. Beautifully she had woven the cloth and fashioned a loose gown. It hung straight and perhaps shapeless, hiding her enlarging figure.

"I don't speak to complain but so that my mind may be at ease. My time, if I have counted rightly, will come in harvest. The services of some good woman will be needed. All may go well—but again—others have had troubles with which we might not be able to cope."

"Much thought has been given the matter, Dolly. If it is your wish to go home to your mother, I will take you in good time. There is a Doctress woman that goes about that busi-ness with proper knowledge. If you wish we will speak for her well ahead of your need."

She thought. "My wish would be to have my daughter born in our new home should the rooms be ready."

He was pleased. "Now I would talk of your ovens."

He explained that in the kitchen and across from the open-ing door into the large parlor whose windows faced the rising sun, he planned to fill the wall with wide fireplace and built-in ovens. Crudely, with his fingers stiffened with hard labor, he drew on brown paper a sketch of tiers of brick ovens. She watched with sharp critical eyes, correcting this line, adding

here and there, for both knew that wall with its great open fire and many brick ovens was to be the center and heart of their home.

Then as the summer days grew long, she went out and looked with eagerness as the chimney rose. On those summer days she rose with the first rays of light for the men must be fed. Often after the evening meal was cleared away, her eager smile, her bright blue eyes, her never-ending chatter seemed to fill the hours with some gaiety that spurred them all on to work until darkness came.

Twice in that early spring Hayes had made long trips through the forest, for no back but his could endure the weight of such loads and no patience and skill but his could lead a cow over that trail.

When the fine creature was led into the small barn he turned to Dolly. "You will now care for her. She is your own." She stood looking into the soft brown eyes of the cow as though gazing at a precious jewel lying in a satin-lined box. Her merry laugh rang out and the men watching her joined in.

Milk. It had been one of her "great needs" and now there should not be one drop wasted.

A youngish man whose eyes often followed her and whose laughter always joined quickly in hers, now spoke thoughtfully, "I make you a promise. On my next visit home I shall return with a pig for you. Should he refuse to follow Hayes' trail I shall carry him all the way in my arms."

"And then you'll build a barn large enough to house all the animals?"

"Hayes has already marked the place."

There came a hot summer day when the roof was protecting her new house. She left her loom to see the first of the wide smooth boards laid for the floor of her kitchen. There soon followed the windows and although there would be no plaster on the walls until the cold should force indoor work, the lower floor was ready for her moving.

From the little cabin they eased through the narrow door her loom and spinning wheel, her clothes were carried and hung upon the pegs in the ample closet. The sun was high in the blue above as Hayes lighted the fire and watched the logs begin to burn. Dolly came in carrying an armful of kitchen utensils. Silently she set them in place; then she knelt before the fire.

Hayes waited but she did not speak. Then he saw she was weeping, her head bent. He laid his hand hard on her shoulder. She bit her lips and dried her tears. "It's only my weakness, Hayes. I am overcome. My time is near."

"The woman shall be fetched. I will start now."

Two days later, he led a white horse up the trail and on it was seated a Doctress woman "full of knowledge." And while the workmen lying in their bunks restlessly listened, a cry, such as only Indian squaws had known before in that wilderness, was heard in the new house. A boy was born and in the kitchen the first "eaglet" lay in the cradle Hayes had fashioned, while the woman "full of knowledge" washed and comforted and finally walked to the cabin door thinking to wake Hayes. The cabin was empty. When she returned to the house, she found him fully dressed looking down at Dolly.

She held the fine boy for him to see. His stern mouth relaxed, his eyes were dimmed with moisture, but all he said was, "I thank 'ee kindly."

They named the boy Jeremiah Copp. They would call him Jerry.

CHAPTER XIII

WHEN COMPARED to the large mansions found here and there along the much traveled turnpikes to the south and toward the sea or compared to fine city houses, this dwelling in the wilderness might have appeared small, plain and poor; however, no ship-owner counting the treasures brought to him over the sea from India or China could have viewed his possessions with more satisfaction than did Hayes Copp and Dolly on these fall days in the Glen.

The harvest had again been beyond his expecting, the better because his good dog had been trained to frighten away the deer that would devour his grain in the nights while he slept. He had paid more of his government debt and with clever bartering for his crops he was buying furniture for his house.

On one fall day, hearing him working outdoors, Dolly opened the front door to watch him. With his prodigious strength he rolled a flat stone into place to form a step to the ground. She had wanted a "door rock."

Now one could step to the sill with ease and enter the little hall. On the south side was her large low-ceilinged parlor. The wide boards of the floor were laid strong and firm. Across one end was the stone fireplace with deep brick ovens. Already, as darkness compelled him to end his day's work on the barn, Hayes had fashioned two fine corner cupboards and on the shelves Dolly's gold-edged china, pewter and silver-set, shone, though not more brightly than her eyes as she cleaned

and polished and set each piece in place, changing and trying it this way and that until all were arranged to her satisfaction. Far enough from the fireplace as not to interfere with those seeking warmth, yet near enough to feel the comfort, she had placed her loom and spinning wheel. There was a small table to hold her tallow dip when she worked at night and close to her feet was the cradle.

After the evening meal was cleared away she often sat suckling the healthy boy, then, after laying him in the cradle, her foot gently and steadily rocked him to sleep even as her hands were engaged with her yarns. She prided herself on her ability to weave and fashion everything they wore.

Across the room against the wall stood perhaps their greatest luxury—that for which Hayes had bargained most astutely—a wide, low bed complete with two mattresses, one made of corn husks, while resting on it, to be shaken and aired daily, was spread a thick mattress made of feathers. A door from this parlor opened out to the side and the two windows allowed the sun to bring in its cheer even as snow piled up to the sills or half covered the small panes of glass. Near the window was set her company table and a few straight chairs.

Behind the parlor were two bedrooms still unfinished. At the moment this space seemed wasteful to Dolly for except when weaving or sewing her busy hours were spent mostly in the kitchen where again was found a large stone fireplace, and deep ovens. At one side stood a plank table and arranged on pegs about the wall were her cooking utensils. Close at hand were her sacks of meal, her tub of maple sugar, for no other sugar would be used for many years. In the small back room was hung their venison, bear meat or game for their fare was still composed of little they did not produce on their rich land or bring in from the river or from the wild life with which the forest teemed.

On the day before the two workmen were leaving to return to Mr. Emery's, they sat with Hayes about the table near

the kitchen windows and slowly, carefully, together they com-puted the debt Hayes owed them. When all were satisfied with the amount, Hayes fetched a leather pouch and counted out the money which each should receive.

When he turned to the younger man and asked the price of the pig, the man laughed but there was indignation also in his face.

"You cannot pay for that pig. If Mistress Dolly doesn't want it? I shall take it home. Moreover, in the spring I plan to fetch her the bees she covets that she may have hives and honey. If they are to be paid for, in Bartlett they shall remain."

There was laughter as Dolly said her pig should be locked in her closet if it proved necessary for her to guard it. Then turning to Hayes she chided him to have the grace to join her in thanking the man for their pig. Smilingly Hayes spoke, "I thank 'ee." Then he added, was there nought they could give the young man to express their gratitude. A gift? From this poor place?

Surprising them, he answered, "With my earnings I am setting up a home. To my girl, I would wish to give one small piece of Mistress Dolly's weaving. If it please her—one small piece like that of the blue that lies upon her new chest."

Quickly Dolly brought the piece of cloth and laid it in his hands. "That I can replace. The pig and the bees are harder to come by."

Then in the parlor she spread a snowy cloth and out of her ovens she took such a meal as they would long remember and from their cabin they brought what was left of a jug of "O-be-joy-ful," as the rum was commonly called. On the fol-lowing morning she heaped their plates with cakes and cov-ered them with maple syrup and soon called hearty greetings to them as they went off toward the south with their packs on their backs.

Now they were left alone to face the winter that was fast closing in. One day when Hayes returned from shoveling a path to the barn she questioned, "Did you not use poor judg-

ment in placing the big barn so far back from our home? It is a journey to reach it and much useless labor to shovel snow every day. Besides, does it not loom up amazing large against the sky?" She laughed, "So mighty in size and so full of emptiness. The cow scarcely knows the horse is at the other end."

He looked at her as a quizzical smile deepened in his eyes.

"Back from this house I see an ell with a shed, large and airy where there will be room for all our supplies; where you will make your tallow dips and store barrels and cases of all you need. Then I see a dairy where there might be the making of butter and cheese and beyond that a shop for working with tools, sparing your kitchen floor. When these stand each in its place, the barn will not be far distant and can be reached from within and there would be safety for man and beast."

Beneath the fair hair parted so smoothly, the blue eyes were raised to his and she laughed, "All that had not entered my dull mind!"

Still he watched her with a thoughtful expression, his face grave. "You find it lonely now that the workmen are gone. The loud talk and much laughter was to your liking."

As though startled, she raised her head and looked sharply at him. There was an edge to her voice as she answered, "You like to look into my head? There are none of my thoughts hidden from you? Why shouldn't I find it lonely? For months there have been many men coming and going, many mouths to feed and fun—much fun—laughing and joking. Now it is all quiet. Don't you know, Hayes, that you are a very silent man?"

He spoke gently, "I have many thoughts but I cannot always put them into words. It is a fault I have tried to mend without success."

When he ceased speaking they sat in silence. Quietly the snow fell, flake by flake against the cold window pane. The baby, Jerry, slept in his cradle; the dog lay with nose resting on outstretched paws. The eternal quiet of the deep forest seemed to pervade the room.

She rose, walked to the window and looked out through the small panes of glass. Yes, again they were alone in the great wilderness. A year ago, there had been the excitement of be-ing the talk of all her neighbors and friends, there had been the romantic dreams of love and adventure, the daily stimu-lus of persuading her parents to accept her decision, the activ-ity as she prepared for her marriage, weaving her sheets and blankets and fashioning her clothes; then the agitation as she waited for the wedding day, the ceremony, the journey.

With enthusiasm she had learned to take her part in his life, though she had hardly become acquainted with the Glen before they were waiting for the sleds to arrive with the planks for building. The spring and summer had been filled with days too short for all the work and excitement she wanted to crowd into them.

Now there would be no sound of many hammers, men laughing, joking, flattering and admiring her skill in cooking, weaving and spinning. She remembered Hayes' own words, "The winter is not short, Dolly. The winter is long."

She turned to him with that sudden sweetness in her smile and voice that enchanted him. "Hayes, have I said one word of complaining?"

"No, Dolly, there has not been one word of complaining."

"Then why do you rebuke me for being lonely?"

Again he looked both confused and perplexed. "Rebuke?" He stared at her. "I spoke only because I do not know what to do to keep you from being lonely."

She looked down at him, a rather wistful expression in her eyes. "Perhaps you will be patient. How many times I've heard my father say that you can change the habits of a man or a beast but never can you change his nature. I've watched you go alone up that great mountain through brambles and thickets, climbing until you are far out of my sight. I have often pondered as I tried to imagine you alone—one man alone tracking a deer or fighting an angry bear. I tried to imag-ine you living alone in this great wilderness, never forgetting

my first night when I would have given all the wealth of the world to have heard another human voice. When I alone you seem to grow stronger. I become a weak thing." She smiled.

"You cannot change my nature, Hayes."

He rose. Clumsily he tried to find words to tell her that he wanted only her happiness, only the sound of her voice; that he would not want her nature changed. "Soon, Dolly, the boy will grow and be lively. There will be work enough in plastering and painting and planning in the house. The days pass quickly when there is work to fill the hours."

She smiled as she watched him fetch his coat and cap. He went out the door followed by his dog and soon she heard his axe ringing against the tree he was felling to clear the road that should some day pass their dwelling," She thought, "He is a patient man."

Because of the many tasks always waiting and their arduous labor they ate their meals, sometimes hastily, on the plank table in the kitchen but when Thanksgiving Day came Dolly prepared a suitable feast. One morning she filled the oven with hot coals. Late in the day she swept them out leaving all clean and yet hot. Into this deep oven she placed great pots of pork and beans, puddings and a wild turkey that Hayes had brought her. Closing the wooden shutters of the oven, she went about her usual tasks, knowing that through the long hours of the night the food would be cooked to her liking.

On Thanksgiving Day she spread her snowy linen, smoothing out the deep fringe, then laid her fine china. On the iron crane above the fire, she hung her kettle to boil ready for tea. Outside there raged a great storm—Hayes had said the snow was already full five feet deep on the level—but there was no trembling or shaking of their dwelling; no bitter icy fingers reached in between the cracks of logs. When they sat down to the great feast Jerry, now three months old, was set in the high chair which Hayes had fashioned for him. Dolly wore, as always, her gold beads but now in her better gown fastened at the neck with her gold pin she sat with folded hands look-

ing across the snowy cloth at Hayes. He spoke with gravity.

"It would be fitting to give thanks."

She nodded, her eyes bright. "And you will mention the good milk? And perhaps ask that the cow and pig, like us, may endure the storms and cold?"

He asked. His words were few and simple, utterly devoid of eloquence but it was in their hearts that there was great thanksgiving for the corn and wheat and oats and milk and the salted fish and the game that Nature had provided so plentifully. Then they fell to and ate such quantities of the food as only healthy bodies could consume.

She had cleared away the remains of the meal, suckled and rocked to sleep their child. He had, on snowshoes, gone to the barn to care for their animals against the increasing cold and at last they lay warm in their wide bed. She spoke.

"If it is God's will on next Thanksgiving Day there will be another with us. I hope it will be a daughter."

He reached out his hand to hold hers. "That is well. It pleases you?"

"It is what I wish."

Now when the storms and cold forced him to remain indoors, he found the hours too short to accomplish all he willed. He plastered the rooms, laid floors, cleverly fashioned more wooden pegs on which to hang various articles. There came a time when paint was applied to walls and this was always planned according to her wishes.

One winter day Dolly was so anxious to see the accomplishments about which she had asked that she followed him through the narrow path which he had shoveled to the barn. Here she expressed her amazement at his handiwork. Some eight inches above the wide boards that formed the floor of the barn, he had fastened a heavy timber extending through the length of the structure. Six feet above this he had fastened another heavy timber and in both he had bored round holes. He had placed poles which fitted into both lower and upper holes perfectly. To keep the poles from slipping, he had placed

a wooden pin below the upper hole. He showed her with some pride how he had fixed a smooth yoke about the pole before setting each in place and now the animal could stand or lie down as the smooth yoke moved up or down. The way the heavy yoke about the cow's neck and the small stanchel yoke were made to slide easily together, how he had used brown ash and bent it U-shape, how he had fashioned the small wooden pin and the large pins—some sixteen inches long— kept her exclaiming. "Why, Hayes, how simple spinning and weaving seem now. Never could I have devised such a thing. It is all so strong and works so well. And you intend to set them all down the side of the barn?"

"Soon we shall need them." Then he drew a long breath and smiled, "Is it not good after waiting so long, to smell cow manure?"

She laughed merrily and wrinkled up her nose, inhaling deeply. "It's good to smell manure in our own barn."

During those winter days her only complaining was when she found her sacks of wool and flax and cotton exhausted. "When the spring planting time comes, I would have a strip of land which I have chosen near the river and on it I will grow my own flax. I know how to raise it and pull and heckle it and spin it on the wheel. I know how to weave it and bleach it in the sun. We shall have more table covers and sheets and cloth for garments against the summer heat. You should teach me to help you shear those sheep. When the wool is clean and carded I shall weave it into thick blankets and clothes of such warmth as we have not known."

He smiled, not at all because of her boasting, knowing it was her way to talk; but knowing also that such linen and blankets would be theirs did she but have the wool and flax with which to work.

So patiently they labored and waited until again the snow melted and the horse was harnessed to draw the plow and the fields again lay ready for the planting. In journeys so hard that only his cunning could devise ways of transport-

ing them, he had brought more cows and sheep and in a shed which he had built were hens for Dolly's care. The young workman was true to his promise and there would be honey and he taught her the tricks of caring for bees. She had given him another piece of her fine linen and, in his short visit, listened thirstily to his news of all that had happened in the towns so far south.

While Hayes was working in his fields, Dolly was intent on a planting entirely of her own. She had roamed through the woods on many days looking with sharp eyes for small apple trees. Now she claimed a generous section of land lying off at the side of the house and reaching toward the barn and in this space, marking each planting by a strong stick, she dug and set her "wildings," or sowed apple seed. Some day she would have apples for cooking, for drying ready to use in winter and for the much valued cider.

When she worked at planting this garden she must devise a way to care for her baby boy. Should she like the squaw strap him to her back? Hayes scowled his displeasure at the notion. Through many generations Indian babies had been inured to such strapping but the white man's child was to grow strong and healthy only when enjoying complete activity. Already the child ran or crawled, never resting until asleep and his legs grew hard and the muscles of his arms which grasped and pulled grew mighty for his size. So Hayes made a harness of those same sort of thongs which strapped an Indian's child, but this was a clever harness and a noose was slipped over a pole and the child could run to his liking.

Slung over her shoulder Dolly carried a horn which she was to blow if there should appear on the horizon anything that promised ill; then she could quickly slip the noose and run to the house with the precious boy. Many sheep could be spared but not their son.

So, watchful, she planted her orchard and dreamed of red-cheeked apples that some day the boy would relish.

Soon, again, she wore the shapeless gown of homespun

even though about her neck was always clasped the string of gold beads. To Hayes' eyes, those beads were more harmoni-ous with the yellow of her hair, the sparkle of her blue eyes and the delicacy of her complexion than with the homely dress but of this he did not speak. Her figure had grown large but often she laughed, "For my own work, I believe, Hayes, my endurance is now as great as yours."

He only smiled and looking over his fields remarked, "Our need is still for more cleared land."

As she walked with him across the clearing, seeing the space which should be her orchard, the larger garden, the fields planted to grain, the fine cleared road in front of their door, she marvelled. "You had only two hands, Hayes. I will tell you this now. Little did I know how mighty a thing is the wilderness. When I first came to your cabin, I feared that forest. Once I dreamed at night that it laughed at you and the wind and storm and trees closed in and choked you and no man knew that you had ever thought to subdue it. Now—the Glen is a rich home." She looked up at the mountain tower-ing above them. "Do you know what gave me courage?"

He waited, listening, his brows meeting in a frown.

"When you told me of the eagle and his strong home. One day I looked up and saw him soaring through the sky. His nest had stood through all the winter storm. I told myself that so should our home. I believe God has given man strength as great as the eagle's even though he lacks wings to fly above the mountain tops. I think he has given you as great courage."

Still he frowned. "Your head is filled with many fancies, Dolly. I like to hear them. Still—I can never clear the forest of bears, and in the spring they will take your lambs. The wolves will scent our young cattle in the fall and cannot be stood off by one dog and one man. Now that you have a poultry yard the skunks and coons and foxes will be your daily visitors. When the sun is still hot on August days, there may come sudden frost to damage our crops."

Her face sobered. "It fills me with anger, Hayes. I would

fight them all. But you can lay more traps?"

"That I will do."

"If one could sleep at night, the other by day—"

"That talk is idle. We will sleep in our bed."

She turned away. "It is still the wilderness?"

"It is still the wilderness."

Fetching her clean buckets she went to the barn to milk her cows. Resting her forehead against the smooth brown flanks of the animals she sighed often and spoke aloud as was her habit. "There are but two of us and the babe to guard, for now he has outgrown long hours in the cradle and there is no mischief he cannot manage to get into. I cannot, like a squaw, strap him to my back and soon his naughty hands will learn to lift the latch on the door, then I shall know not how to deal with him."

She carried the precious buckets of milk to her kitchen and often in the days following she started in the night at the fierce barking of the dog. Often she hardly wakened yet knew that Hayes had sprung from his bed, seized his musket and run out. Many a night she waited to hear the sharp retort from his gun. She sighed with relief when he again lay by her side but she did not question him until the morning.

It was in late June, Hayes said, "I intend to make the journey in the morning. The Doctress woman must have word now that you may be sure of her coming in good time."

Never, when his many journeys to bring cattle had delayed him overnight, had she feared to be alone. Her eyes had grown keen, her ears sensitive to every sound and, though cautious and alert, she was unafraid.

"This time I do not need the dog. I shall leave him with you but he cannot wholly protect you. That you well know yourself."

She laughed. "I fear nothing for myself. For Jerry, I will take care."

"I shall return by morning."

"No, Hayes. All those miles by day and then again all through the night?"

"I will decide that."

Before the sun was above the horizon she had cooked his breakfast and watched him disappear into the dark shadow of the woods.

It was a perfect June day. Overhead the sun burned bright in a clear blue sky. Softly through the warm air came that summer sound that seemed like the humming of all living things. Almost she thought one could see the grain springing up inch by inch out of the rich soil.

Merrily she hummed and chattered to Jerry as the hours wore on and she attended to her many household tasks. Toward noon clouds began to darken the sky and there was thunder. She looked out of the window, telling Jerry, "It is deceitful like an April day." However, only a few drops of rain fell.

Then came the hour when she must go to her milking and feeding of the animals. That a day so quiet, so uneventful could bring at its close an experience that she would tell and retell throughout her life would have seemed fantastic to her at that moment. Yet she would recall that she started for the door to leave the boy locked securely safe in the house when her heart seemed heavy with sudden fear as she looked at him. Obeying her impulse she turned back, picked him up and with buckets swinging in her hands started for the barn.

She was large with child but her strength was great and she carried him easily. Approaching the barn, she charged the dog to bring in the animals. With the barking at their heels the cows docilely meandered to the barn door. She opened and went in. There was one cow missing. Sternly she ordered the dog to fetch the last cow while she went to work after tying Jerry to a post.

As she milked, she heard the constant barking of the dog; then annoyed, she realized that the sound instead of coming nearer was growing fainter. She finished her task and setting

her pails in a safe place went to look for cow and dog. There was no sign of either. Perplexed she took Jerry in her arms and walked toward the river. Anger seized her as she heard the distant barking, for it was coming from the forest beyond the stream. The stupid beast had wandered far. Should the animal go on and on and the dog return without her, the loss would be great.

Some short way down the stream she knew a safe fording place. Holding her skirts high in one hand and with the baby in her arms, she stepped into the stream. The rocks were slippery but she reached the other bank without mishap.

Now following the faint sound of barking she hurried through the underbrush. When fallen logs and heavy branches blocked her way she was forced to turn back, wondering desperately how the large cow had made its way, surely along some easier path. Sometimes she talked aloud. "How stupid I am. If it were Hayes in this forest or any ignorant Indian there would be marks on trees or broken leaf or foot prints to guide them. To me it's still all alike."

Now she began calling in her high, clear voice. "Come Boss, come Boss, come Boss." Harder she fought her way, for now the barking, though faint, was surely nearer. Soon she must come upon them. How long she fought her way through the woods she would not know. Again and again she shifted the heavy boy from arm to arm but still she trudged on. "I could never face Hayes if, gone only one day, he found us poorer by the loss of a fine cow. It shall not happen."

Closer and closer she came to the barking and then through the dense woods she saw the brown flank of the animal. When at last she reached it, she patted the dog and with a firm hold of the cow turned back. Back? Where was back? Then a fear such as she had never experienced since her encounter with the bear, overcame her. To be lost in the woods. With her baby? At night? Nothing could save them if wolves should hunt them down. A terrifying blackness seemed to clamp down on her mind as she actually saw the little limbs being torn

apart by dripping jaws. She would have sunk to the earth in weakness had not the baby begun to whimper as though knowing her fear.

Bitterly she thought, "And I boasted of my endurance..."

She peered up through the trees but the sun had sunk so low that she could not be sure of shadows to help her tell east from west or north from south. Then her hope centered on the dog. He stood beside her wagging his tail, proud of having performed his task of cornering the cow. What should she do? Many times she had heard Hayes order the dog home. She knew that did she but say the word "home," he would run off to obey, leaving her. If she could only talk to him, how cleverly he would take her to the river. She looked at him, patted his head and could have wept. He was her only protection.

There was a dimness coming in the thick woods. She must try to get out. Slowly and desperately hoping to see landmarks, she moved ahead, leading the cow and carrying the baby. How long she struggled she did not know but when she saw darkness creeping in, knew the shadows were growing blacker and blacker, she felt faint and weak and filled with sickness. Still she could not rest or allow herself to weep as she longed to do. More and more desperately on and on she pressed. Over and over she patted the dog's head and said to him, "Take me home, Rover. Take me home, Rover. Home to master?"

Now she let him go ahead and frantically she followed wherever he led. Her little shoes were soaked with water and caked with mud; her dress was torn to shreds but none of that mattered; only to save her child and the cow and get out of the woods.

Her faith was pinned entirely to the dog. When he ran from her to startle some small animal in the brush she called desperately to him and always he returned obediently and she hugged and patted him. Sometimes he stood still and barked ominously as he did in the night when wolves or fox were near the house. Once as he seemed to stand listening, her own ears

strained also to hear. In one such silence sudden tears gushed from her eyes. Surely she had heard it—the sound of running water. Had she only imagined it? With new strength she pressed on. Now she was sure and she could have shouted with joy. Closer and closer it came until she saw the faint light shining on the surface of the water.

Now they were all standing on the bank of the river but surely she knew not where she was, for here the current was running swift and strong and the banks seemed closer together. Which way led to home she had no way of knowing. Should she start in the wrong direction to find the fording place she might wander throughout the night.

Again her only hope was the dog but when she said, "Home Rover," he plunged into the stream and desperately she called and called until he returned to her side.

She must start one way or another; so they made their way along the bank, the baby crying in discomfort. As the river widened she felt sure of a shallow place and carefully, step by step, she found footing, forcing the reluctant animal to follow while the dog barked and turned and returned as though beside himself with excitement.

Now dripping, cold and miserable she followed the dog, calling him when he ran too far ahead and feeling sure he was leading them home.

When she saw the clearing and the house dim in the night-light, she could not control the tears that streamed from her eyes. Angrily she closed the barn door on the cow and made her way to her home. Within, she went straight to her closet and took down a fine piece of meat and patted the dog as he ate. Not until that was done did she undress Jerry and feed him and lay him in his cradle.

She had barred the door and now rekindled a fire on the hearth, for she was cold and wet and far spent.

When Hayes returned, fatigued, in the early morning she had not awakened. The baby lay wide-eyed but happily quiet in his cradle. In a heap on the floor were her torn and wet clothes.

It was he who prepared breakfast and ministered to her. Frightened thinking her delirious, he heard her say again and again, "The cow is safe in the barn. There was no loss." Then again, "There was no loss."

It was not until the baby cried and she must hold him to her breast that she seemed like herself. Then she poured out the entire story of her stupidity.

There was no word of chiding but when he had attended to all the chores he sat down beside her. "The Doctress woman will come in good time. Now you will take some needed rest."

Once she said, "Hayes, it is a fearful thing to be lost in a deep woods at night with a baby and a cow."

He replied dryly, "It is a fearful thing to be lost in the woods."

CHAPTER XIV

THROUGH THAT SPRING and early summer when heavy rains compelled him to stop his outdoor work, Hayes had laid the floors in the bedrooms back of the parlor. He plastered the walls, and in each room there was set up a bed and small chest.

When her time grew close, Dolly spread one bed with her hand-woven sheets and with great pride laid upon it a beautiful cover of her cherished blue. This she had woven with a design in white that caused Hayes to marvel at her cleverness. Again Hayes led the white horse on which the Doctress woman was seated through the woods and their hearts were warmed with her praise and wonder at what they had accomplished.

One night he paced the kitchen floor in great anxiety as hours wore on and ominous sounds telling him of Dolly's suffering came from the parlor. Often he brushed beads of sweat from his own brow, for it was not until the dark hour immediately before the dawn that a cry was heard and soon the Doctress woman told him that another man-child, as she said, "as fine a boy as my eyes have ever beheld," had been born. They named him Nathaniel and now their little Jerry had a brother, Nat, who should oust him from his cradle.

Only once in those hard years had Dolly made the journey to her home but now a messenger, sent by Mr. Emery, came to tell them that Dolly's mother was "poorly" too

poorly for any travelling" and had a "great yearning in her heart" that they should bring the babes and eat with them on Thanksgiving Day.

Hayes discerned the longing in Dolly to see her mother. She had always sternly conquered her spells of home-sickness but Hayes knew those times well when she was wont to chatter of her home and girlhood days.

The winter had closed in early and the snow was deep. Besides it was the season when violent hurricanes had been known to sweep across their valleys and ravines destroying much of the work of Nature as well as the puny attainments of man. That their cows, their sheep, their poultry could not live without their protection, both knew.

Even as she bit back tears, Dolly said firmly that they must not leave the Glen. Equally firmly, Hayes said he would take her and return again for her.

One day he harnessed the horses and attached to it a rude sled which he had fashioned. With many blankets and bear skins, he made her and the babies comfortable and led them through the trail that by now had been so well trodden as to be quite passable. Leaving them at the Emery's, he returned in the night. When the holiday was over he went again and brought them safe home.

It was late in the day when they arrived and soon Hayes had a great blaze in the fireplaces. Out of the deep oven, with a long two-pronged fork, Dolly took the remnants of the tur-key and Indian pudding which she had prepared for Hayes before she left. The babies were sleeping when they sat down to eat. She had walked about the house, going from room to room, looking lovingly at her precious possessions, silent for her, but as she sat at the table she spoke with a deep sigh of contentment. "Hayes, it was worth all the long journey to see my mother's joy in her grandchildren. And my father was filled with pride. He crawled on the floor and played with Jerry like a boy. It was worth all the journey. But" —she looked about and her bright eyes glowed, "it is good to be here. Like the

eagle, I return to my own nest." And she asked little intimate questions about each of their four cows, about her hens, and concerning all his activities, that filled him with a happiness greater than any he had known before.

When the meal was cleared away, she fetched the bag containing all the flax and linen and cotton which her mother had given to her. Happily she sorted, making each ready for her spinning. Then, sitting before the fire, she stretched out her little feet to warm them at the blaze. She still wore her good wool dress with a fine linen collar fastened with the gold pin. The soft gold of her beads shone in the firelight; but now her fingers were nervously twisting and turning the beads and he saw that something was bothering her.

Never had she seemed to his eyes so pretty, so dainty or more alluring, yet there was that in her bright eyes that he did not understand.

She was gazing down at her little feet. His eyes followed hers. As was her custom, she had left her heavier calfskin shoes in the kitchen. Always when she came in for the night she took them off where they should be cleaned of mud and oiled for out-of-door use, then changed to her fine kid shoes which she wore in the house.

She spoke with a show of gaiety. "I left with my father an order which he will, when the occasion arrives, send to Portland—an order for a new pair of shoes. These are well worn. When someone chances to come this way in the spring, they shall be brought to me."

He frowned. Well she knew that the pouch where money was kept was empty and that he had gone deeply into debt for the beds and chests and for the medicines she had purchased and for bottles for feeding Jerry who must now do without her breast and for many useful but, to them, costly articles.

His eyes were stern beneath the frowning brow. "Would it not have been more seemly to have bought a pair of shoes in Jackson? You would pay so great a price for shoes made so fine and to your order when there is no money and shall not

be until after another harvest? I have calculated closely and though I clear more land and plant more in the spring, even a greater harvest will scarcely fill our needs and meet our debts."

She lowered her head and under the fair smooth brow her eyes were fastened on the little feet. Not even in the summer heat would she wear Indian moccasins as did other pioneer women, for that fine arch should not be flattened. "I've ordered the shoes. If you refuse to accept them I shall beg my father for a gift of them. He won't refuse me."

Then, though red stained his forehead, he laughed. "You know quite well, Dolly, the shoes shall be paid for and I shall do the paying. No one else has that right."

She smiled. "Then it doesn't anger you that I gave the order?"

He again looked down at the little feet and laughed. "It gives you great pleasure to go about the house in your fine shoes."

"Doesn't it give you pleasure?"

He rose. "We must sleep. It is late." As he undressed and banked the fire he thought, "There is in her that great vanity. She will work like a man in the field or in the wood or in the barn. She will care for her poultry yard and shear the sheep or kill and dress a turkey but there is also in her some great love of her silver set, her china, her gold beads, her ring and her gold pin and even of her little feet and fine shoes."

When she had suckled the babe and at last stretched out in the soft bed, she spoke pleasantly. "If you had forbidden the shoes, Hayes, I would have made no complaining."

In the darkness he smiled but he was too perplexed for answering.

In the depth of that hard winter, word was brought to them that her mother had died. So deeply she grieved that he knew not how to console her. Alone in the house with her babies, she sometimes bent her head and wept. There were brothers, some married and living off on their own farms, one gone to the city, one left to carry on with her father but was

she not the only girl-child? Should she not have been with her mother to be by her bed and give what only a daughter can give of love and understanding in that last hour? Sometimes the great privations of the frontier pressed too hard on the hearts of women. The only girl-child. How her mother must have loved suckling a daughter at her breast. She must have loved fashioning little dresses and knowing the companionship of the kind that only a daughter could give.

She did not try to explain to Hayes why her grief so overwhelmed her. Neither did she try to explain when she took her father's death in the spring. Side by side they would be lying in the small family graveyard but those graves she could not visit. She was a woman of the frontier. More, she was a woman who had freely chosen to share a man's great adventure in the wilderness.

Hayes well knew her great desire for a daughter. Proud of her boys? His delight in them was no whit greater than hers. They were such fine boys, strong, healthy, so full of activity that she laughingly said she could scarcely cope with them. Coming but little more than a year apart they should grow up in a companionship that would be pleasant to see. No sooner was Jerry running about the house on two sturdy legs than little Nat was creeping after him.

In the long summer days they must have sunshine and the freedom of the out-of-doors so Hayes built a strong fence and an enclosure in which they could tumble and run and shout and tussle or quarrel as the mood was on them. However, in spite of the fence, she must be always vigilant against enemies with either two or four legs that might molest them. It was in their second summer. One day Hayes was on the long slope of the mountain with his musket seeking game when his dog began a furious barking. Making his way toward the sound, he found the dog beneath a tree looking up into the branches as he darted first to one side then to the other, wagging his tail violently as his master approached.

Coming close, Hayes peered up and smiled as he saw a fine little bear cub clinging desperately to a limb and peering down at the dog who had treed him.

There was great danger for if the old bear should hear her cub's calls they would have that to deal with for which he was not ready, having come without axe or hatchet or club. Yet, looking up at the small cub, he wanted it.

He decided to take the risk, so he commanded the dog to silence (though he could not silence the squealing of the cub) and laying his musket on the ground he prepared to climb as far as he could go up the trunk. After much slipping he finally got hold of a small branch and with all his strength shook the tree loosening the cub's hold. With a terrified and babyishly angry squeal the cub fell to the ground and instantly the dog grabbed him by the ear and held him.

Taking a thong from his jacket pocket, he tied the cub's mouth, then picking up his musket, he took the squirming little animal up in his arms and hurried down to the Glen. Into the ground he set a strong pole and securely tied the cub with a rope fastened about his neck. Dolly fed him and fondled him. "He is as soft as a kitten," she exclaimed as she and the boys petted and played with the little creature. But that evening, Dolly questioned. "What about the mother bear, Hayes? Is it not dangerous? Will she not seek her cub?"

"I warned you long ago that I had been watching her tracks."

"I have been vigilant. But doesn't this increase the danger?"

"I do not doubt it was she who took those two lambs in the spring. I have watched for her all summer but could not come upon her. She is a crafty one."

"I don't like it. She angers me. If she were a chicken, I'd wring her neck."

He laughed. "She would not lend herself to such treatment."

The evening chores were done, the meal was eaten and they were ready for a good night's rest.

The kitchen was dark except for the smoldering light from the fireplace which Hayes had banked.

Dolly went toward the little window which was open. Lifting her arms to close it, she paused meaning to lean out and look at the sky where myriads of stars made the night beautiful. As she bent her head and leaned forward, upon the air there issued such a shriek of horror as Hayes had never before heard, for she had come within inches of thrusting that yellow head into the great open jaws of the bear.

Her arms fell trembling from the window but she had, even in that instant of terror, heard Hayes command, "Keep yelling and don't move. She can't get in."

Shriek after shriek rent the air, then above it all she heard a crash. She saw the flash of the hatchet as it struck the back of the bear's head. She crouched to the floor, weak and trembling as to her ears came frightening sounds. There was blow on blow, the sound of scuffling, angry growls and then—when it seemed to her to have lasted for hours—silence.

Now the silence was like something cold and hard pressing on her heart. Weak, she could neither rise to close the window nor move from where she lay. Then, when she heard the door open and saw Hayes enter she laughed and wept and did not know what foolish things she asked. "She's dead?"

"She will not trouble us again. I will leave her lie until morning. Put the child to bed." She had not even known that Jerry had wakened from his sleep and stood beside her.

There was another bear skin for winter warmth. For some weeks they fed and petted the little cub, then one morning Hayes went out early and there was the post and noose but the wild creature had somehow slipped her head through and departed. At Dolly's disappointment he laughed, "The cub has gone home."

"There was always wildness in the little thing."

"Of course. Would you have had me kill her?"

"No, not that cub." Then she too laughed, "She will soon grow up and come for our lambs."

"I shall get her then."

But that night she mused. "One cannot pet and feed and play with a creature and then want to kill—even with a wild thing."

He smiled. "That is truly said."

CHAPTER XV

HAYES WAS PACKING together some dozen traps preparing to go into the forest to set them. A five year old boy leaned against his knee watching each movement with fascinated eyes.

"Mother says that there is a bounty on the sable."

Hayes nodded, "Such a bounty as I never before heard tell of — one dollar for every sable."

"Mother says we would be rich if we could catch enough sables." He was a handsome lad with blond hair and his mother's brightness of eye. "Father," the lad coaxed as he often had before, "If you would give me a gun I'd go into the woods and bring you the sables Mother wants."

It was Nat speaking and now his brother Jerry, over a year older, looked at him with a knowing smile. "To get the sables, you first must kill all the black-cats. Isn't that so, Father?"

Hayes explained to them as though talking to grown men, telling them how the fisher which they called the black-cat, ate the sables and how that same fisher was so cunning that he even followed the line of traps and ate the sables after the trap had imprisoned them. How the fisher leaped from tree to tree, so ferocious yet so swift, so knowing, so wily that he seldom was caught with either trap or bullet.

The little lad's face was sober. "Would he hurt *her?* Would he come near and leap the fence and take *her* from her cradle?" Jerry answered with decision. "Nothing is ever going to hurt her. We watch *her.*"

For a moment Nat's lips quivered, then there came that

flash that was not unlike that seen so often in his mother's eyes. "When I get my gun, I'll take care of her."

When Jerry said, "Nothing is ever going to hurt *her*," he spoke more truly than he knew, for in that cradle lay something so precious that the entire household seemed to exist only to serve and love her—a tiny girl-child. After five years, when hope for a daughter had almost vanished from Dolly's heart, the little girl had been born.

On the night when Hayes had come to the bedside to look at the infant lying in her arms, he knew that never before had he seen such an expression in Dolly's face. Tenderly, with the baby cradled in her arms, she bent her head and pressed her lips against the downy head. "I never stopped praying for her, Hayes."

As he went about his work, he too was reverently thankful. Now there would be no more loneliness in the long winter days, for when the boys grew and went with him to forest or field there would be the daughter by her side—the sweet companionship she had hungered for. Not that he understood. Had there been only daughters born to them, he would only have worked the harder, waiting for the time when sons-in-law would come to carry on and inherit the place. Curiously, he thought of the baby girl as somehow connected with the silver set, the gold beads and the fine shoes he paid dearly for—her vanity—adorning her pretty feet.

As the infant thrived, day by day, he watched and was thankful for Dolly's great happiness. Now, as her hands were busy with mending or sewing or causing the knitting needles to flash in the firelight, her foot again rocked the cradle and her eyes often left her work to rest on the face of her daughter, Silvia. They all felt that into that stern, hard household had come something so pretty, so delicate, so fairy-like that Hayes had scarcely touched her and the rough boys stood in awe beside the cradle. No, surely, nothing would ever be allowed to harm her.

It was a stern household and Hayes was a stern parent in

training and discipline. At six years, Jerry tried to do any chore as his father taught him. From early morning until dark he followed close at his father's heels a born farmer and woodsman. That he had inherited the prodigious strength of his ancestors was evident. He feared nothing. Soon he promised to relieve his mother of the milking. When trees were felled and more land was cleared he guarded the fire as the great stumps were burned. And Hayes was content. Jerry had the makings of a good farmer.

There was already a difference in Nat. When he was only three, Dolly had found it necessary to tie him or there would be hours wasted and great anxiety as they sought him in the woods. Hayes told Dolly the lad was "eagle-eyed" and one day with some pride he added, "and with the ears of a dog."

That the boy lived in a world of animal enchantment, Hayes knew well. Into the new shed where he often worked at his crude carpenter's bench, the boy brought strange creatures and talked with what Hayes called his mother's "glibness." When it seemed in the winter months that all living had gone out of the earth, that all was icy quiet, he found the little case which the butterfly had constructed for its winter home. It was his father who taught him not to disturb that tough, silken girdle; taught him to wait until spring when something within would stir and slough off the case. Were his eyes not sharp enough to see the tiny wings folded like a baby's arms? Were his eyes not sharp enough to see all the small cases hanging in sheltered places about the house and under bits of bark on the trees? With wonder making his eyes shine, the boy asked, "All alive, Father?"

"As alive as you are. In the spring there will be moths and butterflies."

They knew no Latin terminology but the boy learned such nature lore as no school could teach because he lived and breathed in a world of nature's witchcraft.

"You say the seed down under the snow is not dead, Father?"

"As alive as you are. It is taking the food from the earth

ready to make a plant in the spring."

"I dug and found the moss as green under the snow as in summer time. Does it never freeze?"

"The snow keeps it warm."

The boy smiled. "The snow is its overcoat."

One day he confessed, "I dug where the moles were far under. I knew the place. I found them all living but I could not find where the woodchuck was sleeping as you told me."

Sternly Hayes rebuked him. "Would you like to have a giant come in the night and remove the roof from your house to see where you were sleeping? You are a meddler."

As Dolly heard the many questions and Hayes' answers, she spoke her surprise. "You never spoke of all these many wonders, Hayes, until the boy questioned you."

He answered dryly, "The boy does much talking."

The boy, Nat, did more than talking. Often he tried her as she said, "sorely," coming home with torn breeches after hours in the underbrush or with clothes soaked to his skin as he again fell into the river while learning how the beaver made his home, or while following the footprints of deer. Twice he had tangled with a skunk which sought to steal food in the poultry yard, with results that brought severe punishment. Ashamed, he had no answer as Hayes asked, "Doesn't the dog know better?"

She wove the tough homespun and made all the clothes but the legs soon outgrew the trousers and the arms hung awkwardly below the sleeves. When Nat was ten years old, from the same pattern she cut trousers and shorts for the two boys and said that Nat would too soon be wearing socks as large as his father's; but, as to strength, the boys might always be equal. True to the eternal ambition of parents, true to the dreams that fill minds and hearts, when she asked, "Will they equal you in strength? Will they have backs to bear such burdens as your back has borne?" he answered gravely, "If need be." They both understood that to be able to bring home a deer or possibly another human being was one thing, but to load a back with household furniture or lumber, making a pack horse out of a man, was another matter. The latter they wished to spare their boys.

So sternly they admonished the lads to "straighten up" and the backs were strong and straight.

There was another stern duty which gave them many anxious hours. Often in the little towns of the frontier it was the minister or some better educated woman who gathered together the children and established a school. Here in their isolation, there was no such group to be reached, so in spite of all their other tasks they set themselves to teach their children to read and write and "figure."

On winter days about that plank table in the kitchen, the tallow dips were lighted. Before them Hayes' Bible was laid. On slates which Hayes had purchased, the stubby fingers, letter by letter, wrote the alphabet. When they could call aloud the twenty-six letters almost in one breath, they must learn to form them swiftly on the slate. Patiently they combined them until dog and cat and cow and sheep had added to them wolf and bear and beaver and skunk, painfully progressing to the words found in the Book.

It was Hayes who chose the places for beginning. Did he not know well that which had stirred him and quickened his own heart-beats? Now, in clear, high-pitched voices a boy learned to read, "At that time, Jesus went on the sabbath day through the corn; and his disciples were an hungered, and began to pluck the ears of corn, and to eat."

Their eyes brightened, for they understood. "But when the Pharisees saw it, they said unto him, Behold thy disciples do that which is not lawful to do upon the sabbath day." Yes, they understood when they read, "For the Son of man is Lord, even of the sabbath day."

What stories! About fishes, about bread, about the sun being darkened, about vineyards and husbandmen, sowing on good soil and on rocky soil, about armies and generals and the sick and poor, about money and traitors and life and death

and love—love of man and love of God.

They never dreamed that some man called an "educator" would have been amazed at the speed with which they progressed from the easy stories to the pages with long, hard names; that the "educator" would have said there was not one dull mind in that sober group.

It was a living Book, filling their minds with rich imagery, delighting with stories that came close to their own daily experience. Had they been told that learned men would dispute for centuries over the meaning of some few of its words, they would have been puzzled. To them, the moral code, the instruction, the commands were clear. Lying, stealing, murder, adultery, bearing false witness, envy and hate were forbidden. It was plain and it was God's will.

Thus Hayes Copp and Dolly, poor and hard-driven by their arduous labor had merely done that which they thought their duty, never dreaming that they had bestowed on their children a priceless gift—the ability to read the printed word with a fluency that gave them pleasure. Besides their mental capacity to understand they now had the skill to follow with ease the story, the exhortation, the dreams and deep thoughts.

Once when Jerry was reading aloud—"—He maketh me to lie down in green pastures—" he stopped and looked up at his mother with a smile, "He says it pretty, doesn't He?" That it was God speaking he did not doubt.

As to figuring, they could add to and take from and multiply and divide and what more did they need? There would come a day when books of history, books of botany and books about great people would be brought to them and by that time they would be ready for that knowledge and eager to acquire it.

On summer days their bare toes sought crevices in the rocks, their strong fingers clung to tiny shelves and they ascended sheer cliffs on the mountains. They waded in mountain streams and played and shouted beneath the foaming waterfalls, or they swam naked in the river seeking the trout and Hayes was not more skillful in baiting his hook, casting his line and bringing in the speckled beauties which Dolly cooked in pork, never counting the numbers consumed.

That for many of the flowers they had no names troubled them not at all. They found strange delicate flowerlets blooming in the early spring close to shelves of ice in the ravines. Hayes called them "Alpine." They watched cunning, wicked spiders weaving their marvellous webs; like their dog, learned not to trouble the porcupine who could afford to take his ease, never hurrying because of his knowledge of his means of defense. Seeing the first robin in the spring was an event that warmed their hearts. Now there would follow many birds building nests and laying eggs, and all the myriad insects. In the woods Nat's sharp eyes discerned a tiny branch but he was not fooled. He poked it and saw it walk away—the marvellous walking stick.

He knew the bullfrog closed its eyes when he dived into the water; knew why the lizard could walk upside down on the ceiling in search of flies and wished he could grow little sucking disks on his own toes.

From both father and mother he had imbibed, almost with his milk, a great love for the mighty eagle. Now he was sternly for bidden to try, but some day he would climb way up into that giant pine and look into the eagle's house and see eaglets.

He lived in a world of enchantment but still that which he most coveted was denied him—a gun. Hayes' old musket was outworn and now stood in a corner of the shop although the time would come when, like many pioneers, he would fasten it above the mantle at the fireplace. There were new guns in use and closely the boys watched as their father loaded and fired and when some day permission should be given, there would be no need of instruction.

One by one the coveted sheds had been built connecting the house with the large barn and Dolly had her place for making cheese and butter. At an outside fire there hung a brass kettle and here she made her own tallow dips ready for the winter's use.

There were many losses. Now and then a hen, but it was the defenseless sheep disappearing that angered her most because she needed the wool. Often toward night, the boys herded them into the sheltering shed provided for their protection but as both knew and often remarked, they were stupid creatures and could not be taught to discern the approach of wolves. Jerry said they had eyes to see and saw not, ears to hear and heard not, and noses to smell but were too dumb to scent the enemy.

One evening Hayes was far in the woods to the north working on his road which would soon be ready when the road from both north and south should come to meet it. The skies were clouded and the dusk deepened early. Dolly and her little girl were in the kitchen preparing the evening meal, Jerry cleaning his buckets after milking, when Nat heard something strange outside. Running to the door, he saw a frightening sight. The sheep had wandered far into the woods and now were coming home, bleating piteously, while from the dark pockets of the forest there emerged a pack of snarling wolves that surely would overtake their prey before the sheep could reach shelter.

Barking furiously, the dog ran out, directly toward the pack. They stopped, turned from the sheep and with low, terrifying snarls advanced toward the dog. The dog had no chance against so many. Nat did not hesitate. He took one of the loaded guns. At the kitchen door, Dolly gasped in terror as she saw the boy step out into the yard, lift the gun, aim and fire. The wolves stopped and one fell dead. Another shot and the pack ran back into the shadows as Nat commanded the dog to return.

The boy walked directly to the kitchen and Dolly saw the sweat in beads on his forehead and for once she did not know what to say or do. He waited. He asked tremulously, "You'll tell Father?"

"He must be told."

"He will punish me. The gun is forbidden."

She frowned. "You showed great courage, Nat. That's all I can say."

He repeated, "He'll punish me. Could I take the dead wolf from the yard?"

"You will leave it where it is."

But already there were steps in the yard and Hayes was standing, looking down at the dead wolf, then examining the many footprints.

The boy looked imploringly at his mother. She spoke sternly, "You will go out, take the gun to your father and tell him everything."

Walking slowly, his eyes opened wide and staring at his father's back, the lad approached, still holding the gun. With careful accuracy, shunning one word of exaggeration which he knew his father would instantly detect, he stated the facts. "I was afraid for the dog."

Hayes looked at the dead wolf. "You brought him down with the first shot?"

"The second missed because they were running. That one was wasted."

"No—not wasted. It frightened the pack."

Hayes took the gun and silently put it in its place. He washed at the well and soon they sat about the board.

In the evening, Dolly heard the lessons and Hayes disposed of the dead wolf. All went to their beds and still Hayes had taken no action. Dolly did not question. It was a man's affair.

Sometime in the night, Hayes wakened to hear a sound. He rose and in bare feet approached the kitchen. The door was open into the outer shed. He quietly went nearer. There on the floor was Nat in his nightgown lying with his arms about their dog, his head pillowed against the neck of the animal.

Hayes coughed and the boy jumped to his feet. Seeing his father, tears gushed from his eyes and he sobbed, "I did save Rover's life."

Hayes' arm was laid hard about the small shoulders. He pressed the boy against his side. "I care more for that than for the loss of many sheep. I saw the footprints. They were too many for one dog. Now you will go to bed and sleep. Soon you shall have a gun, but until that time, you will understand that I forbid your touching mine, unless to save a life as valuable as that of Rover's. Now go to sleep."

For a minute the boy clung to his father's hand, then ran up the steep stairs to the small bed where he slept beside Jerry.

CHAPTER XVI

THERE WAS an amazing sight on the road in front of the home of Hayes Copp and Dolly—two teams of oxen, drawing great logs and the wherewithal to smooth and widen the road. They had come through from the north and now the farms in all the countryside about the town of Randolph could be reached with what they called "ease." Toward the south a bridge made of heavy logs spanned the river and soon, when more money and more workmen could be found, the Glen House at the foot of Mount Washington would be accessible.

The boys could scarcely restrain their excitement. Around and around the oxen they circled, examining the beasts from teeth to tail, running their hands up and down the smooth yokes and finally obtaining permission to "drive them" which seemed to he mostly a matter of yelling at the top of their lungs.

All through a summer day, they widened and smoothed and when night fell, five men weary of camping in the woods or taking the long trek to their homes, came to Dolly and asked if they might find shelter in one of the sheds.

They were a mud-spattered, unshaven, rough looking crew but she knew them for what they were—farmers or farmer's sons and farmer's helpers, all giving time to complete the needed road. Her eyes smiled at them and with her light laugh she told them that not only should they have shelter but they could keep their food for another day; tonight they should have a hot meal.

They stretched out on their backs before the house, lazily

enjoying the mowed grass, the boys hovering near them when not engaged in errands for their mother. Soon—in so short a time as to cause them to exclaim in astonishment, such odors reached them as made their mouths water.

In the outdoor fireplace Hayes had logs burning, for the nights soon grew cold. They sat in a circle about the fire as the boys ran in and out bringing the chunks of meat and the fresh cooked vegetables. Never had they tasted trout so delicious, each browned bit covered by a piece of salt pork. Then came Dolly's famous Indian pudding and the hot tea.

When all had eaten and the food was cleared away they drank of their O-be-joy-ful and found the world a good place in which to be alive.

Dolly had put her little girl to bed and now she joined the group to hear news of the road's progress and although she was not the dainty slim girl who had once arrived in the famous "bridal car," she was still so bright-eyed, so easy in her chatter, so delighted with company that the eyes of the men followed her with admiration. They told her that they had heard tales of her magic in cooking and now they too must spread her fame.

She laughed easily. "Men's tongues are made for naught but flattering. Their great wisdom lies only in their stomachs."

One answered, "It is our stomachs that tell the truth. From there we get no lies."

Another, growing merry on many returns to his mug of rum, took out his jews harp and, setting it against his teeth, pleased them with tune after tune. They grew merrier and now they urged a young fellow to get out his violin. He went to the wagon and returned with a shabby, well-battered case and soon was twanging the strings, turning the little pegs, and screwing tight his bow.

While he was tuning, one asked, "Would you see such jigging as was never the like of seen in these parts before?"

As it was growing dark, Hayes suggested the kitchen.

The tallow dips were lighted and about the room they

disposed themselves leaving a clear space in the center. The violinist sat on a stool, one long leg stretched out, and whether it was more fascinating to watch his nimble fingers race up and down the strings or see the flourishes of the bow or keep one's eyes fastened on the stretching, twisting, jumping, tapping, or many other antics of that long leg, the boys would never decide.

Other feet were tapping in time with the merry tune, but finally the expert jigger was prevailed upon to take the center space and go to work. He was an old fellow, red-haired, red-faced, not improved by a fringe of red-white beard about his chin. There was little of flesh on his angular bones and soon it appeared that all the joints which held those bones together must be well greased. The old legs moved so fast one could scarcely follow the steps; he bent and twisted in contortions beyond belief but always the feet tapped and shuffled in perfect time to the tune.

Hilariously, they clapped and asked for more when he finally stopped. Out of breath? Not at all. There was another jig tune, more tapping and more O-be-joy-ful.

There came a time when Hayes spoke sternly and the boys tore themselves away and slowly mounted the stairs but when in their nightgowns they stealthily lay on the floor of the upper hall, listening, Dolly knew but said nothing.

As there were no extra beds, Hayes, having finished but the one small bedroom below where the little girl was now sleeping, he gave them blankets and the men, now mellow and sleepy, rolled themselves up and soon quiet descended on the house.

Before the sun had risen above the forest treetops, the boys were up ready for their chores, watching the line of men take turns at the well and bend over the basin of water that Dolly had placed outside, snorting and washing and wiping, ready for such a breakfast as would sustain them for a hard day's work.

Now they must pay for their meals and night's lodging.

Indignantly, Hayes refused to accept payment. It was his privilege to be host, for years of work on his road had made this a day to be remembered.

The head man explained that they were "working for hire" and they were not beggars but were expected to pay for any help received along their route and surely a night's lodging and such meals were "help."

Dolly should decide the price. With her gay laugh she said; "A shilling all 'round."

The head man said, "A shilling for each meal, a shilling for lodging and a shilling each for the cattle." Thus with laughter and good feeling was established a precedent that should adhere to her house for many years.

The money was counted out, the violin was packed away, the oxen were put under their yokes, and with shouts and many expressions of praise and thanks, the procession moved south, leaving them a road that delighted their hearts and promised that what had been only a dream would become reality when such a road should extend not only to the Glen House but all the way to Jackson.

Until that time, there were matters of immediate concern. That fall their losses were heavy. Hayes told the boys that never in all his years in the Glen had he seen deer so plentiful. Many came to the river to drink. However, he also told them that when the deer were numerous the wolves would follow and sometimes in those cold fall nights, it sounded to the inhabitants of that home as though the woods were alive with hundreds of the snarling, growling creatures. A sudden wolfish cry in the night would rouse them all from sleep and then there would come the many accompanying cries of frightened animals and the danger to their livestock pressing closer.

It was Jerry whose brows met in a frown not unlike his father's as he repeated daily, "When we get the harvest in, we'll build more fences."

Yes, they must have more fences and in those few hours

when a man might have rested his aching back, when at last the mowing was done and the hay stacked in the barn, when the shed was filled with the vegetables and other produce for their winter's need, when the woodpiles reached unbelievable heights for they were known to burn a cord a day in the bitter weather—while they were still clearing land, felling trees, chopping up branches, burning stumps—then they must build more fences.

Within the house, Dolly also was finding a need for "more." She had tended her flax in the strip of land she had chosen near the river and now she was weaving more of the beautiful thread into sheets and table cloths. Out in the sun she bleached them until they were as white as snow. About the edge of her table linen she patiently fashioned long fringe and when they were washed and ironed and spread on that parlor table it was with keen pleasure that she set upon such cloths her beautiful silver pot and gold-edged dishes.

There had come an occasion for their use.

One fall day she laid aside the heavy trousers she had been patching, for before her stood her little girl. Here was a gentle child. Surely there was no "good point" of either father or mother which had not been bestowed on the little girl. Over her head was a shimmering of golden curls with a touch of the burnishing red that Hayes still claimed. She was small, slenderly built, graceful and altogether charming with feet so small, so well-arched that tiny shoes were ordered with Dolly's own. Her bright blue eyes sparkled even as Dolly's would always do. Although the mouth was wide and somewhat straight like Hayes' mouth, it was so dimpled at the corners and withal so softly gracious in expression, so often opening in happy laughter that they noticed no resemblance.

She was Dolly's child. Were every day in the year to be set aside as a Thanksgiving day, there would still not be enough days for the outward observance of the thankfulness that was always in her heart since she first suckled this baby to her breast.

Long ago, as she worked in the field or milked the cows or

helped with the most abhorrent task on the farm—the slaughtering—or at her own unpleasant task of soap-making, Hayes had always marvelled at that in her which craved the beauty of snowy table linen, fine china and shining silver.

On the sabbath afternoon she always "dressed" for the evening meal and part of that "dressing" was the wearing of a small white linen collar fastened by her gold pin. So he perceived the happiness and satisfaction showing in her face and every action as she lived daily in the companionship of this lovely little being. That to Dolly the sound of the child's sweet voice was as music to a musician's ears, he well understood, for he felt the same about her although nothing of his feeling was ever expressed in words. Nor even in actions, for she was so completely Dolly's own that he seemed to have no part of her.

Was there something else that he dimly perceived though he could not formulate his thoughts even to his own mind? Did not this woman see something of herself in her child? The lost beauty of her own girlhood? The pretty, laughing, innocent child she once was?

So gradually had the change in Dolly come, day by day, cooking over hot fires, mending, weaving, spinning, milking, making tallow dips—endlessly laboring indoors and out, all the hard life of a woman of the frontier—that Hayes scarcely noticed that her hair had grown thin and bleached in color, her figure had grown heavy, the delicate complexion had changed to one weathered and already showing creases in the skin, lines that would multiply year by year. The hands that accomplished so much were grown coarse, the back, like his, a little bent. Dimly he perceived that all this did not matter when she gathered into her arms the daughter who was more beautiful than she had ever been.

On this fall day, she stopped her work to help little Silvia put on her outdoors clothes. Over the hand-woven dress of the light blue that Dolly so loved, she drew on the warm coat, pulled up the knitted wool stockings and on her head fastened the bright red cap that matched the mittens she delighted to knit.

Opening the door for her, Dolly watched the child run out to play in the autumn leaves, for cold nights warned of the coming of winter. There was no fear, for two stalwart boys as well as Hayes were always keen to see the little red cap and guard her against any evil thing that might come into the clearing.

Dolly returned to her low chair and, one after another, flung aside the garments she had mended. Some time had passed when her hands stopped their busy plying of the needle, her head was lifted as she listened to an unaccustomed sound. Occasionally now a heavy farm wagon passed on their road or a team of oxen, men walking, or, now and then a group of mountain visitors, but in the early fall there had been a fearful storm and a torrent of water had washed away part of the half finished road south of the bridge. Since then there had been few passers by.

Listening intently, she recognized the steady thud of a horse's feet upon the hard road. She rose and walked to the window, waited, and soon a horse appeared with a rider. He pulled in his reins and stopped, looking with evident interest and pleasure at the home, then down at the little girl who was gazing at him with wide eyes even as she retreated toward the south door.

The man turned his horse and rode close to the house, bowing to Dolly, who now stood in the doorway.

Dismounting, he came forward. He was a small man, as she afterward described him "all gray." He wore a gray overcoat, gray cap pulled down about his ears, glasses through which gray eyes peered and surely a gray face showing fatigue and cold.

Graciously she opened the door for him to enter, calling Jerry to care for the horse and tell his father of the visitor.

As he removed his gloves she noted that his hands were not the hands of a farmer. At her invitation he laid aside his coat and approached the fire, telling her how good the heat felt, how delightful to find a home, how comfortable and pleasant was her sunny parlor.

Soon Hayes and both boys arrived as the man explained that he had had much difficulty approaching on the washed-out road, was somewhat lost as to direction and whereabouts and would be pleased to rest awhile.

In her spontaneous, hospitable way, Dolly suggested that he spend the night, for it would be difficult to travel the distance to a northern inn in the darkness.

His pleasure in receiving the invitation was so evident, his relief in finding a shelter so great that he looked from one to another, smiling, and expressed his thanks over and over. Then in a quiet voice he told them that he was a botanist, that he was seeking certain berries and plants which would now be in their fall fruitage—plants said to be very rare but indigenous to this locality.

Nat took a step forward and one could hear his sharp long drawn breath of excitement as he listened. Hayes smiled but was silent. These plants, could he find them, were to be packed in moss and leaves or soil, some to be sent to Boston, some to New York.

Talkative Nat came close with glowing eyes. "My father knows every plant in the Glen and besides every berry on the mountain. In the morning we could take you to find them."

Now Hayes must speak apologetically. "He is quite a boaster, Sir. We claim no such knowledge. If, perhaps we can assist you, we can try when morning comes."

Already Dolly was clearing the table on which she spread her fine linen and china and silver. In the kitchen, even as she prepared the supper, she consulted with Hayes. Above, there was only finished the small room where the boys slept. This was a gentleman and surely they could not offer a blanket and the floor by the fire. So they planned to let the boys come below to the kitchen and speedily, as her dinner cooked, she spread clean sheets on one bed and prepared for the gentleman's comfort.

Yes, this was different. Never before had they entertained such a guest. Seated at the table he noticed and spoke appreciation of the food, asked her curiously how she cooked the trout under its cover of pork, seemingly surprised that one like young Nat could still bring in so great a number. Nat grinned. "We get them in the deep pools. They will be there all winter. Until the ice forms too hard to cut, we have plenty."

From her silver pot Dolly poured the strong tea and their guest did full justice to her Indian pudding.

As they rose, he laid his hand on the curly blond head of the little girl and a great sadness seemed to fill the eyes back of the gold-rimmed glasses. "I shall describe little Silvia to my wife. We have two boys but we lost our girl." Then he looked into Dolly's eyes and she would not know that to himself he thought, "How should I ever be able to describe this mother of little Silvia? This is a wonderful woman. I shall not do her justice in any words."

After the children were sent to sleep, they sat about the fire. He drew from his pocket, a pipe and asked permission to smoke. Instantly Hayes rose and going to the closet brought out a pouch of tobacco. This was costly and hard to come by but he offered it to his guest. However, the gentleman had his own supply. Hayes took down a clay pipe and filled it with the precious tobacco. Then they sat, smoking and talking of the White Hills, of the clearing, of the Glen. To his courteous questions some history of their adventure came clear to the gentleman's mind.

Once going into the little hall, Dolly saw the kitchen door was ajar and well she knew that Nat's ear was pressed to the opening but she made no mention of it for here was talk different from any to which the boy's ears were accustomed. To this visitor these hills were not covered with something merely called a forest. He talked in his quiet way of Balsam Fir, Marsh, Pursh, the Yellow Birch, the Paper Birch. How far up should one be forced to climb to find the Mountain Alder? All this Hayes could answer, knowing quite well that his visitor was purposely abstaining from Latin nomenclature and using the familiar names used by the pioneer.

Found on the lower slopes they discussed the Dwarf Raspberry, the Swamp Gooseberry, the Skunk Currant, the Common Low Blueberry. Could he in the spring find the Downey-leaved Blueberry? And the Small Cranberry? He could. Then came a discussion of the wild flowers, like the asters, and some rare delicate flowers that Hayes could only call Alpine and also the strange flowers found only in the mountain lakes. Nat listening felt a great pride that his father could talk like this to a botanist.

It was an exciting morning for both father and sons, for before dawn they were up getting all the chores accomplished, getting the logs in for the fire even as Dolly was filling her oven with coals, brushing it clean and getting more food ready.

Then hours were spent in the woods, carefully pushing aside the leaves, finding specimens, bringing them into the shed where Hayes made receptacles for them as the scientist attended to the careful packing.

Something which they were pleased to call Indian Summer made the few days beautiful and the visitor each day begged to be entertained one more night and thus a week passed.

On his last evening there was one moment when some embarrassment had descended on them all. Firmly he said he must pay for his lodging. Hayes haltingly tried to express what he felt—that the visitor had brought more than he had taken.

On young Nat's face was registered something like shame that such a thing as payment should be spoken of; however, when their visitor said sadly that he could not come again in the spring to be their guest as he earnestly wished to do unless such comfort could be recompensed, Dolly laughed merrily, "Very well. Before I charged a shilling all 'round and this it shall be."

When the hour came that they tied his packages to his saddle and saw him mount and ride away, they all stood together by the road and waved as he turned in the shadows of the forest road, again and again, until he disappeared.

As they walked back to the house, Hayes said, "I will take one of the boys with me to the town. I shall buy some single beds. Jerry and Nat shall help me finish first the downstairs extra bedroom, then the long room upstairs. In it we will place beds and tables for there will be more guests and it is fitting that there be places ready."

Dolly walked lightly. Her eyes were sparkling.

He looked at her. "This gives you pleasure?"

"It is good." Then she added, "There's flax waiting. I shall weave the sheets and covers. Perhaps, you'll now bring home my clock."

CHAPTER XVII

THEY KNEW THAT, later, sleet would follow snow and more snow would follow sleet until a hard crust formed over all the level land; however, Hayes and his son did not wait for that. As soon as there was enough snow on the road to allow the runners of their sled to glide smoothly they harnessed the horse and started on their journey to town to buy the beds and stands. Nat remained to be the "man of the house," helping Dolly in attending to the cattle, feeding, cleaning, milking and carrying in the needed wood. The boy was entrusted with the responsibility of guarding the clearing should bears or wildcat or wolves appear to harm them.

"If need be, I can use the gun, Father?"

Hayes nodded soberly, "If need be."

For many hours before their departure, Hayes and Dolly had sat together estimating costs and deciding what should be bought. At last wallpaper should be purchased and, although every penny must be counted, they agreed that this paper must be of good quality.

Hayes had reckoned on a day to go, a day for bartering and buying and packing and, if the good weather held, a day for returning.

It was on the third day that Dolly became concerned when, hour after hour, snow fell. By noon time, a bitter wind from the northeast was whistling through the trees driving great drifts of snow against the house and in clouds down the road. Outside, Nat shovelled valiantly, determined to keep a path clear to both parlor and kitchen door, but the snow almost blinded him, the sharp wind howled about his ears and the path filled again almost as fast as he shovelled. At the window, Silvia's face was pressed against the cold pane as she watched, ready to shout notice of the travellers' return.

When at last the light began to wane and the heavy clouds pressed lower and lower, she turned from the window-watching, her eyes wide with fear. "Could they be lost in the snow, Mother?"

With that same fear in her own heart, Dolly assured her children, "Your father will come. They are just delayed some with the drifting snow. He'll know how to get through."

The rooms were filled with the delicious odor of her cook-ing and over the fire a pot of soup simmered. From this she scooped enough to fill bowls for the children and, although they wondered why she did not eat, she would not let them know that she was too filled with apprehension to swallow.

Darkness had descended but Nat wished again to clear the paths. "There's only the wind and drifting now, Mother. The snow has stopped falling."

She set a tallow-dip in the window and again he put on his boots and heavy clothing and shovelled.

Never had minutes seemed so like hours, hours like weeks to her. Rapidly her small foot worked the treadle as she sat near the fire spinning her yarn. Sometimes she glanced up at an empty corner. For many years she had dreamed that some day her precious clock would be brought from her old home to be set in that space that had so long awaited its coming, for never could Hayes transport so delicate, so precious an article with his heavy loads of meal or furniture, lumber or tools.

While they waited and worked and watched, father and son were facing the relentless enemy that had defeated many a pioneer. Had he been alone with his pack on his back, Hayes could have found the old trail and many a shelter; but now with all the false promises of good weather mocking him, with the cumbersome sled piled high with goods purchased by their hard-earned money, with the precious clock, with the frightened, half-frozen horse, and with his son, he faced something with which he, for all his prodigious strength and ingenuity, might not be able to cope.

In the deep forest, darkness descended and only the whiteness of the snow alleviated the blackness. The heavy clouds seemed resting on the treetops, the swirling snow obliterated the branches and only because there was space between their bare trunks could one know where lay the road. Here and there the road was swept nearly clean as the wind whistled through and then the runners moved freely; but soon they were again confronted with drifts reaching to the shoulders of the horse, which stood trembling unable to proceed. For many miles they had progressed slowly with Jerry, wrapped in the fur robes, holding the reins in stiff hands while Hayes went ahead on foot leading and coaxing and comforting the weary animal. Again and again they stopped while he shovelled away heavy drifts making a path through which horse and sled could safely follow.

Mile after mile and the cold became intense and yet he must press on. With frost-bitten hands he shovelled. To give up and stop would be fatal. Sometimes a fear such as he had never known before assailed him. Suppose his strength should prove inadequate to this night's work? Was there perhaps a limit to what one man could endure? Then it was always the presence of his son that somehow gave him renewed vigor. The horse could be sacrificed but not that boy.

Sometimes he went back to the sled and spoke words of encouragement to Jerry, more firmly securing the robes, peering into his face and repeating! "Soon it will be over, Jerry. Breathe deep and often. You will not sleep?"

Always there was a smile and the boy repeated, "Don't worry, Father. I'd like to get out and help you."

"No, Son, keep the robes about you."

"The horse is spent."

"Your mother waits for you and me, not the horse."

"And the clock."

Hayes could laugh at that—and without bitterness—as he returned to lead the horse.

Once he called to Jerry, "The bridge cannot be far now. This is the bend in the road. We will soon see lights and home."

Then as he progressed through another drift something like a sickness in his stomach that brought a taste to his tongue assailed him and his heart grew faint for in the stream he saw logs floating—debris—more and more logs. Another hundred feet and they were where only the wreck of what had been the bridge was left. Ice was floating and the water ran black and cold.

He came to the boy's side. "Jerry, there is that here will test our strength. We are near home but the bridge is out. There is only one place where we can ford the stream. We must go back."

"But how, Father? We can't turn or back the sled."

"I shall go behind and lift the runners and pull and you will back the horse. I am depending on you, Son."

It was not far until they again stopped. Hayes spoke and now it was a command. "You will come down now, Jerry."

The boy threw off the robes and climbed down.

"You will help untie the box. That and the packages holding stuff that would be ruined in the water, we will carry."

With their cold-stiffened fingers they worked at the ropes. When the box containing the precious clock was loosened Hayes spoke and in the night and darkness his voice had a peculiar hollow sound.

"Now you will take great care. We must hoist it onto our shoulders and we—must—not—slip. The water will be like ice on our legs but we will not stop. I will lead. Now steady—steady—steady."

Sliding his feet, not foot by foot, but inch by inch, they descended through the trees to the bank, down into the icy water then slowly, often standing still as each moved a foot cautiously, they progressed. Once Jerry called, "It's well that I know every rock, Father. I've crossed here often. Isn't it the place where Mother led the cow?"

In the darkness Hayes' heart was cheered. The boy would endure. He was wide awake and alert and strong and unafraid.

They laid the box on the snowy bank and returned for the perishable packages. One by one all were taken over. They were shaking with cold and now neither spoke for their teeth were knocking together.

It was Hayes who went after horse and sled, leading, coaxing and finally half pushing both up the low sloping bank.

They reloaded but not with the care of the first packing. Now Jerry should sit on top of all the pile, steadying and guarding that long box with the clock still safe.

Up their own road and there came a glimmer of lights in their house and only Hayes heard the sobs and knew of the tears that were running from the boy's eyes.

❦

The night was wearing on but Dolly had not the heart to send her children to bed. She allowed Nat to clean farther and farther toward the highway.

It was Silvia near the window who called out, "Mother, I think Nat hears them. He has dropped his shovel and is running out to the highway."

Across her eyes and forehead, Dolly's hand was pressed hard and she bit her lips to hold back the tears that threatened.

They were coming to the kitchen door. She flung it open wide and there before her happy eyes were father and son and the horse and the long sled.

Hayes was helping the lad down, calling to Dolly and Nat to take hold of the box. Scarcely was it laid on the kitchen floor when Hayes spoke in a tone of command. "Leave everything. Strip off the boy's clothes and get him into our bed. Get warm irons and hot drinks." Then turning to the lad, "Let me see your hands." To Dolly, "Make poultices at once."

Never had that mother's hands worked faster or more gently as she stripped off the icy stockings and pants. She called to Nat, "More logs on the fire."

Soon he said, "The teakettle's boiling, Mother."

The irons were wrapped in wool and placed about Jerry's body, the hands were poulticed and hot drinks were forced between his lips and soon he slept deeply, not knowing how gently his mother's hands slipped under the bed clothes to rub his legs and back.

With Nat's help the packages all lay piled high on the kitchen floor. Hayes remained in the barn a long time caring for the faithful horse. Silvia and Nat were asleep when Dolly, in her long woolen nightrobe, lay beside the little girl and at long last, Hayes stripped off his icy garments and stretched out in the warm bed beside his son.

There was only the light from the fireplace. Again Dolly stood beside the bed touching the boy. "He sweats well."

"He endured much."

"You drank the hot rum?"

"All of it."

"I had best prepare more."

She hovered over them. "You may sleep, for I'll tend the fires. I needn't rest."

Then she came again. "Let me see your hands, Hayes." When she had seen, she made more poultices. She hung all the wet clothes to dry and made more of the hot rum drink.

With the morning light, Hayes rose and dressed and with Nat and Dolly's help was early at the chores.

All were impatient for the moment when they could finish the unpacking and look their fill at the new treasures. And what a morning it was! The sun rose through bars of blue and gold such as only a northern winter can produce. It shone with blinding brightness on the fresh snow while indoors the logs burned brightly and soon one of the new beds was unpacked and set up in the parlor for Jerry, who must remain in warm blankets until Dolly was satisfied that he dared venture again into the cold. He was so hoarse he could scarcely speak aloud and suffered silently with his frost-bitten hands and feet. However, his mother's home remedies soon brought comfort and Hayes' quietly spoken, "He almost equals me in strength" brought such a glow to his face as must surely have helped with the cure, for in a few days the bed was placed in the little room and the hands and feet and chest were healing.

As to Hayes' part in that bitter night, no one spoke or asked. He always, in his own mind, "reckoned" it was from that night when he waited so long before removing his icy trousers and socks that there started certain pains in his legs and back, which he thought of as "mayhap some rheumatism," although he thought complaining to be useless.

Dolly exclaimed over the careful wrapping of that clock. First, it was covered with rags, then paper, then it was made to lie in such a bed of hay as insured its safety from any rough jogging. Hayes unwrapped it, layer by layer. With all hands helping, it was raised and stood in the empty corner. Little wedges were placed first here, then there, until Hayes pronounced it level and steady. Almost breathlessly they watched him hang the weights and set the hands.

It was ticking! What a sweet sound to gladden their ears. On every hour it would call out its numbers in its clear, metallic voice almost, to them, like another person in the house.

This was no peddler's clock. Accurately, Dolly told them that in 1821, long before her marriage, twelve of these fine clocks had been brought into the town of Jackson. She had bought this one from one Camp. Anthony Vincent and for it she had paid five and one-half dollars although the clocks when they first arrived in Jackson sold for twenty dollars.

With what pleasure her eyes rested on it and with what satisfaction did she hear its pleasant ticking mingling with the sound of her loom or treadle. Not then, but long after when her eaglets were beginning to leave their nest, she wrote the history of the clock on a small piece of paper and pasted it in the case. That its life would be long she did not doubt and

that anyone possessing it would want to know all about it, neither did she question.

The clock in place! She looked eagerly at the pattern of the wallpaper, Jerry waiting anxiously for her verdict.

"It was hard to decide, Mother. There were so many patterns."

Generously she exclaimed, "This is so pretty, I wish to see no other."

Jerry looked at his father and smiled. It had been a momentous question in their minds and had worried them no end. The beds and feather mattresses were just right, the stands were perfect, the little splint-bottomed chairs were strong and really elegant, and now she would make and fit the under mattresses ready for straw.

There was one small package which they were keeping half hidden but her sharp eyes discerned it and she questioned. Hayes opened it and they all watched her eyes sparkle with surprise. Here was something she had long wanted but about the absence of which she had made no complaining—pencils and some paper and a large notebook. She handled them tenderly with her roughened fingers, then said she would place them in the drawer of her little table; but first, while they watched, she wrote the name of their first distinguished guest, the botanist. The handwriting was small and cramped but quite legible. She told them that through the years she would write the names of all their guests.

They watched her place the book in the drawer, sharing in her excitement for as Hayes had said there would be more guests after the spring came and he, with men from the south and helpers from the north, would again rebuild the log bridge and mend the washed-out road. How many times through the years this would be done after the fierce storms or the spring floods, they did not anticipate. That was well; for on this winter morning nothing but happiness and keen anticipation filled their minds and hearts.

The boys were taught to handle tools, to make a stool

without benefit of nails, boring holes and fitting parts and polishing the maple until it was as smooth as silk. Closets were likewise made and smooth pegs inserted to hold clothing. Doors were made of plain planks and likewise smoothed and painted. One by one the mattresses were finished and on them lay the softer ones of feathers. When Dolly smoothed her linen and spread her firm coverlets, it seemed to them the papered rooms were as fine as any a weary stranger could want. That all was simple and plain they knew. Also they knew it was clean and sweet-smelling and comfortable.

With her home remedies she was still doctoring a cough which bothered Jerry and on stormy days she kept him protected against the bitter cold.

On one such day as she worked at her loom; she listened as he told Nat many details of that terrible night.

"To me, Nat, it's the greatest enemy. It's more frightening than the fiercest bear or wolf. You don't know how to fight it. A gun is no use. You can't shoot at the angry sky. You can't hurl a million hatchets at the clouds nor use an axe on the wind's neck. Then too, you are a mere fool ever to trust it. The skies were blue and it was fun going, then it changed so fast. I tell you, Nat, never will I fear anything again but the storm and cold and ice and such wind as knocks you off your feet."

Dolly's hands lay still for a moment in her lap. She bent her head and there was a far-away look in her eyes. She was lying on one bitter night, alone in all the wilderness alone in that bunk feeling the icy fingers of the winter cold creeping through the cracks between the logs.

Yes, when the heavens hurled their fury at little man he knew he was facing his most relentless enemy.

She rose and from the pot simmering on the crane, she scooped up hot soup and smilingly handed a bowl of the steaming dish to each boy. Then she piled more logs on the fire until the blaze crackled and flames shot merrily up the chimney.

CHAPTER XVIII

BETWEEN THE HOURS of plowing and planting, everyone gave time to the road and bridge and soon the highway was again in use.

Would the botanist return to examine the rare spring flowers? There was never the sound of a horse's hoofs upon the road that Nat did not watch until the rider disappeared.

Pouring down from mountain side the streams were swollen and never was the music of cascade and rushing rivulets so plainly heard night and day at the house. The river rose high, spilling over its banks and Hayes, working near, pronounced it a "brawling stream."

One chilly day the "little gray man" rode into the clearing. Finding the house empty and no response to his knocking, he rode around to the barn and soon discovered the busy family, each hard at work on various fields or in the sheds.

He was cordially received and Dolly went back to the house and established him in the extra bedroom on the first floor. The long room above should be kept for transient guests. He praised the improvements, admired the wallpaper and asked all the questions about the clock that she was delighted to answer. While he unpacked, she had the kettle on the crane boiling and soon set a cup of tea before him.

He tried to express his appreciation. "It is like coming home." His eyes rested on the little girl and back of the gold-rimmed spectacles one saw the affection in his eyes.

Even before the hearty dinner was ready, he walked through

the new grass to examine her "wildings." He prophesied that with the care they were receiving, she would soon have strong apple trees and excellent fruit.

As Hayes was in the midst of his hardest spring labor, it was Nat who was allowed to accompany him day after day into the forest and up the steep cliffs. The boy carried his new gun and often, while the botanist worked, he wandered into the woods and then there was heard a sharp retort and presently he would return with some game slung over his shoulder.

When the supper table was cleared at night, the scientist worked with his specimens. Sometimes he wrote many strange long names attaching them to the small boxes and the boys watched with amusement, grinning and sometimes spelling out the letters. That their little Downey-leafed Blueberry was properly called, Vaccinium Canadense; that their common Low Blueberry was something else again—Vaccinium Pennsylvanicum; that the small Cranberry was known to the little gray man as Vaccinium Oxycoccus, on and on, as he carefully labeled box after box, afforded them both excitement and wonder. Sometimes Nat looked at his small head covered with carelessly combed gray hair and thought of it as a box stuffed full of Latin words. Yet they were always delighted with his questions and his interest in everything concerning them.

There were three days of such rain as brought the small streams pouring down from the mountains into the Glen in noisy torrents. All day and all night there was a steady patter on the roof, the roaring of the "brawling" stream, and the fire felt good at night. He asked, "I expect all these streams are named for early settlers, excepting those, of course, which bear Indian names? For instance, this Peabody?"

They turned to Hayes and he told them what the boys had not before heard. He told them that a man named Peabody came up from Andover, Massachusetts, to see these White Hills. One day he was climbing on the side of the mountain when night overtook him. He made his way in the dusk, hoping to reach the Saco River, when he came upon an Indian's hut. He begged shelter for the night and the friendly Indian took him in and treated him with great courtesy. In the middle of the night all—the Indian, his squaw, his children and the white man—were awakened by a loud noise. Following the Indian's leading, without question, they all rose and rushed out of the cabin. They had had time scarcely to escape when their hut was washed away by a torrent of water rushing down the mountain side.

With what blankets the Indian had saved, they passed the night of driving rain in the shelter of a cliff. When daylight came they reconnoitered and found that this torrent had burst out suddenly from a spot where there was no spring before. Hayes smiled, explaining that the Indian knew the land about his hut as Dolly knew the contents of her closet.

He ended, "The stream has been flowing ever since and forms the branch of the Saco which bears the name of Peabody's River."

Thus the sunny hours were filled with work and on the rainy days they were busy in the shed until after supper when they all gathered about the fire. Here the little gray man, courteously but insistently plied Hayes with questions which brought forth stories of his father's and grandfather's struggles in settling the new land. Sometime the boys' eyes opened wide in astonishment at some tale of heroism or they shouted with laughter as Hayes, with dry humor, recounted absurd predicaments. Never would they forget those stories.

On one such night as the rain beat against the window panes, there was the sound of voices outside and soon a heavy knocking at the parlor door. Hayes opened and the light streaming out illuminated a strange scene. To their startled eyes it first appeared like a company of Cavalrymen, water dripping from their garments, handsome horses pawing at the earth. The spokesman asked, "Is this an Inn?"

Hayes answered, "It is a farmhouse."

More questions were asked and answered and it developed that the men had become lost on their way to Canada, had fought through washouts on the roads, forded the swollen river and knew not how to proceed through the blackness of night and the downpour of rain and would pay well for shelter and food were that shelter to be but the roof of a barn.

Now Dolly was standing at Hayes' side. "How many are there?"

"There are six of us."

Without hesitation, "You are welcome to food and shelter. The boy will conduct you to the barn."

Now the little gray man watched Dolly with fascinated eyes; her whom he, in his mind, designated, "this wonderful woman."

Her eyes sparkled with pleasure and excitement, her feet moved quickly and directly, there was crispness in her speech as she directed Nat to light the long room above. Then, in her kitchen she set plates on the plank table and out of her seemingly inexhaustible ovens she brought remnants of food. When the men filed into that kitchen and shed their wet garments, they ate ravenously, drank the hot tea, then, as Hayes filled the mugs with rum, their tongues were loosened and they joined the family about the fire.

While they told of their journey, above their heads, the little feet went quickly from closet to bed spreading fresh sheets and, when drowsiness at last overcame their visitors, Hayes conducted them to their good night's rest.

While still in his own bed, the little gray man heard her moving about her kitchen and soon a huge breakfast awaited them all. There were so many they must eat in relays.

When they were ready to mount their horses and depart they laughed at her "shilling all 'round." They had gold and flung pieces on the table, as the spokesman said, "Such hospitality cannot be paid for. We'll remember you, Mistress Dolly Copp."

When Hayes had given them careful directions and they had disappeared into the forest, Dolly "cleared up," then sat at her loom. Tired? She laughed at the botanist's question.

Her eyes still sparkled with pleasure. This was what she loved—people, more and more people, excitement, activity. And the words of praise, even flattery? The many shillings?

Even before the botanist left there were other guests, for the knowledge that food and lodging could always be procured at the Copp Farmhouse was spreading. Dolly recorded their names and the month and year of their visits in her book and smiled as she counted the many shillings.

On one sunny day they again loaded the packages and waved the little gray man farewell. He had promised that some day his sons who were in college, would visit them.

❦

Through the months of springs and summers and harvests, through the long winters Dolly knit larger and larger socks and watched the legs outgrow the oft-mended trousers. In the fall she helped shear the sheep and cleaned the wool and wove more blankets and replaced the worn and mended sheets. The little girl grew and the skirts were lengthened yet all was woven on her looms and sewed and fashioned with her capable hands.

On one hot summer day it was Jerry who called his father's attention to a group of horsemen riding by.

Hayes' eyes followed them. "They look like the men who make measurements and place the marks for farm property. Two of them I have seen before." There was a speculative smile on Hayes' face. "With folks far off hearing of the good road, there may come new neighbors."

"Neighbors? Neighbors here?" Jerry looked incredulous.

Dolly had seen and now joined them as Hayes went on, "Your mother knows what happened down at Bartlett when the long highway was connected with Portland." His smile broadened. "There are those who follow the roads. They come in to settle and build homes when others have made the road clear for them."

Nat raised his blond eyebrows and glanced at his mother. "I'd follow the roads everywhere."

She responded tartly, "To the moon, if others first make the path."

That the boy was so much a rover worried her at times; that Hayes had given the boy a good gun and a sharp hunting knife seemed to her a matter of poor judgment; that the boy should so soon, like his brother, grow to be a man with concerns only for men's affairs left her with a little ache in her heart. That the ache was soon to be healed, that there was that within her that sometimes brought a tremulous smile to her lips, she had told no one but Hayes. When preparing for rest one night, she spoke to him. "You're to go to the attic and bring down the cradle. I'd like it made fresh and prettily painted."

"For that you have been weaving the small blankets?"

"You noticed?"

"I wondered if the time were not near."

Soon he brought the cradle and they chose a bright gay red for the new paint and hardly had they finished and seen it ready with fresh blankets when there followed, to lie on the snowy pillow, a little boy whom they named Daniel.

Silvia was ten years old and would be a second mother to the little fellow, rocking and singing to him while Dolly attended to her work; for the two boys, Nat and Jerry, were as men to feed and clothe, and never, though sorely pressed with duties, did she turn a tired or hungry traveller away from her door.

When the winter days came, a pleasant smile curved her lips, a new brightness was in her eyes as she suckled the boy while her lovely daughter hovered near. The three of them made a picture to Hayes' eyes as he passed through the room to lay logs on the fire. That he had no part in the picture did not enter his mind. With only a deep satisfaction filling his own heart he thought, "She has found new happiness. She might well always have a babe at her breast."

On one such winter morning she stood near Nat watching a large moose come from the woods, cross the field and go to the river's edge. Still low in the east, the sun from out a sky of cloudless blue shed a dazzling light across the whiteness of the snow. The ice on the river looked forbidding but the animal stepped down an easy slope of the bank, tapped the ice, broke it and placed its two front legs in the water as it drank. There was something of magnificence in the sight and neither father nor son went for a gun. They merely watched and smiled as Hayes said, "They are peaceable creatures if let alone. They neither molest man nor any small animal. I have startled one close by and sensing I meant him no harm, he merely walked away."

"Yet they're terrifying if angered, you say."

"I would rather have it out with a she-bear. If you were surprised without a gun and angered the animal, those tree-horns on his head reach far forward and he would get at you and tear you to pieces, for there is no chance of your knife reaching him."

When the moose had drunk his fill, he lifted his stately head high, leisurely stepped across the snowy pasture, and soon was lost in the depth of the forest.

But Dolly would not have understood that deep love of the forest and all its creatures that bound this father and son together in sympathy.

One summer day, Nat entered the shop where Hayes was working.

"Father, I have never been allowed to spend a night alone on the mountain. I know the shelters you've pointed out to me. I'd like to take my gun and knife and a pack on my back and have permission to hunt high up and see from the top-most bare rocks the views you've spoken of."

Hayes' brows met in a hard frown. "You are still young though grown nearly to man's stature and you are often careless and imprudent."

"I'd be very cautious. I'm not afraid of darkness or being alone."

"Always a boaster! Do you not know that only a fool is without fear? Are you such a fool?"

Nat laughed. "I know what you mean. I promise to be cautious."

"The venison is low. Your mother would welcome more, though she would be angered at your sleeping in the forest."

The boy's eyes glowed. "Then you give permission?"

"I would see you tested."

"I'll go when I've finished my work."

"You'd best talk to your mother. She will say what food for you to take."

There was a mischievous gleam in the boy's eyes as he hurried away.

It was at the supper hour as Dolly was placing the food upon the table that she said, "Someone has neatly halved this cake and taken generously from the fried chicken. Was the dinner so small?"

It was Hayes who looked as guilty as though he alone had emptied the dishes she had prepared for the supper. As the boy did not appear it was he who was forced to offer explanations, he who braved her anger, not being able to put into words that which had seemed of importance to both him and his son.

Also it was he who slept badly that night, waking at every unusual sound; then, in the morning light, casting his eyes often toward the great mountain, hoping to see the blond head appear and now wondering if by chance it were he who was the fool as Dolly had suggested.

Had he known the predicament in which the boy had spent the night, he could not have slept at all.

With his gun and knife secure, the pack fastened to his back, Nat had climbed up the path whose lower reaches he knew well. Eagerly his strong hands grasped ledges of rock and he pulled himself up almost perpendicular surfaces, determined to reach one high bald spot from which to view what promised to be a fine sunset. At last, stopping in an open space he turned to look around him. His heart beat hard with the exertion and with the pure joy of the adventure.

A vast scene lay below. This was what he had long wanted to view. The river was but a silver ribbon, the fields were little patches of different colors as they were sewn of oats or wheat or corn or barley. The distant mountains were like friendly neighbors of this one on which he stood. Slowly the sun was sinking and over all the earth was a glow of such pink as seemed of another world. That was it. Another world filled only with beauty and grandeur and with no cramping boundaries. Now great bars of crimson were splashed across the sky. He breathed deep and felt only a sense of liberation and pure happiness.

However, there was just time to descend to the spot where he knew of a suitable shelter before the cold and darkness should come.

Thrilled with pride in his strength and dexterity he slid and ran and slid again until he had reached a small clear lake. Not far from here there was a great pine and in the morning he might climb to examine the eagle's nest. His father had told him that it measured two good yards across.

After one long slide he sat a moment looking about to make sure of his direction. Then, quite by accident, his eyes rested on some leaves and dainty flowers close to his feet. Was this perhaps the flower the botanist had sought and been unable to find? Could he with great care take it up, wrap it in soil and leaves and send it to him? As he started to dig in the earth he lifted a sizable stone and flung it away with more strength and violence than he was aware of. Instantly there was a terrifying growl and looking up he saw coming toward him a great moose which he inadvertently had struck hard with the sharp stone.

Only a few yards away the angry animal was plunging at him with those great tree-horns lowered. There was not an instant to lose. Somewhere near he had carelessly laid his gun but to take time to reach it and load and fire would be fatal. Knowing at last the terror that can grip a man when threatened with death, like a cat he sprang for a tree near and with a desperation that gave him strength and agility, he climbed. Higher and higher until he was safe from the horns. Now furious, the beast seemed to fairly thunder against the tree trunk.

Nat was clinging desperately to his none too safe perch when suddenly above his head there was such a commotion and such frightful sounds as he had never before heard. What had he done? Climbed a tree in which a young eaglet was precariously perched and here was the mother bird screeching above him. What he said would have shocked his mother's ears.

How long the din lasted he was unable to determine but presently he realized that it was growing dark in the forest and he neither dared descend nor move. Then, in that summer night the woods heard a sound so unaccustomed to its silences that many a small animal's ears must have twitched with alarm—a boy's laugh ringing out again and again. Surely here was a predicament that was funnier than any tale he had ever heard.

He shouted epithets to the mother eagle above; he hurled all the names he could think of down at the moose and then he called himself a few more. When his laughter had relieved him he began wondering how many hours were in a night? Would that beast wait there through the darkness? Could he ever know? The branches were heavy and the leaves were thick and a great animal can move through the forest as silently and softly as a kitten.

So he sat and so he clung, sometimes talking aloud, sometimes singing softly to himself to be sure he could not sleep and fall and break his neck.

Fortunately, the days were long and the nights short at this time of the year and when his sharp eyes could pierce through the darkness, he began a quiet descent. At last he could see the ground now torn and well trodden where the angry, injured moose had stood. With fast beating heart he

dropped to the ground and ran for his gun. Ready now, he crept downward until there was much distance put between him and his night's lodging.

Ravenously he ate his supper and breakfast in one and then decided to hunt in earnest. He had discerned deer tracks and with the stealth of an Indian he followed them.

Late on that afternoon his father saw him coming down the trail long before he reached the clearing. Over the boy's shoulder was flung a deer which he proudly laid before the barn door.

Though it might, as his father had said, prove that he was careless and imprudent, like his mother, he must talk. So at the supper table that night, even as they ate of the fine venison, he told how he was "treed" and the boys roared their laughter and even Dolly joined in. To Nat, discomfort was forgotten and there was left in his mind only the excitement of the adventure and the pure fun. Of the beauty and grandeur that had thrilled him to his soul, no boy could speak.

That night Dolly turned to Hayes earnestly: "Don't you see that the boy can't be trusted? How often I have heard you tell them that a hunter and his gun and knife must never for a moment be separated."

He frowned. "No hunter lives by rules. There was but a moment for his decision. He did the right thing in springing for the tree."

She sighed; and then she laughed for pride in these men who feared not forest nor animal nor to be alone on the great mountain.

CHAPTER XIX

ON THAT SIX MILES of road cut through the north forest connecting the small town of Randolph with their clearing there was something happening of great moment to the family, bringing wonder and excitement and furnishing conversation for every meal.

They were to have neighbors. From the north-country came oxen drawing away the trees which lumbermen cut and loaded. On the cleared land a small frame house was built by men hired from the town and into that shelter moved a family of English descent named Barnes.

On the day when Nat came in from reconnoitering to tell his mother that father, mother and children had come with all their household goods on an ox-cart, Dolly's feet went swiftly back and forth from her "victual room" to her ovens and in the evening there was packed in the two strong Indian baskets, food such as she alone could prepare. Jerry and Nat were well loaded and sent with the gift to the new neighbors, returning with accurate news of many a detail concerning the family. On the next day Dolly, in her homespun gown, went up the road to welcome them and offer all her warm hospitality.

It was not an uncommon sight now to see Mr. Barnes seeking Hayes in a field, standing long, as he asked advice about planting or examined Hayes' fences or his cattle or his various tools.

It was not an uncommon sight to see Mrs. Barnes approach Dolly's kitchen door carrying in her arms a baby that was ailing, seeking Dolly's help or accepting thankfully of her remedies. About this baby Dolly worried as though he were one of her own. Often she reported to Hayes after an early winter visit, "He is wasting away. The mother is weak and the child doesn't thrive on her milk."

"Their cow is scarcely sufficient for so many. Could we spare milk?"

They spared milk and butter and cheese and many cakes of Dolly's baking but, in spite of everything there came a day when a girl came running to the house, knocking wildly on the door. Could Mistress Dolly Copp come at once?

Dolly outdistanced the girl as she ran up the road to find the baby stiff and blue. She laid him in a hot bath, her sure fingers rubbing, her eyes watching closely until he breathed normally and his color was pronounced "right." She sat in the half furnished room, her feet on the bare, cold floor, for the husband's outdoor work gave him little time for keeping up the fire. Her head was bent over the baby in her arms but often she glanced about with keen eyes, watching the tired, half-sick woman. Finally, she spoke brightly, cheerfully and there was authority in her voice. The woman was too hard pressed with sickness and journeying and settling and she, Dolly, would bundle the little fellow against the cold and carry him home and 'tend him as one of her own until such time as he was able to play and eat and sleep as did Daniel.

Neighbors.

Hayes nodded his approval as the child was laid in Daniel's cradle. Nat and Jerry watched the little fellow through the winter days and Silvia 'tended him through the busy hours and often sat by the fire rocking him until he slept. As they accepted the truth that there was heat from the sun, so they accepted the truth that there was magic in their mother's hands. Did she not make plants thrive? Already were there not growing by the corners of her house lilacs of great strength? Were not her "wildings" growing into strong apple-bearing trees? When a seed brought forth a sickly plant did she not, with the same magic, bring cow manure from the pasture and feed and pet it until it grew strong like others in the row? The winter months passed and that the sickly boy was growing pink and rosy, grasping his mug of milk with sharpening appetite, creeping after Daniel and laughing in new health, did not surprise them.

One spring day she took the little fellow home and the bond of neighborhood friendship was so great a reward that her eyes sparkled with pleasure as she walked back alone down the road.

Hardly had that family begun to thrive on what was to be a prosperous farm than another house was built bringing a closer neighbor, Mr. Culbane, and across the river there came those who were to remain their friends for many years—a farm cleared by one Frederick and Sally Spaulding. In this house were four children and now all told there were four families—neighbors—warm friendship, visiting, fun-making among the young, consultation and advice among the elders and more and more prosperity for all.

That the commodious old Copp house was not only the center but the strength and inspiration of this neighborliness no one would have thought of questioning; that it was becoming the goal of many a day's hard travel to weary ones caught by darkness, to others merely stopping in mid-day to assuage their hunger, was also true.

The occupants of the home watched with interest the change in the vehicles that passed. Sometimes it was the slow-moving ox cart, more and more often the farmer's creaky but sturdy wagon; but, now and then they looked with frightening eyes at handsome carriages and before too long they were to see something that was beyond their wildest dreams—a coach carrying mail from the new Railroad Center at Gorham down the valley to the beautiful new hotel called the Glen House or farther down to Jackson and Conway. Not regularly, no one would expect that, but now and then; and the man representing the Government, conscious of some subtle quality of his cargo far outweighing any dollar value, drove into the enclosure, rested his horses and ate his midday meal at the Copps'. When there was a rare letter from a relative or friend it was read aloud at the table and everyone joined in discussion of the news.

On one fall day, a man who had come to the Hills to renew his failing health, announced that he was opening a school and soon with laughter and excitement, curious home-made vehicles were seen passing, carrying children of all ages to be "educated."

Hayes had fastened on a pung, a circular seat constructed from a cross section of pine, hollowed out to make a snug place for the children. In this, on snappy cold mornings, one saw the red caps and red cheeks of the laughing children as Hayes drove them to school over the hard crust of snow, leaving them with their lunch boxes to return for them in the afternoon. Of the fact that his children were fluent readers from the Book, that they wrote legibly, he was justly proud; but now they were to learn much else. Soon on the parlor table there appeared other books, treasured and studied by young and old. There were a geography and a history and one that became perhaps more quickly worn with use—a speller.

Here was fun for all. Often on winter nights the neighbors came, sometimes on snowshoes from their farms, and before Dolly's blazing fire there was conducted a spelling bee and the triumph of some oldster who spelled down the over-confident youth was greeted with hilarious laughter.

While they eagerly welcomed these bright spots that enlivened the days of arduous labor, always they must be wary. A family returning in the night from such a party, a mother carrying an infant in her arms as other little hands tugged at her skirts, kept close to the father and grown sons whose ears were alert to every sound emanating from the surrounding forest. A moving shadow might be a hungry bear. Harmless until frightened, they knew this fellow must be passed quietly. No one spoke and, huddled close together, they proceeded cautiously over the snowy road. Dark lines streaking across the edge of tree trunks might be wildcats. When there was a wolf cry, followed by many growls, they hurried, fearful for their sheep or pigs. A din in their poultry yard meant that the hated weasel or skunk or cunning fox was foraging to satisfy his hunger.

Their losses were sometimes heavy but the larger plantings, the more extensive grazing pastures increased their harvests and they prospered and grew in strength.

It was in the fall when the harvest was stored in barn and shed, before the snow became too deep, that they now felled more trees. With the community of spirit in the neighborhood, the farmer with oxen lent his double yokes to him who had none and soon great piles of heavy logs awaited the lumber man who came with cash in hand to hawl the wood away. In the winter after every frightful storm, it was necessary to "break" the roads. Here, heavy "stone boats" were used, sometimes with hook-ups of six or eight of the slow moving but powerful oxen.

Now there was something troubling Hayes—something as inevitable as the course of the seasons. It concerned Jerry, the stalwart, steady farmer. From boyhood he had quietly taken on a man's responsibility. That he had year by year become as "his right arm," Hayes knew well.

Dolly, throughout the summer months had said, "He goes often to see this girl. We shall lose him. I wish I could see her and know what the wench is like." But Hayes, watching the lad as they worked together in the fields thought quite differently. Always he only smiled and nodded assent as Jerry asked for the horse on Saturday nights. There was a bashful turning away of his head; a flush on his face and—as Hayes saw clearly—a light in his eyes. On such nights there was scrubbing and cleaning and dressing in his good suit. Off he rode, returning in the early hours, hardly with an hour's sleep before daylight when he was up and taking his usual part in the morning chores.

Hayes watched silently and thought, "He is in love. The mother will rebel and grieve but when it comes time for the eaglet to leave the nest, he must go. A whole man comes to the time when he must have his own life, own family, own home."

One cold January day, Jerry drove away with his trunk in the back of the sleigh. Two days later, while a neighbor cared for the cattle, Hayes, Dolly, Silvia, Nat and Daniel drove to the wedding.

Then the bitter winter closed in in earnest and often for weeks the families were, as Dolly often said, "jailed in." With the snow six feet deep on the level, with drifts banked against the windows closing some to any view of the outside world, the inner passage from house through the sheds, was a boon to man and beast. On nights when the temperature dropped to thirty and forty below zero Hayes stirred uneasily. The house was snug, the fires kept up, but there was danger for the cattle. Dolly would waken to say, "You take your rest. Nat will be up."

Then they listened to the footsteps coming quietly down the stairs as Nat passed through the hall and kitchen, going to the shed where he secured a stiff prong. Out in the barn they heard his voice angrily shouting at the hogs as with long prong he stirred them up, forcing them to move about before they should be frozen to death. After looking over all the cattle and being assured of their safety, he returned and they listened as he stopped in the kitchen for a hot drink, then slowly ascended the stairs to shiver in his bed until the feathers warmed him.

❦

It was in late March and though the snow still lay deep in the woods, the bitter storms of winter had passed and now they could almost feel the sap rising in the maples.

At night they were often awakened by the sound of snapping and booming as the ice broke up in the river. In bright daylight they raised their eyes and smiled to see the wild geese flying high. Soon the great eagle would return to his home and the birds would nest and the woodpeckers would hammer and a restlessness seize upon the young; when the blood coursed through their veins and they felt, without understanding, the strange mystery of life.

However, the farmers knew that in those three or four short weeks beginning at the end of March, there was heavy work to do for the sap ran only once in the year and the sugar must be made sufficient in quantity to last through all four seasons.

Often Nat would ask about the time when Hayes had first come to the Glen. Did the Indians use the sap?

Hayes nodded. "We learned from them." While, out in the snow not far from the shed door, he drove into the ground forked posts, then placed on them a strong pole where should be hung the huge kettles to hold the syrup, he told the boys how he had seen the Indians drive small wooden taps into the maples, gather the sap in bark cups, then pour it into large wooden bowls. Skillfully they boiled it down by first getting small rocks red hot in a fire, then dropping those rocks into the sap. Hayes laughed as he added that neither Dolly nor the boys would have liked the looks of that sooty blackish syrup nor cared for the finished product, for the Indians mixed bear's grease into this dark fluid. At their meals, they dipped in venison or corn bread. They all laughed and Dolly said she wanted no such sooty mixture.

That their method of making the syrup, although differing from the Indian's, was still primitive, they were unaware. Now, Nat tapped the trees with sumac stems and the syrup was caught in small home-made wooden buckets. Hayes emptied into large wooden buckets hung on the shoulder yokes of the stalwart boys who carried the liquid to be poured into the great kettles over the fire.

It was to be a long remembered night for a party was planned for the "sugar brush." Young folks were invited from far and near, and Jerry was to come with the "pretty wench" who had stolen his heart, now his young wife.

By late afternoon, the sleds and wagons began arriving and red-cheeked young men with their girls dressed in pretty wools filled the parlor with laughter and much chatter. When Jerry's wife, Susan, came to Dolly, she flushed to the roots of her hair. Dolly laughed and welcomed her but the girl did not miss the shrewdness of the appraisal as the sharp eyes of Jerry's mother looked her over.

Hayes had long since pronounced her "a comely, wholesome lass" but Dolly was not so easily mollified by a sweet young face. That young thing had come like a thief in the night to steal her son and leave an emptiness in her heart.

It was well that she little dreamed that among that company was one who would deal that heart a far greater injury.

Above, in the open sky, there was a full moon and out in the snow the young folks watched the white liquid turn to golden syrup. With wooden dippers they poured the syrup into the snow to harden and when they were gorged with sweets, they ate sour pickles to renew their appetites.

They crowded around the kitchen table as Dolly and Silvia served heaping plates of pancakes and over these the syrup was poured as young men ran in and out, bringing it in dippers from the snow.

The table and chairs were finally pushed back and the floor cleared for dancing. The visitors had brought their fiddler who went to work with a will and as the lilting tune of the jig filled the room young feet began to tap, and the girls flushed, looking up with bashful eyes as they waited to be invited to join the squares.

Near the fireplace stood lovely Silvia and often Dolly's eyes rested on her. She wore a pretty dress and only Dolly knew the fineness of the stitches that had fashioned the floating ruffles, the delicate lace at throat and sleeves. That she was, with her blond curls and bright eyes, a vision of beauty in the pale blue dress more than one farm boy had discovered. However, as soon as the fiddler had struck the tune a young man who had come from Maine—a stranger to them, though a relative of their neighbor—stepped up to claim the lovely girl. Others followed quickly and soon all were swinging and laughing as the fiddler "called" the numbers.

Out in the snow Hayes tended the crackling fire and into the clear air rose the clouds of steam from the boiling syrup. Hayes knew there was a jug of O-be-joy-ful in the shed and some cider that could not claim to be "fresh," that some of the farmboys repaired there often, but there was no excess and he only smiled at the gales of laughter that greeted jokes they cracked while sitting around between the many dances.

Only once a year could there be such a party in the "sugar brush," only once a year came that breaking of the winter and the advent of spring. That the blood was flowing more tumultuously in their bodies than any sap in the trees he knew, and vaguely he knew that through all ages man had celebrated the "rite of spring." The men of ancient times in their way, the Indian is his way and now the farmers in the White Hills in the "sugar brush."

At last, reluctantly and with much loitering they prepared to leave. The girls bundled up in their warm furs and wools although some blushingly knew that young men had other ways of warding off the cold when huddled in the big farm sleds. So busy was Dolly watching Jerry say goodbye to his Susan that she entirely missed another scene that would have frightened her.

Silvia stood back in the parlor shyly bidding each one farewell while near her hovered that youth who had claimed her for most of the dances. She felt his eyes always on her face. When he was left alone he came in front of her and daringly placed his finger under her chin and raised her face until their eyes met. What she saw compelled her to try to shield her sweet blue eyes from his gaze. In a low voice he whispered, "You know? I'll come for you tomorrow. Will you go driving with me?"

Faintly she whispered, "Yes." Then quickly he bent and touched her lips with his and in a moment he was gone, jumping into a moving sled.

The young girl ran quickly to her room. When her mother called, she answered, "I'm changing my dress."

She must help with the cleaning up. Taking off her pretty shoes she slipped into her workaday clothes but her hands fumbled. Before she left her room, she walked to the little window and her hands pressed hard on the sill as she looked up into the night sky where that fine clear moon was riding high. Her cheeks were still hot and once she touched her lips with a delicate finger. The kiss seemed to be still burning there. Would it show? Would her mother's sharp eyes see?

CHAPTER XX

OFTEN IN THAT SPRING PLOWING Hayes stopped his work and stood with bent head looking down at the dark, moist earth. For some time he was lost in thought, then, again resuming his task, he sighed for there was in his heart a "great pity for the woman."

In the house he sometimes heard snatches of their conversation.

"You're too young, Silvia."

There was in answer a merry laugh.

"Why, Mother, I'm nineteen years old."

Was there some boldness in the laugh? Was there that in woman that makes for boldness in matters such as these? Was it near thirty years ago that the mother had taken things in her own hands at a certain meeting in his cousin's house? How cleverly she had brought things to a head when he fumbled stupidly for words, choosing all the wrong ones.

There was no chattering now from Dolly's lips. She could not lightly say, "No, you're not a woman, nineteen years of age. You're a new-born babe—always—a girl-child suckling at my breast. You are my daughter, my loved companion. From the time when I outgrew my dolls there was always a hunger in my heart for you. I wanted my sons. I loved my sons—yes—still—was it not for you I waited? When I had given up hope of your ever being more than a dream, you came into the world. Nineteen years! It is but one short bright day. It will be dull and dark when you are gone."

Instead she said testily, "It's a pity you could not have chosen one of our fine young neighbors who have looked on you with favor. In the Glen there is rich ground and everyone would have been glad to lend helping hands—if you had chosen to stay with us."

There was a moment of silence, then a merry laugh rang out. "Mother, did you choose to stay on the great highway by your father's house? Wasn't it you who left behind all that was safe—home, friends, neighbors—journeying far into an unknown wilderness?" Now there was sweet coaxing in the young voice, "Doesn't it gladden your heart to know I go to a home in a fine town?"

Dolly sat with compressed lips, head bent over her work. She suffered, for the blow had come all unexpected. There had been no preparation. On that spring day when the young man had come to their door with his horse and sled, she had looked from one face to the other and what she saw in both pairs of eyes had filled her with sudden terror but after the sled had disappeared up the road, she denied it.

Worry showed in her own eyes as she went about her afternoon's work. A short ride? No, they were gone several hours and when they returned there was that in their faces she could not deny.

He prolonged his visit, coming day after day and, when they stood one afternoon before Hayes and Dolly, saying they wished to be married in the fall, they were not asking permission, they were stating their decision.

Her daughter. That lovely, gentle girl. Had there only been other daughters to wear the pretty bonnets and flounced skirts, to be always at home. She had been as a flower growing in their rough field. Oh yes, she was capable. Dolly had taught her to spin and weave and cook; and her needle was guided by slender but strong fingers as she sewed; and beautifully she knit. However, no one of the family would have suffered her to engage in the rough work of field or the distasteful labor in soap making or slaughtering.

Never to see those deep blue eyes sparkle as she looked up into her brothers' faces and listened to their tales of the hunt? Never to hear her sweet voice singing as she went about the household tasks?

Often in those spring nights, Hayes knew Dolly slept not and he thought, "she grieves."

With the road again clear and the days warm in June, the postman turned into their enclosure and smiled at the girl waiting outside the door. Always there was a letter and she read aloud the part which told how her new home was being built. There were parts she did not read aloud but learned by heart in the privacy of her room.

One night lying in their bed before they slept, Hayes said, "About Silvia. We must do well by her." There was only a deep sigh for answer.

He pursued, "I plan to make for her a splendid trunk. I plan to make it strong of wood and cover it with leather and fine trim of brass. I have seen hatboxes and would make the same. The foundation shall be strong and you will cover it neatly with wall paper and knit of a pretty color, ties and loops."

He waited and there was no response. "It would be fitting if into this trunk were placed fine sheets and table cloths and many towels and such useful and pretty clothing as you can fashion."

By his side Dolly wept. At last she said, though her voice was hoarse, "I will fill the trunk and boxes."

The coming marriage was accepted. Never had the girl's voice sounded sweeter or merrier as mother and daughter worked at wheel or loom. Out in the shed Nat helped his father as they fashioned such a trunk as would endure for a lifetime.

There was more than preparation for weddings to occupy them through those summer days. One July morning a splendid carriage turned into their enclosure. There was a driver, a gentleman and two young ladies. One quick glance and Dolly knew they were of "high station." The gentleman alighted and approached smilingly, expressing his surprise at seeing the good farm and house. "Could this possibly be Dolly Copp?"

She acknowledged her identity and then he explained that some years before he had visited at a hotel down at the Great Notch with much benefit to his health and with admiration for the beautiful country. Since, he had travelled in Europe where he and his daughter had climbed many peaks in the Alps. At that time of his visit in these White Hills this section of the country had been a vast impenetrable wilderness. Now with the new road opened he wanted to show his daughter and her friend this, their native land, and climb the most famous Mount Washington. At Gorham he had been told that an excellent meal could be had at the home of Dolly Copp.

All this was explained as the two young ladies alighted. In her hospitable way, Dolly invited them all into her parlor, dispatching Silvia to find Nat that the driver and horses might be cared for.

To her questioning she found they were planning on an extended stay at the Glen House. Whether it was from the odor of food being prepared in her deep ovens or from the ladies' delight in examining her beautiful woven spreads or from some simple enticement in the place as a whole, it mattered not, for they were soon making plans with Dolly for a night's rest. They must eat at her table and sleep in her inviting beds.

Soon Hayes appeared in his rough muddy clothes. With his usual dignity he greeted the guests but soon left, seeking Nat in the barn. Placing a gun and hunting knife in his hands he smiled, "You may find a partridge or some duck."

As the ladies in the downstairs bedroom and the gentleman in his room above, unpacked and made themselves comfortable, Silvia set the table. That the ladies' eyes opened wide in surprise at the snowy linen, the delicate gold-edged china and beautiful English silver, Dolly noted not without both inner amusement and some satisfaction. That they exclaimed about the flavor of the food and offered their plates for refilling, did not surprise her. She had come to expect that.

Throughout the afternoon their pleasure in everything on the place became evident. Although she had many other tasks waiting, she nevertheless spun for them and worked her loom. If at times she was a little scornful in her heart at performing as an "exhibition," she only smiled for now she was quite used to these city folks and their many questions. About her cunning with that heavenly blue dye, however, she divulged no secrets.

As the hours wore on they became more completely at home and won the hearts and sincere admiration of their hosts. The man was tall and handsome and dressed in excellent taste. His shirt, open at the throat, was simple but Dolly rightly gauged its fineness. His heavy trousers were tucked into high calfskin boots. The young ladies were similarly dressed in harmony with a mountain journey. They were courteous and asked permission before going into kitchen, shed or barn but their real interest soon enticed Hayes to leave his work in the muddy field, clean his boots and conduct them about the place.

Nothing was so large or so small as not to claim their attention and elicit intelligent questions. The irons at the fireplace, the crane and kettles and frying and baking irons, the wooden shutters at the ovens all were of interest. Dolly swept and made an oven ready for the night's cooking. She told them the history of the clock.

Through the sheds they went with Hayes. Minutely the powder horn was examined, the wood-plugged base, the stopper to keep the powder in. At last they would be aware of the difference between a noggin and a skimmer. The gentleman asked, "You say basswood is not prone to split? Why, this shell is of little more than an eighth of an inch in thickness, yet how durable, for you say you have used it for over twenty years. Amazing. But for milk, must there not be a special way of cleaning it?"

"It is scoured day in and day out, year after year, with sand and a stiff brush."

They learned the uses of the noggin but it was when catching sight of the great demijohns and carboys of crude glass that they exclaimed in admiration. They handled the little kegs and large barrels for cider or rum. The gentleman spoke of the wonderful harmony of proportion and size. When they came to the large barn Hayes must explain the clever yokes and all his home-made contrivances and there was deep respect mingled with their admiration.

The gentleman spoke to Hayes: "You were blessed with four fine children?"

There was a quizzical smile in Hayes' eyes. "Thank 'ee." Then slowly, "Yes. Four children with good reason and proper shapes."

As they passed through a shed the gentleman's eyes were caught by a row of mugs, some rather small holding perhaps a pint, others large enough to hold a quart of liquid. Cider mugs? Fashioned entirely by hand? Hayes explained that in winter days when there were hours that might be wasted in idleness, they sat by the fire, fashioning these mugs from the wood of wild apple trees found in the forest. The cup and handle were carved out of one piece of wood and as the gentlemen balanced one on his hand he expressed wonder at its beauty and perfection. "Apple juice to be drunk from apple wood."

Then followed the story of Dolly's orchard and the fine growth of fruit-bearing trees developed from the "wildings." That orchard they must examine. So unafraid of some mud, for there had been recent rain, the young ladies followed through the orchard, then on to the river, hearing of the endless supply of trout.

Back through the buildings they journeyed, then stood on the grass before the house while the gentleman looked about him. He turned to his daughter. "Here about us in this Glen is a kindly beauty; in those dark gulfs and ravines there is a somber beauty and only lift your eyes to the great mountain top and there is a sublimity, a majestic beauty. I can't even in imagination picture the work in breaking this road, clearing, planting and making a home. My feeble words will never do justice to the lives of such men as this Hayes Copp."

The girl turned to Silvia, who had approached. "My Father is a writer of essays and poems. I am sure many will he written from the inspiration of this day's visit."

As they sat about an evening fire, Dolly wondered at the daring of the young ladies in planning to climb the great mountain peak. It was rough and treacherous, often defeating strong men. The ravines would be filled still with ice and the storms and clouds were frightening at the summit. The wind might blow with such violence that even the guides could not endure it.

Hayes spoke. "Never have I known trouble save when the climbers did not heed the guides. Their horses are sure-footed; their warnings of storm or danger must be heeded."

They assured him they would stick close to the guide and do nothing he advised against.

It was a pleasant evening and in the morning, although they remonstrated against the smallness of the price, the "shilling all 'round" was paid.

The carriage was waiting as Hayes came in from the shed. In his hand he carried one of the finest of the apple-mugs. With simple dignity and friendliness he handed it to the gentleman. "It would give me pleasure if you cared to accept this."

With evident sincerity the man replied, "With many thanks. It will be one of my treasures in our home." Then with promises to return, they drove off.

Dolly was closing her book into which she had entered their names. She placed it in the drawer of her little table, then looked up at Hayes.

She spoke thoughtfully, "They were the finest guests we have ever entertained. Ladies and a real gentleman. Hayes, the Glen House has many guests. I hear that people are coming from as far away as London to see and climb these White Hills and at the hotel they make long visits. Already I've made more butter and cheese and gathered more eggs than we can use. Wouldn't it be well to find a market for all that is above our need? Couldn't we send Nat with such and, if the Glen House wanted to buy, would it not add much to that in our pouch?"

Hayes stood long, seemingly lost in deep study. That it was study of the "endless ambition of the woman" she did not guess. At last he replied, "Nat shall be sent if that is your wish. Soon Dan will be old enough to trust with a horse and then he can go."

It was her work, her province. Like her weaving and spinning and cooking and like her orchard, it filled him with pride and often with amazement.

Nat was sent with beautiful large jars of butter and cheese and eggs. When he returned his eyes were bulging to match his pockets as he handed her the many shillings. "They want all you can send, Mother."

She laughed quietly as she put the money away. Dolly had established an outside market in which to exchange for money the many products produced by her capable hands.

Through that summer many guests came to their door and left with words of appreciation of the hospitality of that home.

In spite of the coming separation, they were good days, bright days. They were prosperous. Besides all the produce coming in from their garden, there was money to use for the purchases which Dolly and Silvia planned.

As they worked one day, Silvia said, "Mother, for this wedding you must have a pretty gown and father a fine suit. I don't mean it to be only a good gown; I wish it to be special. Can't we go to town and purchase a piece of silk for you and order for father a splendid broadcloth coat?"

Dolly smiled. "If that is what you wish."

"That isn't all. You won't deny me this. Together we will sew the gown and when it is completed you will wear it. Then we shall have pictures made of you both. It will mean so much if I can take such pictures with me to my new home."

Dolly was pleased and soon a journey was made and all the silk and trimmings bought and Hayes' coat was ordered and in due time was delivered to their home.

There was much other purchasing for new clothes must be planned for the two sons and many pretty and useful articles to place in the trunk.

So, day after day, Silvia and Dolly bent over their work and by the middle of September all was finished and the photographer was sent for. Thus it was that because of Silvia's urging, a fine picture of both Hayes Copp and Dolly was to be made, pictures that posterity would treasure beyond their imaginings.

There was both dignity and perfect ease in her posture as Dolly sat on the splint-bottomed chair. Her hair was parted severely in the middle, slicked down, but with soft puffs over her ears as was the custom. She wore a delicate head dress with rather long ribbons hanging below her shoulders. The black silk skirt was voluminous, the basque buttoned closely-up the front. Over this basque she wore a beautiful black silk shawl, the collar was trimmed with two rows of narrow black velvet ribbon, while the same velvet ribbons edged the bottom which was finished in a heavy knotted fringe. There was a little white linen collar, beautifully embroidered. At the front a black velvet bow and the same gold pin that had come with her to the Glen. That it would not have been Dolly without the gold beads they all knew, so carefully Silvia pulled them outside the collar to show.

Yes, the figure was heavy, the mouth firm, the face showed the hard life endured for many years; but there was also—and no country photography could dim them—the wonderful eyes—deep, brilliant, humorous, intelligent and still looking directly at life—undaunted.

It was a trying ordeal for Hayes, though he wore his fine black broadcloth coat with the silk-faced lapels with easy dignity. He made the best he could of feeling comfortable in the starched white shirt with its turn-down starched collar and large black satin tie, knotted and hanging down far over the lapels of his coat. His fine head was still covered with heavy hair, parted far to one side and forming curly bunches over his ears. There was the stern face, unsmiling, brows knitted, the strong chin, the wide mouth drawn down a bit at the corners—a weathered face but a fearful directness in his gaze. Like the eagle's eyes, his had peered into far distances, into dark forest shadows. It was the face of a man who "would endure."

With a tender smile, Silvia wrapped her pictures in soft cloth and placed them in her trunk.

Now they were ready for the wedding—for the parting.

CHAPTER XXI

BY THE MIDDLE of October, often the summits of the great peaks were covered with their winter whiteness. In the early morning as Hayes went about his work, he watched the mists slowly disperse; then, as the sun poured its brilliance on them, the white domes seemed sheathed in mother-of-pearl.

Two young men, part of a group of travellers who had spent the night and breakfasted, stood outside the kitchen door. There was something like awe in the voice of the younger as he asked, "Is it always like this? Every fall?"

Hayes answered thoughtfully, "It may be uncommon bright this year."

"So you call this Indian Summer?"

There was now a quizzical smile in the eyes beneath the knitted brows. "Folks call names according to their notions."

"What do you call Indian Summer?"

He thought a minute. "There comes a time in November when the trees are bare of leaves and both man and animal have dug in 'gainst the cold—dug in for the winter. Then there comes a spell of near summer heat—lasts sometimes about a week. Out come the squirrels, rabbits, deer—all the animals—and out come the Indians to catch them." He smiled broadly. "Many a settler—'til he learned—got caught then with no leaves to hide him. Those few warm days got to be called Indian Summer—with good reason." As his listeners laughed, he finished, "Up here Indian Summer comes in November."

All the family would have agreed with him. In those mountains November was winter but the October days, the harvest days, the days of glorious beauty were called fall.

Sometimes they spoke of them as "rustling days." The corn had been cut by hand and now, gathered in shocks, stood in straight rows and there was music in the fields as a gentle breeze rustled through their tops. There was a silvery dew on the pumpkins scattered along the rows. The last of the apples hanging on the trees were waiting to be picked and the morning sunshine enhanced the crimson of their cheeks. Sometimes the branches were bent low with the weight of the fruit that so richly rewarded Dolly for her years of nurturing them.

Silvia came from the river where she had been watching Daniel cast his line for a string of trout. She wore boots and an old work dress as she walked across the russet grass and joined the group

The young man was excitedly calling to a girl within, "Do come out. Look! Right up there." He was pointing to the stone face on the mountain. "I've always heard about that stone face but I never saw it so plainly."

Silvia smiled, "Some say that from this spot, by our kitchen door, there is the best view of it to be found in all the Glen."

"What is it called?" It ought to have a beautiful name."

Both she and Daniel burst into laughter. "Ask my mother. Long ago she named it The Imp."

Dolly stood in the doorway, her arms folded across her chest. They turned to her but she only laughed, "That's what it looks like to me. An Imp."

It was when they were packed and ready to drive away that the girl called back, "We'll hope to come back some time and see Dolly's Imp again."

Silvia was laughing as she turned to her father "Wouldn't it be funny if the name stuck? Dolly's Imp?"

Then he told her of the famous Copp's Hill in Boston, the old Copp's burial ground, the Copp's Bridge in Maine, their own bridge now always called Copp's Bridge.

"And now you think there might be Dolly's Imp?"

"It might be."

Her laughter gave way to thoughtfulness "Father, I'm going to miss our mountain. That peak does sort of belong to us, doesn't it?"

He nodded. "Your mother has word that the artist is coming again to paint the fall colors."

Their eyes followed that color across the lower slopes—orange, masses of pale yellow and russet brown mixed with evergreen, stretches of purple and spots of scarlet so brilliant as to be unbelievable. Silvia drew a long breath. "Why does anyone try to make a picture of that? Nature takes up miles and miles to make her picture and no two places are alike Besides, it changes every hour of the day. I think an artist must be rather conceited to think he could put it on a little piece of canvas."

"Guess there's no harm in their getting their fun trying."

"But really he doesn't get it at all."

Nat passed them carrying a ladder which he set against the apple tree. She turned toward the orchard. "I'd better be getting to work if we've to get the packing done before the party."

Throughout the day all worked, for the products of garden and orchard and field were being stored in cellar and shed and barn against the coming of winter.

It was to be Silvia's last party and this was to be a neighborhood affair. Toward the end of the day they came in groups from across the river, from up the road, fathers, mothers and all the children from the four farms.

In the parlor, the light in the room was rose-colored and the faces within glowed with that unearthly beauty as the sun moved westward, flooding the entire Glen. There was a bounteous supper and then about the kitchen fire there was the apple stringing.

The winter crop would be stored away; apples would be stewed or beat into light sauce or baked in the deep ovens where the maple sugar and nutmeg gratings had seeped through and through flavoring the fruit to Dolly's satisfaction. Now with expert fingers the women and girls pared, carefully extracting the cores until neat round holes were left. Cutting evenly they strung these slices, tying the loops which would be hung on wooden pegs to dry the apples for midwinter use.

Outside, there was a hand-press and as boys brought the apples they were dumped into a rotary bladed grinder where Nat and Hayes took turns, for it was arduous work to turn the grinder crank and press the fruit into a watery pulp.

Out came all the apple mugs and from them were drunk quantities of fresh cider. That such a party should end without a dance or a spelling bee was unthinkable. As the night grew chilly, more logs were heaped on the fire and the women relaxed indulging in good talk. At last the sleeping babies were bundled up, the little children yawned and shivered as the groups, one by one, went out into the darkness to make their way to their homes.

On the morrow, the house was cleaned and put in order. Every bed was freshly made, every chair put in place and into the deep ovens went the quantities of food that would be needed for the wedding guests.

Reluctantly, Dolly turned away transients, for there would be relatives of the groom, friends from distant farms and from the towns, and many would remain for days.

On the wedding morning, long before the rising of the sun, the men were finishing the chores, the early breakfast was eaten, the dishes washed and put away and when the first carriage appeared in the enclosure, Silvia with trembling fingers was buttoning the basque of her pretty wedding dress, and Dolly was laying the beautiful shawl-cape about her shoulders. Hayes frowned as he suffered the torture of the starched white shirt and cramping stiff collar, the boys were scrubbed and self-conscious in their new suits. Then the parson arrived with the Book in his hands.

In the barn already stood the new carriage that Benjamin Potter had driven in. Long since Hayes and Nat had placed in the hack the handsome brass-studded trunk.

When, in the beauty of the fall coloring, the couple repeated the sacred words that bound them "until death do us part," there was a hush in the room. Hayes' eyes rested not on his daughter but on Dolly. Her head was slightly lowered and she was biting hard into her lips but there were no tears.

Silvia Copp and Benjamin Potter were man and wife. Now the room was filled with a babel of voices. There was laughter and bustle and the men pulled out into the center the already set table. Silvia ran to her room to change the lovely blue dress for one suitable for travelling and soon the wedding breakfast was served. In the parlor, in the kitchen, out on the grass they stood in groups, for they must eat in relays. No table could seat so many.

From the barn, Benjamin drove the horse and new carriage, He waited at the door. There were quick embraces, a kiss on Hayes' weathered cheek, one moment of clinging in her mother's arms, then with many goodbyes, the boys lifted her lightly into the seat beside her husband. They shouted good wishes and waved and waved until the carriage disappeared into the forest road.

Soon, those coming from long distances departed and only the relatives remained. Dolly took off her finer new clothes and in her good homespun resumed her usual occupations as hostess and cook, but not until the week's end was the home quite back to normal.

What her feelings were as she changed the room in which Silvia had slept from babyhood, one could only guess. Now it would serve as another guest room. For weeks she was short in temper, sharp in speech, irritable, silent when she had always chattered pleasantly. It was an unpleasant surprise for father and sons.

One day Nat spoke to Hayes. "It seems there is no pleasing her."

Hayes rebuked him. "You will be patient. She suffers deeply."

"But we didn't carry Silvia off."

Sternly, "You will be patient. It is a great loss."

"But we feel it too."

Hayes had no answer. Did they not all feel that the house was dull and heavy and work-laden without the girl? He looked at his son, remembering that he too would some day marry. "When you come on trying days, Nat, it's you that must have patience. A fester doesn't heal by complaining about it. It needs a little time. Just now your mother needs a little time."

Nat watched his father walk away. How bent and old he looked, how weathered, how grim of visage. He murmured to himself, "He's a patient man." He had been patient with Jerry and with him and now with Daniel, and yet often they must have tried him with their carelessness and blundering ways.

The artist came and brought with him a fellow painter. No sooner were they established, unpacking all their canvases and boxes than there came an arrival who developed into something like a rainbow in a dark, cloudy sky.

One morning there appeared at their door a curious looking old fellow with a large knapsack strapped to his back. His face was the color of old red leather and not unlike it in texture. About his cheeks and chin was a fringe of white hair—more than appeared to be left on his bald head. However, one soon forgot his lack of comeliness in observing his eyes. They were light blue with the curious far-searching expression so often seen in those of men of the sea; and this he proved to be—an old sea captain. When Dolly opened the door, he reached to his shoulder and swung around an enormous horn covered with black baize. The small end he inserted in his ear. It seemed he was deaf and one must talk into this black baize.

"Is this a tavern?"

Dolly spoke into the horn. "Not exactly. Do you want food and lodging? We offer it."

"What's the price?"

She explained about the shillings. He thought awhile.
"The food good?"
"The best."
"Beds?"
"Comfortable."
"My corns are hurting. I'll try it for a night."

She had received guests in many ways but never before had one within the hour sat before her kitchen fire as she placed a basin of hot water on the floor and ordered him to immerse his bare feet even as she poured some dark liquid into the pan. He was paring the corns as Hayes entered.

Above the old man's head, Dolly's eyes were filled with laughter as she told Hayes how to talk into the horn.

That night they all sat about the fire, the family, the two artists and the old man and never had there been such bursts of laughter as followed the captain's stories, the sallies, the jokes. Before he slept he mixed his own toddy. When Hayes offered rum he fairly bellowed, "Take it away, man." Then he poured in whiskey from his own flask and Hayes dryly remarked to Dolly, "He will have no knowledge of the hardness or softness of the bed."

The artists packed their canvasses—with more humility than Silvia could have imagined—and departed but the sea captain said, "I'll stay the month."

One night when all had been fed and gone to their beds, Dolly sat alone by the fire. Her shoulders sagged heavily. Her hair had grown so sparse that now against the cold she wore a wig. There was a sad drooping about her lips. Long she sat gazing into the burning logs, her elbows resting on her knees. Silvia was gone. Jerry, Hayes' "right arm," was gone. More and more strangers would sleep in their beds. She rose, went to the closet, took down one of the clay pipes. She filled it with tobacco, went back to the fire and sat puffing. It soothed and comforted.

From the big bed Hayes questioned, "Would you sit the night through?"

"It doesn't trouble me."

His eyes rested on her with deep affection, for, to him, she looked what she was—a great pioneer woman. Would the heart that had never quailed before the hardships, the gruelling labor, the disappointments of *building*, accept without flinching the changes that must come? The partings?

The eaglets grow strong and must seek to build their own nests. Never, by day or night, had she spared herself in feeding them, nursing them, ministering to their every want. Had "the woman" never realized that there would come a time when they would no longer want to cluster about her knees?

He watched her sitting sadly drooping, gazing into the fire, puffing on her clay pipe and he thought, "How deeply she grieves."

CHAPTER XXII

BEFORE THE OLD sea captain left the snow lay deep on the ground and Nat drove him in the sled to the railroad station for his return to his home on the Massachusetts coast.

Nat called into the black baize, "We've enjoyed your visit. Come again."

The old man bellowed back, "I'll be up next summer. By then your cider should be fit to drink."

As December followed November, folks began to speak of the cold. The snow lay deep, the storms increased and it was with difficulty that Daniel, now approaching his eleventh year, could be taken back and forth to his school. Never before had the complete "jailing in" come so early and it was well they did not know that they were to pass through one of the most severe winters ever to be endured by the scattered families of the White Hills.

Sometimes in the short day, the sun hardly broke through the heavy snow clouds. Night closed in early and there were long hours when Nat became restless as his father sat at a table, reading the Book by the light of his tallow dip, his mother speaking little as her foot pressed the treadle. The young boy slept.

They carved more mugs, made stools, mended and painted and yet there was time on their hands.

Only four of them, for now visitors were few. Once to Nat's complaining Dolly replied, "Jerry could have brought the girl here. He knew there was plenty of room. We would have received them with pleasure."

"A girl may not want to be subject to another's ordering."

Dolly relapsed into silence and Nat thought his own thoughts as he polished a fine piece of maple.

So gradually did another change come that Dolly had scarcely taken note of it. Less often did Hayes shoulder his gun and go into the forest in search of food. Nat had become the hunter. Sometimes accompanied by young Daniel, more often alone, he roamed far and near, seeking game.

In that winter, of which tales of hardships endured would be recited for many years, January came with winds and storms so terrific that the strongest heart might quail contemplating the scenes outside their windows. The snow banks grew mountain high and though their livestock was housed and sheltered, they feared that the barn and sheds might be swept away in such gales.

Hour by hour the logs were laid on the fires and not without misgivings did Hayes watch the great piles diminish. Had they ever before endured quite so terrible a season?

In her "victual room," Dolly also watched some lowering of her stocks of salted food, some emptying of her sacks, yet daily she told Hayes they "would endure." There would be plenty.

There came fine winter days with clearing and over all a sky of such blue and sunshine of such blinding brightness that one could scarcely endure the brilliance. On such days Nat, skimming lightly over the crust in his snowshoes, surprised some small game and brought it in to add variety to their simple meals.

It was late in the month when for three successive days he hunted, bringing in small game but of the venison he sought he could find not a trace.

On the fourth day of his hunting he prepared shortly after his breakfast to go forth again.

Dolly, seeing him fastening his snowshoes, cautioned, "The storm is increasing and it's bitter cold, Nat. It's far too menacing for a man to venture far from his warm fire."

"Wouldn't you be grateful for some venison?"

She shook her head. "I would be grateful if you were less adventuresome. In such weather I'm only fidgetted until your return."

"I'll come back in good time."

"You promise?"

"I promise."

Hayes had been listening in silence. Now he spoke. "It is below the zero mark and falling. It is a time for caution." Still he knew that in as great cold he had sought deer in that white forest when hunger had driven him. His son was possessed of that same prodigious strength and at twenty-four years of age, he had proved himself a cautious and successful hunter.

When the door was opened to allow him to go out, there was a violent gust of wind that swept through the house and it was with difficulty that the door was again closed. They watched, as with remarkable speed he passed through the orchard, over the field and was lost in the white woods.

Daniel came in from the shed looking his surprise. "He has gone to the hills today? If he went with the wind, he'd be blown to the Notch without taking a step; against it, I doubt he can go far." In spite of their remonstrance both father and son may have felt a slight envy of the young man there in the storm fighting against that gale. Daniel added, "He told me he'd seen deer tracks up on the slope."

All returned to their many tasks and the hours of the morning passed quickly. Dolly was placing the dinner on the table, her eyes constantly raised to the window and it was with relief that she called "He's coming from the hill."

That there was a glow of triumph in his face, they all saw at once. He turned to his mother as he unfastened his snow-shoes and removed his heavy clothing. "It was because of my promise I returned. I killed a deer. In the morning I'll fetch it. Perhaps then the storm will have passed."

It was on the last day of January, the fifth day of his hunting. Eagerly he wakened and dressed in his heavy wool. Scarcely could he wait for his breakfast, so eager was he to get to the hills and bring home the wanted food. As he had hoped, the storm had abated but with its decreasing, the cold had grown greater. Now Hayes scowled and spoke his warning seriously. "The cold is threatening. Already it is far below the zero mark and falling."

Nat grinned. "Better than that wind of yesterday."

Hayes still scowled but was silent. That the lad would not rest with deer waiting on the mountain side, he knew; so he did not argue with his son.

Well clothed, breathing deeply of the cold air, Nat skimmed lightly over the snow, up and up until he came to the prostrate animal. From certain marks on the trees which he knew well, he figured the snow in level places must be full six feet deep but the crust below the last fall seemed as solid as their kitchen floor. Above, the sky was now a burning blue, the sun so brilliant that one avoided glancing upward.

Carefully, he tied his thongs about the animal and started the long trek homeward. How far was it? For eight miles he dragged the deer. Later they found it weighed two hundred and thirty pounds but he only exulted in its great size as he pulled it through the snow.

Not very far from home he discovered new tracks in the snow. Seeing them, for a moment he hesitated. Should he follow the tracks and perhaps be rewarded with more game, or should he first take this home? He decided it was best to return first with his deer.

About noon time he came again into the clearing and now the entire family waited at the shed door as he entered with his prize. Hayes and Daniel would prepare the good meat and Dolly returned to her cooking. Each being busy with his own tasks, no one noticed that Nat had again departed. Daniel wondered, "Could he have gone back to follow those new tracks?"

Dolly was worried. "To go again without stopping for food or drink? I think he would have spoken had he so intended."

But in her heart she felt quite otherwise. Too well she knew his daring, adventurous spirit. She sought Hayes. "Did he speak to you about returning to the forest?"

"No. You are sure he has gone?"

Daniel searched through the house and sheds and barns. "He's gone. His gun is here. He has taken only his hunting knife."

They cut and dressed and hung the meat and soon the bright sun was sinking below the western mountains and there was silence and bitter cold but no sign of Nat.

The supper hour came and although they ate big chunks of the venison there was worry which was not good seasoning. The mealtime passed and darkness fell and conversation ceased. Faces were sober and eyes avoided meeting other eyes, for now there was foreboding in all their hearts.

Only once did Hayes speak. He entered the parlor where Dolly sat at her wheel. "It has dropped to thirty-four below zero."

Her foot slipped from the treadle, her lips bitten hard as she looked up into his face.

His eyes looked into hers as he said, "I must act. Daniel will keep up the fires and you will be ready for that which may be."

❧

It had been about one o'clock when Nat, avoiding what he surmised might be argument to deter him, started back to traverse those miles to the place where he had seen the fresh deer tracks.

He found them in the soft layer of snow and began to follow. On and on he went sometimes losing the tracks, then filled with excitement as he found them again. He was so intent on the excitement of the chase as to be almost unconscious of the passing of time. At last, he realized that there was a dimness in the forest but seeing what he thought might be the same tracks he went on.

Again he had lost them. He turned and looked about. Where was he? How far from home had he wandered? That he had lost all trace of the deer he now knew; that he had lost all surety of his own whereabouts caused him to be first incredulous, then rather amused. He, Nat Copp, to be lost? Never before had it happened. Soon he would see land marks, for like an Indian's eyes, he could discern the slight markings of a familiar trail; but he realized quickly that this darkness among the bare branches was not because of clouds forming overhead, for the sky had been clear. It was dark because the sun had gone down.

It was only for a moment that he stood still, for now, with perfect composure, even with coolness, he told himself that never before had he been conscious of such bitter cold and he must move. He must keep moving, for to rest was fatal. He had walked steadily for many hours, and at last to rest awhile, to sink down into that soft bed of white would be so good, so welcome. Calmly he told himself what would follow. At first there would be that moment of delicious comfort, then a slow stupor, then an eternal sleep. Keep moving, keep moving; take one step after another and keep on and on and on, never mind in what direction, merely keep moving.

He had been "moving," taking one step after another for several hours when he became conscious of a brightness overhead. He raised his eyes to view the moon. How beautifully it shone above the bare treetops but how cold and far away. It afforded him a little light but no warmth. Then suddenly among the shadows he saw a moving creature. Approaching, he leapt upon it and using his sharp hunting knife cut the throat of a deer. He dressed the animal, took out the heart which he placed in his pocket as a trophy, but there was now nothing he could do with it.

Finding the cold increasing, he left the deer lying in the snow and staggered on. Never would he live to eat venison again were he to let himself sink in the snow.

Sometimes he found himself fighting his way through the thick underbrush, climbing into ravines, creeping up the banks and out again into deep forest, into open country, over frozen brooks, on and on, never stopping, keeping his head clear, cool, resolute, determined to live, to defy that wilderness, that devastating cold.

There came a time even as he staggered, often conscious of such fatigue as he had not thought man capable of enduring, when he noticed a lessening of the darkness, then, moment by moment, a brightening sky. Morning came and no matter in what direction he turned his eyes he knew it was to horizons which he never before had seen. All he could do was to flounder through the snow. He was growing weaker. Could that fearful stupor overcome a man even as he moved? No longer could he progress in a straight line. He was plunging this way and that, leaving zigzag tracks in the snow. He floundered, pitched forward, jerked back but never once in that terrible journey did he allow himself to fall. Keep moving, step after step, and you know you are still alive.

The sun was climbing higher in the heaven and he reckoned calmly enough that it was about ten o'clock when he came on a river, but where or what the river was he had no idea.

He emerged from the woods and with fast beating heart saw the houses. With his last remaining strength he staggered up a village street. Through a path he made his way to a door. In answer to his knock a man opened and Nat Copp fell forward at his feet. He had walked for twenty-one hours without a stop.

They took him in, listened to his story, told half incoherently, and put him to bed. As they helped remove his clothing, he managed to ask, "Where am I?"

"You are in Gilead, Maine. You have walked full forty miles."

He did not even hear that answer. He had fallen into a deep sleep.

❦

"I must act."

Young Daniel stood by with wide frightened eyes watching his father prepare to go out into the cold.

Dolly asked wonderingly, "Won't you take Daniel?"

His mouth was set sternly. "Daniel will remain here to care for the house."

His reply deepened the fear in her heart as she divined his thought correctly. If he, too, should perish there must be left one boy or man in the home.

They stood at the window with faces pressed against the pane but it was too dark to see the figure disappearing into the night.

Hayes made his way up the road and knocked at the door of his nearest neighbor, Mr. Culbane. He had scarcely finished stating the case when Mr. Culbane called his hired man, John Goulding. Without hesitation they offered to accompany Hayes and with them they would bring their two great wolf-hounds.

The darkness was intense when they at last with help from the dogs' keen scent found the spot where Nat had killed the deer. Beyond this point they could not by any amount of searching follow the hunter's tracks in the black night. They stopped and built a fire and, huddled around it, they waited six anxious hours until the rising of the moon. In that light they could again discern the tracks and now they followed hour after hour. Surely in some dread moment they would find the frozen body of the lad lying in the snow.

In the bitter cold they fought their way, always with eyes on the snow, watching for the now zigzagging steps. They too struggled through the ravines, through almost impenetrable underbrush where sometimes for moments they felt lost and hopeless, then coming again to an open space, seeing the marks of those snowshoes and forcing themselves on.

The light was waning, but in spite of their suffering they staggered on until late in the afternoon. Now their own footsteps zigzagged through the snow as wildly as did those they still followed. Both Mr. Culbane and Hayes knew their ears were frozen. This was not the frost bite they were well used to enduring. This was complete freezing. Far more serious they felt was now the plight of the stalwart young farm-helper, John Goulding. Valiantly as he struggled he was fast losing the use of his feet. They were frozen. The two friends supported him as he stumbled and fell and rose again to stumble and fall.

They were approaching the little Wild River. They crossed and like Nat, saw houses. And still following the footsteps, they too staggered up the village street, down the path and rapped on the door.

At last Hayes stood by the bed on which his son lay, tossing in delirium. The father bent over the lad. When he called, "Nat, Nat," and laid his hand on the boy's forehead, there was a moment of quiet but no recognition.

CHAPTER XXIII

WHEN HAYES RETURNED to the sitting room where the doctor who had already ministered to Nat was now examining the frozen feet of John Goulding, kind hands reached out to help him remove his clothing.

Grimly and sharply he answered, "I shall endure. I would there might be found someone to drive me home. His mother must be assured. That can't wait through another night."

Could *one* be found? There was not only *one*, there was not a strong man in that locality—for the news of the events had spread already far and near—who would not harness and drive through that cold night when there was such need. The other suffering men begged also to be taken to their homes. However, as the doctor rose from his ministrations, he looked sadly down into the eyes of John Goulding.

The young man spoke anxiously, "Tell me the truth."

The doctor thought, then answered quietly, "Some toes— we will wait and do what we can." He could not utter the dreaded word—amputation. He could not tell this sturdy farmer that both feet would be lost. He could only repeat gravely, "We will wait and do what we can."

There was tightness in many a throat in that room. They waited as a wan smile passed over the young fellow's face. "Could I be put in the sled? I wish to be in my home, if it is also the wish of Mr. Culbane."

Two men would relieve each other in the driving. Two strong horses were harnessed and the sled was brought. They carried John Goulding and laid him on the straw, Hayes and Mr. Culbane sitting beside him. Already women had hot irons and bottles ready, and off into the darkness of a night of bitter cold they started.

The roads were passable and they made good time. At Mr. Culbane's they stopped to carry John Goulding to his bed, then went on to leave Hayes at his home.

It was long after midnight but the lights were burning and the door was opened before the horses were brought to a stop.

When Hayes entered he spoke quickly, "He lives. He will endure."

Dolly sank to a chair and the men looked away as tears flowed down her cheeks; but only for a moment did she betray such weakness. Quickly rising, she asked of their welfare. She would bring hot drinks and food which she had kept waiting and they should rest in warm beds.

Daniel led the men to the barn and the horses were cared for. About the hot fire as they ate, they answered her questions until the entire story of the terrible night was clear in her mind. Nothing was held back. That her son was lying delirious in a stranger's house, that Hayes was spent, that his ears were frozen and would cause him suffering throughout the remainder of his life, the heart-breaking news concerning John Goulding—all this she heard with no outward sign of grief.

When all were at rest, she undressed by the fire. She put out her light and crept into bed. Hayes was in a deep sleep.

After a hearty breakfast and many thanks spoken, the men drove away.

Alone, Hayes' eyes rested on Daniel; then he turned to the mother, "He has done well?"

She smiled at the boy. "He is a man. He milks, feeds and does everything by my side."

"Then I shall return. With the doctor's permission, I shall bring Nat home."

Anxiety showed now in her face. "The ride is long; the

cold increases and I want to be with him."

"I would wish that." He looked at the boy. "But there well might be that here with which he could not deal. There will be some woman there to offer her services."

She accepted the judgment. "I'll be ready for his coming." That there would be many such women they both knew.

Still Hayes looked at the young boy, Daniel, and she knew that there was something on his mind but still unspoken. She waited.

"We will face a hard winter. The doctor with great honesty told me that Nat may not walk again for some three to six months."

Both shock and sadness showed in her eyes. "That he lives is sufficient for the day. We will see what we see. The hours will be long until my hands can reach him."

Sometimes in those long hours she spoke sharply to Daniel. "Come away from the window. Watching won't hasten their coming."

He came to her side. "My ears ache with listening."

"Patience is difficult to come by. It is much easier to work."

Nevertheless it was his eager eyes and listening ears that knew first of their approach. He fairly shouted, "They're here, Mother. A woman but no man except father. I'll help carry Nat."

With firm hold of the blanket on which he lay, the two women, Daniel and Hayes carried him into the bedroom and soon he lay between sheets that had been kept warm, waiting for this moment.

His eyes were clear. He spoke in his strong voice and laughed while looking into his mother's face. "Isn't this a predicament? With a fine deer lying on the hill waiting to be brought home?"

Perhaps relieved of the many hours of nervous tension, Daniel burst into a loud laugh. "He already talks of hunting!"

Nat turned his head to look at the young boy, tried to speak, but wearily his eyes closed and he slept.

Because another furious storm "jailed" them in, a week

passed before Hayes was able to return the good woman to her home in Gilead.

There were days in February when a strange hush seemed to have fallen on the house. It was said that in that bitter winter, there were six weeks when neither the heat from the house nor the sun ever softened the snow so much as to cause one drop of water to fall from the eaves of house, barn or shed. Men measured and found the snow from six to nine feet on the level and once in the short space of twenty-four hours there fell twenty-seven inches of snow. The heavy frosts had come early in the fall and they lasted late into the spring. The corn that summer never ripened but the potatoes, wheat, rye and oats were a goodly crop.

There were tales of men who started out that winter on fair days to make journeys when, overtaken by storms, they were forced to seek refuge, remaining six or seven days before they could go on.

One day Nat tossed restlessly on his pillow for it was not his own suffering that vexed him but some anguish in his heart that was well nigh unbearable. Early on that morning the country doctor, for whose heroism the most grudging were ready to give praise, came with a surgeon. That they would come from the distant town, through half-broken roads, through storms, through rain or snow, night or day, to minister to the sick and dying, giving advice, leaving their good medicine, begging the superstitious and ignorant to throw out the pernicious nostrums sold by the multitude of "fakirs" prowling through the country—that such men were unsung heroes, every pioneer knew. Had they ridden on noble chargers, wearing armour and carrying shining swords, the tales of their exploits and courage would have filled volumes. What were they? Men, weathered, wearing shabby clothes and driving shabbier sleds and carriages, charging fifty cents, one dollar, or often nothing for their visits. Some were from Harvard, later from Dartmouth or New York, dreaming of hospitals, sanitation, education—fearless men who loved the great hills, the wide valleys, the men, women and children of the frontier.

Silently the family waited until the examination was completed, breathing deep sighs of relief as the doctors agreed that Nat needed only time. There would be complete recovery but there would be required much patience and nursing, rest and quiet.

They repacked their bags, put on their great coats, covered their ears with fur laps and were ready to leave.

Nat's eyes beseeched them. "I must know. You go from here to John Goulding? I must know about him."

The silence was painful. "To save his life, his feet must be amputated."

Nat closed his eyes and did not speak again. Throughout the day he scarcely opened them and food was distasteful to him.

Could they go about their work and forget what was happening in the house up the road? Had not the happiness of one been the happiness of all? The sorrow of one, the sorrow of all? Scarcely had the doctors' sleigh disappeared into the forest when Dolly and Hayes pulled on their heavy boots and warm clothing and, after giving careful instructions to Daniel concerning Nat's needs, went out into the falling snow. Strong men would be needed to hold a man undergoing such an operation.

Not until night did they return, Dolly's face lined and drawn and pinched. She spoke little and when the fires were banked, she crept wearily into her bed.

Daniel, alone, had done the milking, performed all the night chores, warmed the food which Nat could not eat, then, in every spare moment, sat silently by the bedside watching his brother.

❧

Many times in that hard winter, Hayes spoke of the younger boy. "He does well—beyond his years."

He was fine looking, grown tall for his age, broad-shoul-dered, proud of his man's strength. Folks jokingly spoke of the red in his cheeks, as ruddy as the cheeks of Dolly's apples. When Hayes thought of hiring a man to help with the spring plowing and planting, Daniel was indignant. "Father, didn't you and Jerry do everything?"

Hayes replied, "There was Nat also."

"Couldn't you try me?"

"To do the work of two?"

The boy could argue. "It wouldn't be the same. The roads are built, the fences only need mending. If you would trust me, I can go alone into the woods and bring partridge, duck and turkey and"—modestly he added, "should I have luck, venison."

Hayes smiled, "And a bear for your mother's need in the soap making?"

The boys smile answered the father's. "I would not boast. You dislike that."

Also through the hard days, as Hayes saw the boy at his mother's side helping in the butter and cheese making, carry-ing the produce to the hotel, and saw Dolly's pleasure in his company, he thought, "He is like a poultice on a wound."

Born ten years after Silvia, he was to them like a gift from heaven to brighten the dull days. He 'tended Nat, using his strong fingers to rub into his back the grease and ointments which Dolly had ready, neither of them questioning the effi-cacy of the herbs which she gathered from the woods.

Rubbing gently and steadily, Daniel would smile, "You have never had a sore." Then, "against orders," when the coast was clear, he agreed with Nat that it was wise to try daily to move, to sit up, to attempt standing. Never discouraged, when the attempts failed he would say, "We'll do better tomorrow."

It was Daniel and Hayes who fashioned the chair, using a stout maple stool, building a back, fastening to this four wheels of their own making. As the days lengthened, as the sun grew brighter and rose higher in the heavens, they washed and dressed Nat, lifted him into the chair and gleefully watched him learn to manipulate the contrivance.

Soon Nat could use his hands and perform many tasks. He mended the large traps, the small traps, the household utensils, and day by day he gathered strength. By the time the grass was turning green he was hobbling about on home-made crutches; then walking, then little by little, so gradually that they hardly noticed, he walked without stumbling. Now, he was daily at the river bringing in fish, milking, feeding the animals and by summer he was first laughing at the illness, then was ready to forget it.

Nevertheless, as Hayes watched the lad, he knew there was something in Nat that had increased rather than diminished during the long illness—his restlessness. It was not that he did not like the farm; it was not that he found the work too gruelling hard, from his earliest childhood there had been something in his nature which differed from the others. Dolly had said, in anger, "You allowed him to wander far. You gave him gun and knife when he was only a child. Nat is a rover."

Yes, Nat was a rover. He would go off to the great peak, Mount Washington, and work on the road being built there. Glowingly, he would describe the stupendous undertaking. "Some day they will reach the summit and carriages and trains will go up easily."

Dryly Dolly would answer, "Some day."

"Sooner than you think, Mother. Now they've run out of money but others will come to complete the task."

"Is it your business?"

He laughed. "It's exciting."

She protested because Hayes always allowed him to use a horse to ride to the towns on Saturday nights. "There is mischief to be found there."

"The lad is not a brawler."

"No, I grant you he's a good lad, but a rover. Doesn't he

often go to Gorham? I hear there's a girl there who entices him."

"We cannot control that. It is his right. He is of the age to marry."

"Marry, yes; but settle down as Jerry has, I doubt."

That she spoke truth, Hayes knew. That she divined in her heart that there was some bond of understanding between father and this son, something that baffled her, he did not know. He knew only that in the fall it was he who suffered silently and she who talked and complained when Nat said at the breakfast table one morning, "I am planning to be married."

Dolly asked many questions. He answered them all lightly and truthfully.

"Where will you live? In Gorham?"

"We think not."

Dolly spoke eagerly. "The Willey family is of an old and honorable name. This Esther is well spoken of. If you leave us there will be no one remaining to us but Daniel. Why not bring her home? She would be welcome. There's room for all—a good home and work not too heavy for a farmer's wife. Little children are like flowers, brightening the days. This welcome we extend to you."

"It's kindly spoken, Mother. I will take your message to Esther."

"*You* make that decision, Nat."

She knew he was evading the issue.

He laughed. "You'll all come to see us married?"

They journeyed up the new road one fall day to Nat's wedding. In their fine clothes, they sat dignified, sad and troubled as the minister read the sacred words. They hurried back, for there were strangers stopping in Dolly's house.

What was there about Nat that left behind such a fearful emptiness in the house? Often the beds were full; at the table were many guests, the work increased rather than diminished;

Dolly chattered to those who came in and went out, always pleasant, always looking out for every comfort, yet there was emptiness.

❦

Daniel grew yearly into a strong man, a splendid hunter and trapper, tireless in field or barn or dairy or carpenter shop.

One day he came in from a trip to the hotel, seeking his father in the field. "There's talk that Nat is leaving this part of the country. It's said he is going West."

Hayes stopped his work, listening, but he only nodded in answer.

Daniel's eyes looked off at the horizon. "Someday, Father, I'd like to see that West of which they talk so much. I'm told that in their clearings the wheat fields stretch as far as the eye can see. There are not the mountains and in many miles there is not a hill. There are rivers wider than the distance between our towns."

Hayes looked at the lad in silence.

"Already large steamboats carry the produce down to the sea. It must be a strange sight."

Hayes nodded. "I have heard so."

"They don't know our bitter cold."

Hayes smiled. "Perhaps, they have forbidden the winds to blow, the snow to fall? Perhaps, they told the heavens to send only the quantity of rain needful for the growing of their crops?"

Daniel laughed. "The tales do sound big."

Hayes turned to his work. Later he spoke to Daniel thoughtfully, "We have prospered on this rich land. We now have many comforts. There are always new comforts within our home. We own all the tools we require. With many hunting, the bears grow fewer in number and our livestock suffers less—our losses from weasel and skunk and fox are fewer. The soil is rich and our harvests increase. Every cent of my debt to the government has long since been paid in oats, wheat and barley." He smiled at his son. "There are those who would call this a rich heritage."

"That's true, Father. I make no complaint. Yet, hearing all, I do not hold it against Nat that he wishes to go there."

"No. There is nothing to be held against Nat. Barring any harm to others, every man has the right to do that which his nature leads him to. When your time comes, you too will make your own decisions."

Daniel looked grieved. "Oh, it was only to *see*, that I wished. This is my place and I want no other. I expect always to remain here."

Always of an inquiring turn of mind, the boy asked, "Father, how did this great tract of mountainous land, extending more miles than I have travelled and containing so many great peaks, come to be called Coos?"

Hayes replied, "Excepting the great peaks called for our presidents, Washington, Jefferson, Adams, Monroe and Madison—all else bear Indian names. Their Indian word was Cowass, meaning 'The crooked place.' The White man said only 'Coos'."

Daniel smiled. "I would have liked to see it when you first came. Mother says the eagle was her only friendly neighbor."

Hayes nodded. "She always watched for his coming in the spring."

"She still does." Again he said with decision, "Here I'll remain."

Hayes' eyes followed the lad as he went off toward the barn with a sack slung over his shoulder. There was more of thoughtfulness than happiness in his eyes as they rested on the tall, handsome youth.

CHAPTER XXIV

MANY TIMES through the years the little "gray man," the botanist, had returned—it was like "coming home"—he always said—and it was known that he had listed between three and four hundred "Alpine plants" in their White Hills.

When a newspaper notice told them of the botanist's death, there was mourning in the Glen and some wonder at the honor attached to his name. He had been like one of them, a little shabby in appearance but rugged, always their cheerful, affectionate friend, and it was with some pride that Dolly knew that her house had been his "home," never the great hotel. Also it was with pride that Daniel knew it was Nat or his father who had been his companion and helper when he sought strange flowers and plants in the lakes high up the mountains or in the deep ravines.

Now there was a new "scientist" guest—a man who studied the forest trees. He rode into their clearing one morning, asking only for bed and lodging but soon he found that much more than food and rest could be had when he sat by the fire after the day's work was accomplished, talking to Hayes, Dolly and Daniel.

Besides the early familiarity with the letters of the alphabet, learning to write, then to read fluently from the Book, Daniel had had "schooling" and while the hours spent in the one room with boys and girls of all ages may not have instilled in his mind a very great accumulation of facts, it has left him something far more valuable—even priceless—an inquiring mind.

The tree-man, as they came to call him, was immediately received into easy comradeship with the two plain farmers who had imbibed a vast store of information, unconscious of the possession. The mountain, with its forests, animals, birds, lakes, ravines, waterfalls, its insects and snakes had been their habitat from birth to manhood.

However, there were viewpoints which the tree-man expressed casually that caused Daniel to lean forward with brightening eyes, drinking in every word.

Like the botanist he thought in zones. "Going up the mountain is like travelling from the temperate zone to the arctic. Now here—" and he referred to his map, "instead of covering hundreds of miles the same vegetation can be studied in hundreds of yards."

He was a tall, spare, tough looking man dressed in clothes not unlike the Copps' hunting outfits. They were rather surprised when he interrupted the talk of vegetation to ask, "By the way—What about rattlesnakes? I have to admit they are the one thing on earth I most dislike. Bad as a girl—"

Daniel laughed, "Plenty here abouts but with caution—"

"I know—caution."

"Nat told us of a picnic party from the hotel. A young girl was sitting on a ledge enjoying the view when she felt something in her lap and looked down to see a rattler coiling himself up kind of cold, I reckon. They always go for heat."

"Holy jumpers! What did she do?"

"Oh—the guide took care of him."

Sometimes alone, often with Hayes or Daniel, the tree-man made his way through forest trails, then—perhaps one of the greatest of surprises to this man—he found Dolly possessed of a curious fund of valuable information. She had always roamed across the lower slopes of the mountain, in swamps, by the river, up the new road, looking for herbs or berries. They called it the *green growth* to distinguish it from the *black growth* or upper forest. Of the highest *alpine region* she knew little, but down here she was expert. She showed him all the fruits which she was used to gathering either to eat or to dry or to preserve for sweets in winter. There was the red cherry, the brambles with their pleasant fruit, wild red raspberries, and the blackberry which she said was so backward that sometimes its fruit didn't ripen "fit to use." There were the purple-flowering raspberry which she pronounced "very handsome," the gooseberry, which she again pronounced more handsome than useful; the red currant, and the hobble-bush and viburnam, which produced excellent fruit. And as she walked she would stop now and then to gather herbs for her well-tried medicines or flavorings.

Sometimes he laughed at her designation of the shrubs and trees, She "tolerated" some, "detested" that hobble-bush where it formed such underbrush as made for hard travel, but speaking with pride of that mountain holly with its crimson berries. The honey which she obtained in the forest had a finer flavor than any from her hives. "The wild flowers have that which is lacking in our garden flowers."

Often, hearing a crackling in the woods, she would stop to listen warily before she proceeded.

"I notice, Mistress Dolly, you have not only eyes to see but ears to hear. Do you never know fear coming alone through the forest?"

She answered dryly, "Hayes tells his children that only a fool doesn't know fear."

He prolonged his stay not only in that first year but returned season after season, until he too spoke of it as "coming home."

No guest was more welcome. They watched him fill in his charts and always found happiness in the company of this college man who, without words of praise, enhanced their inner sense of dignity and intelligence.

Respectfully he would turn to Hayes. "Will you check this? These, at your elevation of sixteen hundred feet, are wanting—no sumachs, the vine unknown, no sassafras, slippery elm? Buttonwood, hickory, chestnut? Beech beginning much higher on this side of the mountains than on the west?"

They all knew that before the Revolution, the English Crown claimed all the white pine not growing within the area of the Towns. The tree-man had seen books of the "royal contractors for masts" mentioning trees forty two inches in diameter and the greatest 264 feet high.

They discussed many subjects that led Hayes to remember old tales told in his family. There was an uncle of his. "He was always running contrary to the law. Seems his land lay part over the Town limits but he told them they'd never get one of those 'sticks' off of his ground. They didn't. Some said he mostly 'shot before he reckoned.' That's what they called the white pine in those days—'sticks for the Crown.'"

The tree-man was smiling. "I guess no one can estimate the ill will caused by the cutting of those trees. It stiffened the resistance of all New Englanders."

Hayes shook his head. "Not so many stumps about here. It's said no man lives long enough from the cutting to see one of those stumps rot."

The tree-man thought of that. "Well, I hadn't heard that saying."

One mid-summer evening it would have appeared to an outsider that the tree-man was the nominal head of a community interest, for six men, all neighbors of various ages, were alternately bending over the table to study the charts or sitting about swapping yarns or discussing the forest trees.

"Always 'twas said, 'thar's gold in them thar hills.' "

"Only it won't be in yellow nuggets." The tree-man could speak earnestly. "You fellows have given your lives to clearing for farms and homes, building roads to make it possible for lumbermen to come in and rob you. They are already taking those gold nuggets right out of your pockets They offer a farmer a few hundred dollars for a stand and make thousands out of the wood they cut.

"Neither you folks nor the Indians ever had to fear fire except from lightning. Already these city campers are dangerous and with roads finished ascending the hills, no guides can watch them. You know old Haskell—been guiding parties up Washington for twenty years—he told me he has gone back a dozen times to stamp out fires where he had seen smoke. You're too busy farming to lumber—I suppose no one can persuade you not to sell for shillings what's worth dollars?"

"It's ready money."

"That's the devil of it."

Some one chuckled, "They won't burn the tops of these hills."

"Fire creeping through the underbrush hardly stops at the snow line."

It was Daniel who asked diffidently, "How do you explain this? The Indian's story of the creation—water everywhere and only the tops of the mountains sticking up—then the water slowly dropping lower as the great Spirit clothed the hills with trees—not so different than what you scientists say?"

The tree-man laughed. "I don't explain it. I don't know for how many years their religion, their stories and superstitions were handed down from father to son, either.

"There's something even more mysterious that none of us can yet explain."

The men looked at his charts where there were already clearly marked so many varieties of trees, shrubs and flowers as to leave the paper as thick with words as the land was thick with trees.

"Along the rivers, the American elm, for four or five miles; up above comes the white pine, red oak, black birch, balsam, white and black ash, beech, larch, arbor vitae, junipers; up into the evergreens hemlock, fir, spruce—on and on besides hundreds of bushes, fruit trees, shrubs of all kinds, trees with fruit, trees with beautiful berries, food, shelter even beauty.

"Now go to the near top—the Alpine region. At four thousand feet there is a close thicket of dwarf trees. Suddenly they come to an end and there are barren wastes with here and there green patches."

Seeing the interest of his listeners for he was talking to these men about that which constituted their "home" as truly to them as did the contents of a house, he smiled. "These green patches to a scientist are not waste. There are flowers not found nearer than the coast of Labrador—the starry white blossoms of the sandwort, the pinkish flowers and scarlet fruit of the cowberry or Labrador tea, the crowberry, the mountain bilberry. I found Lapland rhododendron with purple flowers in July. I could name some dozens—alpine bear-berry, cassiope with its bell shaped flower, the Alpine heath. When we reach the deep ravines on Mount Washington we step on flower gardens. I have listed some dozens here. In Europe scientists have made exhaustive studies of these flowers and shrubs."

After a moment, he went on. "Mount Washington is a giant thermometer of botanic life found again in Lapland, Siberia and Labrador. Now, tell me how did they get there? Siberia, Lapland, Greenland and Labrador might be answered by the wind carrying the seeds but what about getting to New Hampshire or the Adirondacks?"

"Birds?"

"Could the animals help?"

Now they had fun. "What about those icebergs? I've heard they float hundreds of miles."

So the tree-man became part of their life—a man who *asked* more than he *told*.

Still, up and down, through valley and hill the farmers sold their stands of hard wood and the lumbermen moved in and cleared, leaving only wastes covered with stumps; and the wagons loaded with treasure passed up and down the roads and more and more saw-mills were built and soon on the rivers were seen acres of floating logs.

Now, there was something else passing—something that brought a speculative smile to Dolly's eyes. Often, coming from the railroad station at Gorham, great coaches drove by filled with people going to the base of Mount Washington, some for rest, good air, some for mere sightseeing, some to hunt, some to climb and some for love of sheer beauty.

One day such a coach driver drew in the reins bringing his four horses to a stop before Dolly's door. A gentleman alighted and came across the grass.

"Is this the Copp farm?"

Dolly, meeting him at the door, said it was.

"Would you have accommodations for myself and my daughter? Your place has been recommended to us."

"There is room."

He returned to the coach and with much fussing as all eyes watched, his baggage was extricated. There was a trunk and several boxes and bags.

While the driver was being paid, a young lady came toward the house. She was not a young girl but rather mature and singularly frail looking. Dolly thought, "Peaked."

City folks? Dolly could not quite make them out. Not Boston? Not New York? They were somehow different.

The girl smiled and the smile hardly relieved the tired, rather sad expression of her face. "I am Lizzie Drew. I've been ill and my father wants to leave me in the mountain so that I may regain my health. I rather dreaded a large hotel and someone in Gorham said your home was a good place for such rest."

Dolly's smile was warm and her welcome hearty. "We are farmers and there is little entertainment but you may be sure of good food and rest. Come in."

She led her to a bedroom. "This was once my daughter's room. Would it suit you?"

The young lady answered rather indifferently, "Yes, thank you." Then, forcing brightness, she added, "My father can remain for one night only. I shall be left alone. I'm afraid I am naturally rather a homesick person."

Hayes had come to help the father carry in the trunk. After unlocking it, terms were discussed, then Mr. Drew took his bag upstairs to his room.

Dolly had returned to her kitchen, Hayes to the field and

soon the father and daughter were seen wandering about the place or standing in front looking up at the mountains.

That morning Daniel was engaged in one of the dirtiest tasks that could be performed. He had been slaughtering and now, in old clothes suitable for such work, he was cleaning up. It was one of the hot days of early July. His thin, open-necked shirt clung to his body and he constantly wiped away the perspiration which wet his none too clean face. He was startled by the voices of the visitors and scarcely avoided hurling a bucket of water onto their feet.

With a little cry, the girl drew back her skirts even as the father apologized for intruding.

As they moved away the father said something about "a farm hand." He laughed, "That's probably our dinner. Better not look too closely. It will taste better than it looks."

The girl turned back. Her gaze was direct, not unsympathetic in spite of her listless manner. However, she did not speak to the young man. They walked to the river and on their return the father asked coaxingly, "If you'll consent to unpack your trunk and try it here I believe you may come to like the place. Out there in the shade of those trees you can rest and read. If it's too lonely you can change at any time."

"It's so far from home."

"Only a day on the train. If, as the doctor says, there is in this air the health-giving quality you need, you may soon come home restored to health."

"I'll try it." There was more of resignation than hopefulness in her voice.

She was in her room unpacking when there came the call to dinner. If there was any embarrassment none showed it when the "farmhand" was introduced as "my son, Daniel." He had washed and changed his bespattered shirt to another, also open necked but clean. He looked well-scrubbed. In his cheeks blood showed clear through the tanned skin. His deep set blue eyes were mostly fastened on his plate as he ate heartily, as did Hayes, even as Dolly talked and questioned and served.

The father was somewhat anxious. Would Lizzie take kindly to this farmer table? At the moment there were no other guests although Dolly assured them several were expected and many transients came and went.

With her ease in conversation she elicited the information she wanted. They came from Oberlin, Ohio. Now Daniel looked up. Ohio! The name, to them, meant the far west to which the rover, Nat, had gone. But, Mr. Drew explained not without some condescension, that they lived in a fine, even though small city. He laughed, "We think of ourselves as easterners, for though our fathers and mothers came in covered wagons in the great migrations across the Mohawk Valley to the plains, we are essentially all New Yorkers or Vermonters or from Massachusetts or New Hampshire. Way beyond us is the west of the Rockies and California and Utah with its Mormons."

That they lived in a city surrounded by productive farms, though about them were gently rolling hills, and yet came back to the east for virgin forests and mountains, caused laughter and before the end of the meal the cold formality of the beginning had disappeared. Dolly had never yet failed in accomplishing that feat.

With the setting of the sun, father and daughter, who had been walking up and down on the road in front of the house, came into the parlor expressing astonishment at the sudden chill in the air. The girl was shivering and Dolly handed her a warm shawl to wrap about her shoulders.

Again the father explained, "She has been ill—a long siege of typhoid complicated with pneumonia. She is essentially strong and well and the doctor felt that mountain air would restore her lungs and tone up her system."

Daniel made a small fire and the girl huddled close, looking languidly into the flames. She took no part in the conversation which suddenly became animated when Dolly asked, "What kind of a town is Oberlin? There are mills?"

The gentleman's smile again showed a bit of condescension as he answered, "Oh, no. Oberlin is a college town."

Dolly's head was bent over her knitting. She was fashioning a baby's coat of her lovely blue wool. She counted some stitches but she had not missed the quality of Mr. Drew's smile.

She replied, "Oh? A new college?" but her eyes were sharp as she glanced up at father and daughter.

"No, not at all. As I said, we are easterners. My grandfather was one of those who started the Oberlin Colony in 1835. By 1846 it was incorporated by a minister and a missionary as a home for the Oberlin Collegiate Institute which by 1850 became Oberlin College."

The daughter stirred uneasily. "I'm afraid, Father, that isn't very interesting to Mrs. Copp." She glanced at Dolly. "You must have visitors from many different places."

Dolly's eyes were smiling bright with amusement. She spoke dryly, "All kinds. The New York folks pity the ones who have to live in Boston. The Boston folks wonder how anyone gets on anywhere else. We have all kinds."

Mr. Drew straightened his shoulders, bristling a little, for he had carefully avoided describing his city as "cultural." Then he suddenly smiled. "We have one thing in common with New Hampshire. We were all abolitionists. Oberlin was one of the most active stations in the Underground Railway and that meant something in a town where fifteen percent of the population was Negro." His voice rose and he spoke with pride. "We were a religious institution and we practiced what we preached. We were the first college in the United States to offer co-education—boys and girls treated alike. Also"—and he paused, then spoke with emphasis, "we were the first college to accept Negroes on an equality with whites."

Daniel who had been standing back of the group, spoke for the first time. He had been watching the girl, noticing the delicate white hands that still clung to the shawl. "With that large percentage of Negroes don't you have many poor? Many who work as servants?"

Mr. Drew raised his eyebrows. "Naturally. We have problems that could hardly concern a community such as this. As I said, we are a religious organization and we try to deal fairly with every human being. In our college nearly seventy-five percent of our students, white and black, male and female, earn their own way. We not only honor work, we encourage labor of any kind. It is the mental and moral capacity of a person that determines his life. That capacity, whether God-given or man-made, is a problem that causes thoughtful men to wonder if there ever could be absolute equality anywhere on earth—in any country on the globe. Our constitution promises equal *opportunity*, not equal talent or health or wealth. If we in America live up to that we will have accomplished something never before known on this earth. Don't you have farm-hands? Why are you not all farm owners?"

He turned to look up at the young man. He saw a tall, broad- shouldered fellow, strong, handsome, radiating health. He met the steady, deep set blue eyes and smiled in a friendly way. "You might be interested, young man, in knowing that in 1835 there came to our Theological Seminary forty students from a Theological Seminary in Cincinnati after the discussion of slavery there had been forbidden by its board of trustees. That is one thing we have always stood for—open discussion of every question that concerns our country or its people. Come out to see us some day. I believe you would be deeply interested if not agreeably surprised."

Dolly squirmed and spoke quickly and sharply. "Daniel is not a rover. With his father they have no idle moments doing all the work on this farm. We have never needed farm-hands."

In spite of Dolly's uneasiness, long after the girl had gone to her room, Hayes and Daniel sat with the gentleman discussing the farms of Ohio, the produce, markets, weather and all else. Only thirty odd miles from Chicago? They questioned him about that booming city and it was late when the lights were extinguished.

Daniel's eyes did not close immediately that night. He lay

thinking of the girl. Not once had she spoken to him. What a disagreeable impression he must have made on her in that first sight of him engaged in slaughtering. He wondered what she was really like if one came to know her. Somehow she was different. Sick? He had seen plenty of sick people. Proud? He wondered.

For some reason he could not sleep. He felt some anger and he heartily wished she would change her mind and go home with her father. She did not belong here. He had no wish to visit them or their wonderful college town with their infernal goodness, their Negroes and their culture.

Then as sleep came soothingly to his eyes, he wondered if some partridge would tempt her appetite. There were wild berries, also trout. She had hardly tasted the heavy food.

CHAPTER XXV

SHE DID NOT change her mind. Daniel was to drive Mr. Drew to the railroad station to catch the early train. At the breakfast table she raised her eyes and spoke for the first time to the young man. "Would it inconvenience you if I were to go with Father to the station?"

"Not at all. I'll have some errands to do in town. If you won't mind waiting for that?"

She would not mind.

Going to the station, father and daughter sat in the back seat of what Daniel thought must seem to their eyes a plain, rather lumbering farm carriage. He drove rapidly, taking no part in the conversation. Shaking the young man's hand, Mr. Drew renewed his invitation to visit them in Ohio and Daniel thanked him but his tone and manner indicated dismissal of the idea.

Again to his eyes, the young lady looked completely out of place when he returned from his errands to place packages and sacks in the back of the carriage. It was not until they had entered the deep woods far from habitations that she looked up at him with a glow in her eyes that surprised him. "This is lovely. This is what I like—driving under this arch of trees with the sun laying those shadows on the road. Do you know? I had such a good sleep last night. I felt rested when I wakened." She glanced at him, smiling. "I suppose you have no trouble sleeping after doing such a hard day's work?"

He was conscious of being alone with her in the depths of

the forest, hearing the happy note in her voice, conscious of the sweet quality of that voice. He was bashfully, self-consciously aware of her. His answer was short and awkward. "I reckon sleeping never troubles me."

She laughed aloud. "No, I suppose not." There was silence until she broke it. "Before I came here, I read all I could find—it wasn't very much at that—about these White Mountains. I read about the birds and wondered if I would see an eagle; and I was thrilled when I woke early to hear such a beautiful chorus. I felt very ignorant. Most I read concerned terrible warnings of bears, wildcats, wolves, frightful storms and such cold as could hardly be endured."

"I reckon we have all that."

"Oh, don't you love the sound of that water tumbling over rocks? Is it that same river?"

"My father calls it a brawling stream."

She laughed. "It is noisy." Then, "Could we drive more slowly? In that coach yesterday, it was very unpleasant—such a crowd, and we joggled and bumped until my back ached and when I wanted to stop where the view of the peaks was so fine, it seemed that crazy driver went faster."

He had slowed the horses and once he stopped, for he well knew where were the finest views.

They sat silent, then she smiled, "Thank you. You mustn't let me bother you or take your time. I see you are a busy person."

He started the horses and looked straight ahead. She did bother him. He was uneasy. He felt singularly tongue-tied and awkward and yet he suddenly knew that he did not want to end the drive. Her presence disturbed him. She was different this morning alone with him on this forest road...

Daniel had sometimes wondered why he could not find the right girl for a wife. He had driven with many. He had danced with them, flirted with them, kissed them and—left them. He intended to marry and bring a wife home to live with him on this farm. That would please him as well as please his father and mother. However, though he had more than once come near the decision, he had never quite asked the fatal question.

As he went about his work that day he often smiled and found himself hoping that she would not go until she was really strong.

He brought the trout and Dolly had already found the berries and discovered the girl's liking for milk. Soon choice game appeared on the table and day by day a change came on her behavior as well as in her appearance. On the day that she first passed her plate for a second helping, Dolly laughed, "You must write your father about your appetite."

"He might say it is time to come home. My month is up tomorrow."

For one quick second her son's eyes and the girl's met and Dolly saw something that again frightened her. Not then, for there were many guests at her table, but later she spoke irritably to Hayes. "I wish that Lizzie Drew would go back to her home. Her father wants her to return. It would be seemly. There is something about her I don't like. With her book reading, her poetry, her airs and sweet manners, it's likely she'll turn Daniel away from wanting a good country girl for a wife. Like his puppies, she is always at his heels. Yesterday, they sat by the river while she read to him from one of her pretty books. She plays with him as a cat does with a mouse. It will mean nothing but harm to him."

Hayes listened, gazing gloomily at the floor. "I see naught to do concerning the matter. She grows in health and strength. She was like a faded flower when she came. Now she blooms. She takes great interest in the spinning and weaving and you have taught her to knit and sew. She is changing."

"If she was changing less it would concern me less. She grows pretty, There is that which brings bloom to a woman and harm to a man."

Hayes walked away knowing Dolly had not seen half of what his eyes had inadvertently rested upon—Daniel's hands on the girl's as they sat too close on the river bank, he teaching her to cast the line correctly. He had heard music in their laughter as she followed him to the high pasture to bring in an errant cow. That happy laughter had fallen heavily on Hayes' heart.

On Sundays, when they went to the Meeting House, she sat in front with Daniel and their shoulders touched as they bowed their heads in prayer or shared the hymnal.

And Daniel? The world seemed to be whirling dizzily at his feet. His sleep was troubled. He could hardly wait for the dawn when she would come from her room so sweet and fresh and shyly smile her good morning. Each time the postman handed her a letter a lump rose in his throat. Would it be a command that she return to her home? He wondered what she put in all those letters she wrote to her folks.

The second month was drawing to an end. The great August rush of visitors was lessening and often Lizzie was the only guest at the table. One day she wandered up the mountain trail, alone. Now she prided herself on finding her way, cautious but unafraid.

Sometimes she stopped merely to feel the delicious sense of quiet in the forest. Wary of snakes, she looked about for a place to rest. She had sat there some time when there was a curious sound and like a streak something seemed to shoot past her. Then before her eyes, not twenty feet away, she witnessed a battle so terrible, so blood curdling, that she was transfixed with horror. She could not move even had she known which way to go. A wildcat—and she knew him well but only from seeing his pelt or pictures of him—was tearing a smaller animal to pieces, ripping the throat amid such anguished cries and horrible growling sounds that made her weak as she listened.

Would the beast—and many times Daniel had told her it was the fiercest and most dreaded of all their enemies—would it turn on her? Should she run or stand still?

She prayed. Once she opened her eyes but the sight of the bloody food being devoured sickened her. When she took courage to look again the great cat had gone. Which way? If she moved would she startle it?

She was trembling, uncertain, afraid to run, afraid to wait.

It was when her straining ears first heard the distant call—his voice hallooing that she began to cry. She answered, clearing her throat to call louder and louder. He was coming nearer. She ran down the trail until she saw him. She brushed away the tears and smiled as he came close.

"What frightened you?"

She told him. "It was not because I willed it that I didn't move. I couldn't move. I didn't know what to do."

"The cat was sated with food. I wish I'd got him. He escapes any trapping."

They stood in the gathering shadows. "You must not climb so high unless I'm with you." He begged, "You will promise me never to venture so far again?"

They stood looking deep into each other's eyes. He breathed heavily and something in his throat half choked him.

They started down the trail, her hand tight in his. Once she stopped. "I want so much to see these woods in their autumn color. They tell me it's a glorious sight. When is it loveliest?"

"In September and early October." He gazed into her face. "Would you stay until then?"

Her lips trembled as she whispered, "Do you want me to?"

His answer was the old, old answer. As Dolly would have said there was that glow in a woman and something in a man that could do him harm. The harm was done but it was a harm they gloried in. About them the shadows thickened and they only held one another closer.

That the harm was done neither father nor mother had to be told when they came in late for the evening meal. Still there was no comment.

The autumn days came and went and she would see the snow. Now, as he drove to the hotel with produce she always was at his side, looking always prettier and prettier in the red hood that Dolly had taught her to knit. One day he spoke nervously, "Lizzie, you know and read many books. Doesn't my lack seem very great in your eyes?"

She leaned against his shoulder. "Shall I tell you the truth? From the day I first came here, I loved you and I always feared you would find me an empty vessel. Like my lessons in school I determined to know all you knew—birds, animals, hunting, fishing and—people. I studied harder than you might guess. But it was you who was the hardest to study."

"And I will tell you the truth. The very first night you came, I couldn't sleep. I was afraid you might not stay."

He took her to the country dances, she entered into all the apple paring bees, the church suppers, and by the time the snow lay deep in the level, all in the Glen knew about Daniel Copp and Lizzie Drew.

It was in December that they were married in the little Meeting House. Hayes and Dolly sat in the pew and listened They were old and bent and sad.

Daniel was to go home with Lizzie to see her family—and Oberlin.

Dolly and Hayes bade them good bye and did not even ask how many days would pass before their return. Perhaps in their sad hearts they felt the truth.

They never returned to live in the Glen.

CHAPTER XXVI

WITH SINGLENESS OF PURPOSE, Hayes rose before the sun could be seen above the forest trees. As its rays reached high enough to shimmer on the river, his brawling stream was turned into a silver streak that blinded the eyes. When his early morning chores were accomplished, he returned to the kitchen, removed his coat and took his place at the breakfast table where the bowl of hot porridge was waiting.

Throughout the meal no words were spoken and except for the crackling of the fire the silence was as great as that outside the walls of their house where now the snow fell softly, adding to that already deep on the fields.

When, some time later, he returned from the shed dressed in his rough hunting suit, Dolly had not moved but still sat, elbow on the table, chin resting in her hand, gazing through the small panes of glass at the great whiteness.

Now she turned, her sharp eyes resting on his gun.

"I thought I might find a wild turkey for our Thanksgiving dinner."

She nodded and, though he waited, she did not speak. Her eyes followed him as he passed through the door then they turned and rested long on the breakfast table. Two bowls, two plates, two sets of knives and forks, two saucers, two cups. She did not move to clear up but sat gazing, the hard lines drawing down the corners of her mouth.

Thanksgiving. The end of November and then would follow December and twelve months would have passed since Daniel and his Lizzie had gone to see her people in Ohio.

At first, in spite of the ache in her heart, in spite of the premonitions that darkened her mind, she had hoped. The letters came almost daily, always from Lizzie, letters filled with descriptions of their journey, inconsequential mishaps told with wit and clever phrasing that made them laugh, her people's admiration for her Daniel, his delight in seeing their fine town and countryside.

Then the letters came regularly once a week; then fewer and fewer arrived with half the space taken up with apologies. Dolly happened to be alone in the house when the one came in Daniel's handwriting. "We have, with Mr. Drew's help, purchased a farm."

Alone, she read to the end. She did not weep; did not shed one tear. She sat stony-faced with the letter lying in her lap. She gazed down at it. It was not a thin piece of paper; it was a weight lying on her knees, something to heavy for her hands to lift and return to the envelope.

She let it lie and when Hayes returned and saw her face, he picked it up and read. Quietly he placed it in the envelope, saying only, "I feared it."

He went about his work daily hoping she would weep or call out in anger or berate Lizzie or blame Daniel—anything, anything; but she neither cried nor stormed and he knew then there was a sickness in her that would not heal.

It was planting time and she asked, "What are you planning? You will find a good helper? There seem to be many young fellows about looking for work as farm hands—strong young men and the wages are not too large."

His brows met in a heavy frown. He stood with eyes cast to the floor. When he raised them he spoke with decision. "I will make out."

"You mean you won't hire help?"

"I will make out."

She did not argue with his decision but she watched him toiling early and late at his many tasks, eating heartily, sleeping well. And once she said, "Hayes, so many years ago—so many I can't count them—I saw and told you what is still true."

He waited, but she did not finish until he asked, "What did you tell me?"

"That alone—you grow strong. Alone—I am a weakling."

He still liked to hear her fancies though he thought them mere nonsense. She the willful, the headstrong one! She whose boundless ambition, activities, cleverness—charm? (he did not use such a word but it was the meaning his mind groped for) —whose glib tongue, warm heart, love of company and excitement, had made her name known far and near . . . She, a weakling?

It did not occur to him that in all those long years—except for mere hours in the first months—she had never been alone. It did not occur to him that there might be truth in what she said.

He "made out" and through that first summer he planted as usual. Barring early heavy frost, there would be a good harvest. Standing at the window, she watched one summer day when a neighbor led away and paid well for a large number of the troublesome sheep. He put the money in their pouch.

The harvest was good and he marketed it at a fair price. When he returned and laid the money on the table she looked at it but did not speak.

The snow had deepened early and on a November day, after he had gone out with his gun, she sat a long time gazing out at the whiteness as flake after flake fell until it began to pile up in a soft bank almost obliterating the panes of glass in the window. At last she rose, shivering a little for she had let the fire burn low.

She went about her household tasks and it was nearly noon and yet he did not return. Had he seen tracks and perhaps sought venison?

She went to the window in her parlor and her eyes brightened as she saw the sleigh and the postman. Before he reached her door she had opened it and stood smiling. There was a little pleasant chat and then sitting in her low rocker she tore open the letter. From Silvia. She read rapidly, eagerly. The roads were safe, the weather still good so could not they, Father and Mother, come to join them in a Thanksgiving Day party?

It was as usual a long letter, filled with every little detail about her life, items of news concerning each child, news of each of her friends, the minister and the church, the school and the weather, plans for this and that. It ended with sweet words of love and devotion to "my mother."

Dolly bent her head over the letter and tears streamed from her eyes. Oh, to be with that daughter, to help her in the many tasks, the problems concerning her growing boys and girls, to be close in times of illness and trouble, to nurse, to comfort, to rejoice in times of gaiety. The years were as nothing—now they appeared to her as merely a void which she had filled with tremendous activity which had never obliterated but only deadened for a while her hunger for that sweet companionship.

She laid the open letter on the table and was preparing the dinner when she saw Hayes returning on his snowshoes across the open field. He smiled as he laid the fine turkey down for her inspection. It was not until he later entered the parlor that he saw the sheets of paper. She watched him, saying merely, "Read it."

Slowly he turned the pages, a tenderness showing in his countenance as he finished the sweet words at the close.

"I wish to go."

He looked up at her in great surprise. "I could not leave."

There was no sign now of the tears she had shed. The lines were hard about the tight corners of her mouth. In her weathered face the blue eyes gleamed sharply. She repeated, "I wish to go."

He walked silently into the shed and much later when he returned he spoke gently, "I see your need. You would not be afraid to drive so far alone? The weather is uncertain."

There was something of scorn mixed with eagerness in her smile. "Have I not taken the journey many times?"

"In the good months only."

"The roads are well traveled. I'll leave in the morning. I would like to be there to help Silvia prepare for so many."

It was not the same woman who had sat at the breakfast table without interest even to clear away the dishes. Lightly and swiftly her little feet went back and forth. She dressed and stuffed the turkey, cleaned and heated her deep ovens, placed in them a fine pudding and a great crock of pork and beans.

From the attic she brought down her bag, dusted and cleaned it, brushed her good coat and laid out her dresses. At her old black velvet hat she frowned. "I'm afraid it will shame my daughter. I don't even know how far out of the style it is."

"I would think your warm hood would be suitable for the drive."

So she packed the hat and in the morning, she wore her hood and warmest coat. He brought around the low-slung sleigh with the good carriage horse and placed her bag and bundles, insisting on more robes than she would have taken.

The sun had hardly risen above the forest trees when she lifted the reins. For a moment she sat immobile. Then she turned to look into his face. "Perhaps you could have found a man to care for the place."

"I'm all right. I will make out."

She drove away. The day was fair, even mild.

He wondered a little at his awkwardness in cooking his meals; still, he got along very well and ate with good appetite. Nothing had been said concerning the day of her return but when the weather remained fair and mild he looked for her some few days after Thanksgiving. The week passed; then another week. Neighbors learned of his being alone and scolded. Did he not know that any home would have welcomed him for Thanksgiving dinner? He thanked them and went about his daily tasks, refusing invitations as gracefully as he could. Some days he found himself—rather foolishly he thought—watching up the road toward evening, hoping she would not be caught in darkness or sudden storm. He was rewarded, not with sight of Dolly but with a letter on which he instantly recognized her cramped handwriting. When the postman handed it to him, Hayes caught a curious expression on the man's face. He asked a few courteous questions about Dolly's visit and Hayes answered civilly but nevertheless some anger surged in him as he closed the door. Throughout all the years of his life, in the faces of all men he had seen respect, even wonder or admiration, but never something he did not name but knew as a combination of curiosity and pity.

It angered him and red mounted to his forehead as he opened the letter. It was short—only a few lines One of the boys had been ill with a sore throat and it had been well that she had been there, knowing exactly how to treat it. Now it was so near Christmas that she had decided to remain until after the holiday. She hoped, and had no doubt, that he was making out all right.

He continued to "make out." There were terrific storms in January and brief notes told him of her reasons for delay. The month passed. The farmers' sleds and light sleighs were skimming easily over the hard crust of snow in February and, when the shadows were beginning to lengthen at the end of one short day, and he had no thought of her coming, she drove into the clearing.

For almost a week after her return, the change in her more than repaid him for all his loneliness. Her entire countenance was filled with a happy brightness, her tongue never stopped as she recounted all the activities of the town and in Silvia's home. Proudly she showed him her fine new hat and all the alterations in her dresses. She moved about the house tirelessly, cleaning and putting to rights all that he had neglected.

Almost daily with her heavy shawl over her head, she made

her way to the houses of neighbors, carrying with her pictures of the children, recounting every cunning action, each bright saying, bragging of their smartness in their studies, describing the fine school and the activities of the church, the stores and all the social life of a town.

Now the letters to Silvia were written even more often and the answers were awaited with even greater eagerness. That this sweet intercourse was almost the food she lived on, Hayes knew; but he saw it all only with thankfulness. Was not this happiness due a mother who so loved her daughter?

That there had been gossiping tongues he did not surmise. That wise women looked at each other and shook their heads and grew sober in thought, he never knew. When, through the seasons, a pattern was being set, with some misgivings and yet with a vague feeling of inevitability, he accepted it. In her urgent letters, Silvia always included her father in her invitations, at the same time remarking that she understood, of course, that he could not and never would leave the farm.

Always he "made out." When a terrific hurricane swept through the country one November, in many places his fences were in kindling wood. In his spare hours he mended them all. Often he went into the forest to set his traps and there was no lack of trout for their breakfasts or venison for their dinners. When Dolly was hard pressed, he, silently but efficiently, helped in the dairy.

In the winter days his hammer could be heard in shed or barn. He painted, mended, polished and "fashioned" everything that was needed. When the sun had gone down beyond the high hills, he ate his supper with good appetite, brought in the logs and 'tended the fires, then sought his bed. In all the seasons, mild or severe, he avoided naught but that which he most abhorred—idleness.

Seeing Dolly's loss of interest in sending her produce to the hotel, Hayes sold more cows, disposed of other livestock; but from his fields he still produced rich harvests and bargained astutely, making a profit in the market.

The changes in the country interested and often amazed him. With new roads opened and old roads improved, there was steady travel, more settlers in the towns, more inns built and operated and a greater influx of summer people. When a night traveller saw a gleam of light in the farmhouse window and sought refuge, he was always made welcome, but such travellers were fewer and fewer for railroads now operated regularly while coaches carrying loads of sightseers passed their door without stopping.

The large room with the many beds for transients was almost never in use. In the "jailed in" period of winter, the upper floor was closed to preserve heat and, as season followed season, there was more and more of silence and the lines etched themselves more deeply in Dolly's weathered face. The heavy homespun wools hung loosely on her figure and her light chatter gave way to a strange stillness, though beneath the brows the deep blue eyes held their brightness.

Once, because of Silvia's urging, he hired a man to look after his cattle and accompanied Dolly to spend a week in idleness. To find himself a useless old man expected to sit quietly by the fireside, irked him beyond his understanding. The household was well organized and there was no work for him to do. He must rest. True, he was treated with respect— and with tolerance. At the Thanksgiving Day board, he was requested to ask the blessing and his tongue seemed tied and his speech faltered and he was conscious of embarrassment. He admired and loved his grandchildren but felt he had no part in their lives, but he saw how Dolly had become in an hour's time the very center and inspiration of all the activity in the place. It was wonderful how Silvia turned to her, seeking her advice, heeding her every word, leaving the preparations for the great feast entirely in her hands. He noted with anxiety that Silvia, at her mother's admonition, spent much time on her couch. When, on their journey home. he questioned Dolly, she answered cryptically, "There are periods when many women suffer 'weakness.'"

He frowned. "She was a strong girl—always well."

Still, from overhearing women's talk he knew that there were some who purchased first this nostrum then that, never recovering strength and sometimes going into what were called "declines"; but he could not accept that a child of his could be so afflicted. When she saw his deep concern and worry, Dolly reassured him, "It is naught. It will pass. For a time she must get more rest and in that I can help her."

Reassured, he spoke warmly, "Yes, you must help her."

It was good to get back into his old clothes and resume his daily work. A useless old man to sit idle by a fireside? That winter, besides all his other tasks, he worked on an old sleigh, mended, cleaned, recarpeted the seats and polished the whole until it was as beautiful and bright as new. When it was finished, he searched for more extra work to do.

Dolly became a great letter writer. In her cramped but legible hand she wrote weekly to Jerry who lived in Littleton, to Daniel and Lizzie in their happy Oberlin home, to Nat when, as did not occur often enough to please her, she was reasonably sure of his address. Angrily she would throw a "returned" letter into the fire, muttering, "A rover—gone somewhere else."

The letters came and went to Silvia with amazing regularity. For each baby she knitted coats and bonnets, wove little dresses or caps and mittens for boys. Blankets and fine table cloths were sent with linen towels of great beauty.

In afternoon hours of leisure, she fastened her heavy shawl about her shoulders, tied on her hood and with such letters or pictures in her hand, either going up the road or crossing the river, she sought out her women friends. Her eyes shone as she related the small incidents of Silvia's life. She seemed to know not only what the distant family did but what they said and how they said it.

If Hayes wondered at the patience of the woman in sitting for hours writing those letters, he wondered more at the indestructible love that prompted them.

Through the rooms where fiddles had scratched out merry tunes, where feet had skipped lightly through the intricate square dances, where voices had risen in gales of laughter at jokes and sallies, where the large table had groaned with food— now there was silence.

The daily work was well done. Nothing was neglected. The seasons came and went. On Sundays, dressed in good clothes— for there was no lack of means—they drove to the Meeting House and offered their contributions with pride and dignity.

Sometimes in the evening Hayes sat at the table and read again from the Book. On one such night Dolly was in her bed suffering from a "bad back." He had ministered to her, bringing very hot wool blankets to lay beneath the place she indicated. She was unable to move without pain and, like all who were unaccustomed to physical suffering, accepted the affliction with lack of grace.

Querulously she asked, "What are you reading?"

Hesitantly he answered, "Of the shepherds."

"Wouldn't it be better to get into your bed and repeat the words? If you stumble, I can prompt you."

There was mockery in her tone. Tongue-tied, he sat with bent head. He could not tell her that never in all his many readings had he so felt and understood the words before. In a religious paper for which Dolly subscribed—though she seldom looked into its pages—he had read an article written by one who had visited the Holy Land. Now, he was not thinking of comforting words written for people like himself who might feel the need of a Shepherd. He was thinking of the real men in that far off country who actually cared for their sheep on far distant lonely hills. That shepherd knew where were the green pastures, where to find the water which was scarce. There were treacherous ravines over which he guided his sheep one by one every lamb precious in his sight. The timid sheep, the bleating lambs crowded about that man who would feed them at Nature's table even in the presence of their enemies.

They were helpless, stupid animals and yet goodness and mercy followed them all the days of their lives.

This was reality to a farmer. The words sang in the mind with something of unearthly beauty.

He sat long, gazing beyond the Book. Dolly slept. Had she opened her eyes to look at him, she would have seen naught but an old, bent, grim visaged man, grown unattractive to female eyes. The gnarled hands with their swollen knuckles were still prodigiously strong and now they closed the Book.

He rose, saw to the usual routine for cat and dogs and doors and fires, then lay down to sleep. The old eyes looked into the darkness as he repeated, "Surely goodness and mercy shall follow me all the days of my life; and I will dwell in the house of the Lord for ever."

CHAPTER XXVII

SHE LIMPED ABOUT for a few days and then the pain and stiffness passed and both resumed their usual tasks and their usual silence: but Hayes knew that the sickness that had entered into her heart and soul on that day—seven years ago, only seven years—when they had received the letter from Daniel telling them of his purchase of a farm in Ohio, had slowly permeated her whole being. Here was a poison for which there was no antidote.

When a letter came urging them to visit the farm in Ohio, Dolly's refusal was curt and decisive and addressed to Daniel. As she had stopped answering Lizzie's lengthy epistles they had ceased to come and seldom was her name mentioned by Dolly. She had robbed them of the stalwart son who was to have been the inheritor of this rich farm.

One late October day when the last of the gold leaves were dropping from the maples, falling onto the light snow that covered the level land, she went to the well, drew a bucket of water then, with back turned to the warm sun, she sat down on one of the flat stones placed there so long ago by the friendly Indians. An old woman, wearing a worn homespun dress, shapeless and hanging loose, a frowsy wig slightly awry, shoulders drooping wearily as she rested her elbows on her knees, head bent as she seemed to be studying the cold, wet snow. Was that all Hayes' eyes discerned as he approached from the shed? No, he knew that in the stony face, the eyes still held their brightness and could glow and burn as though some inward fire were consuming her. All that disarray, shabbiness and neglect could be sloughed off like a serpent's skin, or discarded like the chrysalis enveloping a butterfly did the real Dolly within but wish to emerge.

In the long hours and days throughout that fall when he had harvested and sold his crops, working alone in the fields or driving alone to the market, he had been not only uneasy but sometimes filled with a vague sense of fear as he watched her and worried about her and desperately tried to find some way of helping her.

As Nat had complained when Silvia had left them; there was no way of pleasing her. To meet her silence with silence was wrong and yet when he spoke she turned away, not with anger but with something far worse—indifference.

And then there had come clearly to his mind a great understanding. He remembered the moment when the news had come of the birth of Daniel's first baby. She had stood by the red cradle as tears filled her eyes and said, "He should be lying in that cradle." How different it would have been had the babies been born under this old roof; had girls and boys filled the rooms with shouts and laughter and had Daniel and Lizzie and all their friends turned to her for advice, for nursing, for food, for the products of her loom and wheel.

In a flash, he saw the picture complete and in all its small details. Had she not been—he did not use such a word and yet it was the thought he groped for—a "prima donna" throughout her entire life? In the bustling days of her girlhood on the great Highway—a belle. In her home, adored by parents and brothers, the favorite. He saw her through the years, so slender, beautiful, admired, talked-of, envied. Her name and fame had spread far and near. Visitors had heaped praises on her. Flattering tongues—had she not thrived on the flattery? But Hayes did not deceive himself for he knew any flattery did but small justice to her. No casual visitor could gauge the strength and vitality and ambition of the woman.

An understanding of her need for the many visits to Silvia

came clearly to his mind. There, in Silvia's household, she became again a dynamic force. Was it not true that sometimes to a woman her grandchildren were dearer than her own had been? About her, at Silvia's home, were the growing boys and girls, the need for fine dinners, the full life of church and town.

A weight of sadness could fall on his heart as he remembered his misery when he visited there. A useless, unneeded, tolerated old man, keeping out of the way, homely—to his own mind, "ugly"—not even an ornament. He had never repeated the visit and never would. He also knew that Dolly had no wish to see him there.

Sometimes as he worked alone at his carpenter's bench, he stopped, bent his head and closed his eyes as something— was it a prayer or a yearning for light?—filled his heart. He subscribed for a city newspaper and sometimes he had read of great actresses or of a beautiful singer at whose feet whole nations seemed to bow. What happened to them when they no longer received the applause of the public, when their talents were useless, when they grew old, lonely and neglected?

Now, he slowly came from the shed, his deep-set penetrating eyes fastened on the figure resting by the well. In his mind was a clear picture of her whole life, in his heart was a deep understanding but all he found to say was, "You are tired?"

She raised her eyes and anger flashed in them. "I am never tired." She picked up the bucket but stopped on the path and turned to him. "You drive to the town tomorrow? There are some few things I wish."

"You will write them down? I sometimes forget or perhaps you will come."

"I will make a list."

"While I am busy you might visit some friends."

She looked off toward the roadway. "The old friends of our age are mostly gone. If I visited some of them it would be in the cemetery. The younger men and women and boys and girls have no need for an old woman."

"Except your own and Silvia's boys and girls."

"To them I am not a useless old woman." She smiled almost tenderly.

Suddenly the muscles about her mouth twitched and tears stood in her eyes. "Hayes, you are content with nothing more than work. Is that not true?"

He frowned. "A man might well thank God for work to do and strength to do it."

Again she looked off toward the highway. "I sat here thinking of the days when you came here, living alone first in your leanto, then in your cabin. Alone. How many times I have thought that alone you seem strong. You have neither fear nor want. For me, loneliness is worse than death."

She turned and walked rapidly into the house before he could collect his thoughts or find words for an answer.

She was setting the bucket down on the kitchen floor when she saw the postman turning into their enclosure. She walked to the parlor door, opened, held a few minutes of pleasant chat with him then turned with the letter in her hand.

From Jerry. She sat in her low rocker as she read, then read again. Slowly she folded it and sat a long time without moving. The old clock in the corner ticked steadily, the only sound that broke the silence in the room. There was a strained look in her face then, as if her thoughts had clarified, her lips set in a hard straight line and an expression of determination changed her entire countenance. She pressed her shoulders against the back of the rocker and awaited Hayes' coming.

He entered with arms filled with logs which he emptied into the wood box. Long afterwards, pondering over the events of the weeks that followed, he would remember being conscious at that moment of a strange atmosphere in the room. He noted the expression on Dolly's face, the jerky motion of her hand as she pointed to the letter the sharpness in her voice as she said, "Read."

He read slowly and when he finished, he smiled, "It is a nice thought."

Surely there was nothing here that could cause that baffling light in her eyes. Jerry had written that, if he had calculated right in the following November would occur the fiftieth anniversary of the wedding of Hayes and Dolly. Would it not be fitting to gather together the family for such an occasion? He had learned the whereabouts of Nat and had written him. Also Daniel, who had replied that he and Lizzie would journey from Ohio for such an event although they felt it best not to bring the children for the snow might be deep and the weather cold and it would break into their schooling. About Silvia, there was doubt. Jerry was puzzled because she did not seem to be sick yet thought it best not to plan for the trip. However, she would be sure to send presents and love and be there in spirit as she never had ceased to be.

It was a long letter, a tender, loving, appreciative letter and when Hayes laid it down there was moisture in his eyes. He said simply, "It is a nice thought. We will welcome them."

Dolly sat gazing straight into space. Suddenly she rose. "I'll prepare everything. There are not too many days to count before they come."

She walked to the fire and held out her hands toward the heat. She spoke in so low a tone that Hayes hardly heard her words. "It may be that I'll give them a surprise." She repeated, "A great surprise."

He wondered a little why the letter seemed to effect her so strangely. Why did she not express happiness? He looked toward her but the back of her head told him nothing. Perplexed he asked, "Will you write at once to Silvia? She would be sorely missed."

For some time she was silent. He waited then repeated his question. "You will write to Silvia and urge her to be here?"

Her voice was low but every word was spoken with decision. "I don't want her to come. The joggling of her back would make her ill." While he stared at her back in amazement she added, "I would not have her here."

He frowned and spoke sharply. "You always go to her.

Could she not come to you for this one occasion?"

Now she turned and lifting her head looked into his face. There was sudden shrillness in her voice. "I do not wish her here for this occasion."

He stared at her. Curiously, at that moment, many vaguely felt misgivings, suggestions that had always been angrily dismissed from his mind now seemed to clarify into definite meaning, even into certainty. Did this mother actually foster this supposed weakness in her daughter so that her own strength should always be needed? Did she want Silvia to be dependent on her?

He could not express such thoughts in words but he repeated, "You will surely write to her? This once, she should come to you."

"I will decide that." Her voice was again low in tone but there was that in her manner of speaking, in her face that told him the decision was made.

For a moment a great anger surged up in his breast, even into his throat like some living thing that would choke him. He walked out of the room, busied himself for some time in the shed then, as slowly the anger gave way to a sorrow that filled his heart he laid down his tools. He must not let this pass without trying to come to an understanding.

He returned to the room where she was again sitting in the rocker, her shoulder again pressed against the back, her hands lying idle in her lap. He stopped beside her. "It is not easy for me to find words to express my meaning as you know; but there is something I feel and would try to say. Is it not fitting for a woman, as for a man, when she grows old to accept life as it comes to her? Thankful for her strength and for a good home and means for comfort?"

She bent her head and looked at her hands as he stumbled on. "There is a kind of woman who always wishes to have a babe suckling at her breast or cradled in her arms. You are such a woman. You might always wish to see your house filled with many people dependent on you, drawing from your great strength. You might always wish to hear praise of your food, your fine dinners, your great hospitality." He stood rigidly beside her as though he were using every ounce of his strength to find and use the exact words he needed. "Your sorrow when Silvia left you was deep and any mother with but one sweet daughter could understand; but," he now spoke very slowly as though weighing every word, "but, it was when Daniel did not return that—" he floundered, stood silent for some time before adding— "you became a different person. You turned to Silvia and in her life and in her home and with her children sought the life denied you here."

With startling suddenness she raised her head. Tears streamed from her eyes as she cried out, "And did not God send me my daughter and her children? Does He give me health and great strength to use sitting idle by the fire? Lying in bed? Stupidly waiting through the long months of winter merely for the end of snow and storm?" She brushed away the tears and now he marveled at the glow in her eyes. "It is nothing to you. You work through all the days. You are strong, and alone you become stronger. You do not need me. You cannot understand. Your talk is idle."

Need her? He turned away. Yes, his talk was idle. He fetched his gun and some traps and went off into the forest. Not need her? He scarcely saw the path as he climbed. Why could he not say the right words?

"Not to cook my food or mend my clothes. *That* is not a man's need after fifty years."

He returned with game and they ate their supper in silence.

Lying in his bed, he thought, how dull he was never to have thought of the anniversary. Fifty years! How like eternity it seemed in length! How like a moment or the shortness of a day it also seemed!

When he thought her asleep she suddenly spoke. "I harbor no ill will toward you, Hayes. I will do what I purpose to do and there will be no wrong."

Vaguely he wondered what was in her mind but knowing

questioning to be futile he did not speak.

The days passed quickly until heavy November snows covered the ground. She filled the hours with activity. One morning she polished every piece of silver. A little later, passing through the room, his eyes opened and stared in astonishment as he saw her placing the tea set, each piece carefully wrapped, in a box which was already padded with straw. To his questions, she tossed her head and spoke lightly, "My grandmother passed these on to my mother, my mother to me and now I shall pass them on to Silvia."

"Of course. That we expect; but why do you pack them now before your party?"

"The china will do well enough for the party. My mother gave them to me when I came here to make my home. Silvia should have had them long ago."

From cellar to attic there was cleaning, putting in order, polishing, preparing of food from her choicest recipes. Yet there was always time for her writing. Letters to Silvia seemed to go back and forth almost daily.

There was something else. He heard her opening boxes and trunks and though he knew her to be orderly and scrupulously clean yet he wondered why even so good a housekeeper should be watching in such things for damage or dust when the days were growing fewer before her family would arrive.

As they finished their dinner one day, she spoke of their money. Would he bring the pouch and, with her, carefully calculate the wealth in the house and that in the town bank? That was easily accomplished although he saw no reason for figuring up the exact sum. He spoke to reassure her if any future lack could be worrying her. "It is a good amount and each harvest adds to it." She did not raise her eyes to meet his but kept them turned toward the figures as she said, "Then half that amount rightly belongs to me?"

He frowned. "Why waste time in such talk? We share together."

A full week before the party, a man alighted from the stage, walked rapidly down their drive and Nat, without knocking, stepped into the parlor. It was a moment of rejoicing. The lad, who was now a middle-aged man, was splendid to look at. Ravenously, he devoured and praised the good dinner and Hayes, watching the clear eyes, the ruddy complexion, was happy as he told himself, "A rover, yes, but no brawler."

Hardly was the meal completed when Nat asked for a gun and hatchet. Would Hayes want to go with him to the forest?

He turned to Dolly, "Wouldn't some venison be welcome?"

Together father and son hunted for days until there was all that could be used even for so many.

In the early morning Nat was up, brushing them aside. "I shall do the milking and feed the cattle."

Already there was a festive air as his hearty voice and infectious laugh filled the rooms.

Two days before the event, Nat drove to the station to meet Daniel and Lizzie. In her pleasant voice and with her usual fluency, Lizzie exclaimed as she named the familiar peaks and praised the beauty of the forest road. Nat cordially agreed and kept the conversation light and merry even while he was conscious of Daniel's silence, of the tense expression in his brother's face and even of the curious knitting of his eyebrows so like that of their father.

When the sleigh turned into the driveway, Hayes opened the door. With some nervousness, he glanced at Dolly who was walking slowly across the room. She wore a fine wool dress, her gold beads and pin, while at her neck and wrists one instantly noticed the beautifully embroidered collar and cuffs. With poise and dignity she stood waiting but some slight quivering about her lips and an added intensity in her eyes told Hayes how difficult the moment was. However, he never questioned her endurance.

She received Lizzie's demonstrative hugs and kisses pleasantly but it was she who laid her hands on Daniel's shoulders and for a moment bit hard on her lips to hold back tears. It had been seven years since her eyes had rested on that loved face.

The weather held fair. The snow lay deep on the fields; the sun shone and there were no storms. Although he had not been expected so soon, Jerry, Susan and their large family arrived a few hours after Daniel and Lizzie had become settled in their upstairs room.

Now there was a sound that to Dolly Copp seemed the sweetest music she would ever hear—the calling, laughing, even shouting of young voices as the boys raced toward the sheds and barns and the girls seemed to be "everywhere at once." Had she prepared beds enough? Up and down the stairs, into the kitchen, back and forth from the victual room her little feet stepped lightly and quickly. Once she was stopped on those stairs as Jerry's youngest child wound strong arms about her neck and whispered, "I love it here, Grandma."

She would not understand the moisture in Dolly's eyes as she replied, "You do?"

"Yes, and I heard my Uncle Daniel tell my father that next summer he would bring all my cousins here for a long time and we would all have a good time together."

Dolly loosened the arms and went slowly toward the kitchen where a supper was being prepared with the aid of the two young wives.

Once, while helping to prepare vegetables, Jerry's wife, Susan, laughed, "Why, Mother Copp, you seem to be as strong and active as on the day I first saw you when Jerry brought me here. I never shall forget how frightened I was. Imagine how scared any young girl would be in trying to cook for a man who had sat all his life at your table." They all laughed and she went on, "Are you really as well and strong as you appear to be?"

Had she blundered? Asked the wrong question? There was an awkward silence as Dolly's face changed. She jerked up her head and answered tartly, "I have nothing to complain of except" as her sharp eyes looked from face to face— "except when I have no use for my strength—no need for filling my ovens—no reason for rising in the morning no way of passing the long day."

It was that ever-clever Lizzie who had lived with her longest and knew her most intimately who spoke sympathetically, "It must be very lonely when the eaglets all leave the nest, all grown too large to crowd in and all wanting nests and eaglets of their own." She continued, "Perhaps Nature planned better for the eagles than for the humans. When we are old and finished with one brood we can't start another."

Dolly's eyes were sharp and bright and a light flashed in them as she replied, "I am not old and I am not finished. I shall not sit like an old pot in the shed to rust in idleness until it is thrown out."

They all might be middle-aged people, living their own lives with dignity and efficiency, but they could be made to feel infantile, commonplace and even weak when they found themselves pitted against the restless spirit and inflexible force in this woman. They would watch their tongues and speak pleasantly of impersonal matters.

When Lizzie went to the drawer to fetch the tablecloth, she noted, not without some wondering, that the drawer seemed to contain few pieces of linen though it had always before been well filled. Dolly stepped to her side, selected two small cloths and in her sharpest authoritative voice said, "Put these two together. They will do very well for tonight."

When the younger woman asked for the silver set, Dolly answered crisply, "We'll use the china." Quietly to herself Lizzie wondered, "Has she given all her handsomest linen and her beautiful silver to Silvia?" Dutifully she set the china in place; then, with hands holding a pile of plates, she stopped in the middle of the floor and stared through the door at Dolly who was now moving quickly back and forth in the kitchen. A shocking thought had entered her mind. "She spends so much time with Silvia—long visits—Susan has told me how she leaves Father Copp alone—weeks—months—could she be planning to follow her treasures? Even the blue coverlets have disappeared from the beds." Slowly she set the plates as fear clutched at her heart. Susan had written that Father Copp would never consent to sit useless in another home—idle— how he abhorred idleness! Was there something besides fear clutching at that heart? Why did this feeling of guilt plague her through all the years?

Surely it had been a natural and expected event when Jerry had married and sought possession of a farm and home of his own. And no one could have expected Silvia to refuse to marry and join her young husband in his own home. One could not expect Nat to change his roving habits; but had not she, Lizzie, enticed and argued and finally persuaded Daniel to do that which he had never dreamed of doing—desert his father and mother and leave this home he had loved? As she set the knives, forks and spoons in place she thought—not knowing she was repeating Hayes' question—"Why can't Silvia come to her mother? And bring the children here, making this loved home the center for them all." She, Lizzie, would bring her own for a long summer visit.

After the supper, Dolly warmed and cleaned her deep ovens, and into them went the whole wild turkey, the jars of pork and beans, the Indian pudding and all the delicious dishes she knew so well how to plan and cook.

About the great blazing logs they gathered, happy in looking into each other's faces, listening to the well-known and loved voices, laughing, telling of their childrens' problems, of their education, of schools, plans, dreams, health, reverses and prosperity.

It was growing late. The darkness of night enveloped the house without, but Nat laughingly piled more logs on the blazing fire. He was in the shed and long before the sound was heard by those chattering before the fire, he stepped to the outer door as the music of sleigh bells rang clear on the night air. His sensitive ears told him they were not common bells but those tuned chimes that were such a delight to hear as the runners of the sleds passed noiselessly over the snow. He waited for them to pass the house wondering who was abroad so late when—no—yes—the chimes rang closer and closer and the sled turned into their drive. He ran around the house and was at the parlor door when it was opened and a-blaze of light disclosed an astonishing sight. There was Benjamin Potter holding the reins, while by his side, so smothered in furs and rugs and hood that her bright eyes and blond hair were almost hidden from view was Silvia; and from the back of the sleigh were emerging from what had been a huddle, her tall sons and young daughters.

Quickly the bags and bundles were fetched in, and Nat drove the horses back to the barn.

What a hubbub! How they laughed and questioned and gazed as Silvia untied the hood, threw off the heavy coat and stood gazing at one face after another. It was her husband who turned to Dolly. "She was brokenhearted, Mother Copp. After she read Father Copp's letter, I thought it would be better for her to die of a broken back than drown in tears. We took it easy, made two night stops, and here we are. Can you feed and house us?"

Many eyes were turned to Dolly who stood erect and strangely quiet as she looked from one face to another then turned the piercing brightness of her eyes to Hayes. "So—*you* wrote to Silvia?"

He nodded. "It seemed fitting."

Dolly turned to Silvia as they all seemed to wait breathless. Then out in the room from that daughter came the happy, infectious laugh they had all loved to hear. No longer could Benjamin's hands span the waist as they had when he had carried away a mere slip of a girl. The blond hair showed a little gray, the bosom that had nursed children was full and womanly but the blue eyes still sparkled and the laughter was still merry. "You have not answered Ben's question, Mother. Can you feed and house so many?"

For only a moment Dolly's lips quivered then she tossed her head and spoke crisply, "I have housed and fed many more—but not all my own—under this roof."

It was Susan who fed them in the kitchen while upstairs Lizzie fairly ran as at Dolly's bidding they prepared beds, spread sheets and opened trunks and boxes for extra blankets.

When at long last all were comfortably bedded and slept, Dolly was still moving, sometimes in the kitchen, sometimes opening drawers in her parlor chest. More than a little worried, Hayes listened to her footsteps. He heard her open the shed door and waited. When the minutes lengthened he rose and went out to remonstrate with her. His eyes rested on a strange scene. She was opening the box and carefully setting each piece of her silver on the shelf.

She raised her head and for a long moment they looked deep into each other's eyes. She half whispered, "Will you carry those in for me?"

At last by the light of the fire she undressed and as she stretched out by his side something that was half sigh and half groan escaped her. Then she seemed to be laughing as she said, "The old bones ache. I'll never hanker to run an inn again."

Then he knew she was crying and he wondered why, after fifty years, he did not quite understand why she laughed or why she cried.

When morning came even Nat could not get dressed and downstairs before she was moving about. Dutifully all helped in preparation for the dinner. Now her handsomest cloth was spread and with her own hands she smoothed the fringe. The same hands set the silver set in place. Two tables had been set together and with merry jests and much laughing they found chairs and silver enough to accommodate so many.

What odors were emanating from those ovens as they all took their places about the board. Napkins were tied about the necks of the youngest children, the turkey was set before Hayes, and then there was a pause.

There was that which touched every heart as they turned toward their father. His face was lighted with the happiness of looking into the faces of his three fine sons and that loved daughter. He had not picked up the carving knife and now with

a tremulous smile he spoke, "I believe God knows of our thankfulness without our speaking and yet I think it would be fitting—" he bent his head— "to thank Him for His mercies."

The prayer was not eloquent but he asked for a continued blessing on them all. When he spoke thanks that Death had never taken one from their midst, there was an uneasy moving. Each one would have insisted that there could be no ignorant remnant of superstition in any mind—yet an evil should not be mentioned. However, when they raised their heads there were only smiles and happiness in their faces, and they ate as only hearty, healthy, hungry men and women could.

When the delicious desserts had been consumed and duly praised, the dishes washed and returned to the closets, they sat about the fire smoking or cracking nuts.

As the brilliant light of sun on snow diminished, the flames from the crackling fire grew brighter. It seemed they would never want to end the good talk.

Daniel, who had been going about from barn to each shed, up the stairs and down into the cellar, again took his place by the fire. He spoke to his father. "There is scarce a crack. You built well, Father."

Hayes smiled, "It is a good house."

They slept. In that night a great peace seemed to descend on the white world without. The moon rose clear and across the clearing, over the old farmhouse and across the Glen, its silver light turned all to cold, bright beauty.

The End

Publisher's Note

When *The Pilgrim Soul* was first published in 1952, The Peoples Book Club of Chicago and J. B. Lippincott Company of New York simultaneously published two slightly different editions of the book. The Peoples Book Club of Chicago published the book that you have just read. The edition published by J. B. Lippincott had a different, but more historically accurate, final chapter. This second "final chapter" follows. Otherwise, there are no differences between the two editions.

—J. T. B. M.

CHAPTER XXVII

SHE LIMPED ABOUT for a few days and then the pain and stiffness passed and both resumed their usual tasks and their usual silence: but Hayes knew that the sickness that had entered into her heart and soul on that day—seven years ago, only seven years—when they had received the letter from Daniel telling them of his purchase of a farm in Ohio, had slowly permeated her whole being. Here was a poison for which there was no antidote.

When a letter came urging them to visit the farm in Ohio, Dolly's refusal was curt and decisive and addressed to Daniel. As she had stopped answering Lizzie's lengthy epistles they had ceased to come and seldom was her name mentioned by Dolly. She had robbed them of the stalwart son who was to have been the inheritor of this rich farm.

One late October day when the last of the gold leaves were dropping from the maples, falling onto the light snow that covered the level land, she went to the well, drew a bucket of water then, with back turned to the warm sun, she sat down on one of the flat stones placed there so long ago by the friendly Indians. An old woman, wearing a worn homespun dress, shapeless and hanging loose, a frowsy wig slightly awry, shoulders drooping wearily as she rested her elbows on her knees, head bent as she seemed to be studying the cold, wet snow. Was that all Hayes' eyes discerned as he approached from the shed? No, he knew that in the stony face, the eyes still held their brightness and could glow and burn as though some inward fire were consuming her. All that disarray, shabbiness and neglect could be sloughed off like a serpent's skin, or discarded like the chrysalis enveloping a butterfly did the real Dolly within but wish to emerge.

In the long hours and days throughout that fall when he had harvested and sold his crops, working alone in the fields or driving alone to the market, he had been not only uneasy but sometimes filled with a vague sense of fear as he watched her and worried about her and desperately tried to find some way of helping her.

As Nat had complained when Silvia had left them; there was no way of pleasing her. To meet her silence with silence was wrong and yet when he spoke she turned away, not with anger but with something far worse—indifference.

And then there had come clearly to his mind a great understanding. He remembered the moment when the news had come of the birth of Daniel's first baby. She had stood by the red cradle as tears filled her eyes and said, "He should be lying in that cradle." How different it would have been had the babies been born under this old roof; had girls and boys filled the rooms with shouts and laughter and had Daniel and Lizzie and all their friends turned to her for advice, for nursing, for food, for the products of her loom and wheel.

In a flash, he saw the picture complete and in all its small details. Had she not been—he did not use such a word and yet it was the thought he groped for—a "prima donna" throughout her entire life? In the bustling days of her girlhood on the great Highway—a belle. In her home, adored by parents and brothers, the favorite. He saw her through the years, so slender, beautiful, admired, talked-of, envied. Her name and fame had spread far and near. Visitors had heaped praises on her. Flattering tongues—had she not thrived on the flattery? But Hayes did not deceive himself for he knew any flattery did but small justice to her. No casual visitor could gauge the strength and vitality and ambition of the woman.

An understanding of her need for the many visits to Silvia

came clearly to his mind. There, in Silvia's household, she became again a dynamic force. Was it not true that sometimes to a woman her grandchildren were dearer than her own had been? About her, at Silvia's home, were the growing boys and girls, the need for fine dinners, the full life of church and town.

A weight of sadness could fall on his heart as he remembered his misery when he visited there. A useless, unneeded, tolerated old man, keeping out of the way, homely—to his own mind, "ugly"—not even an ornament. He had never repeated the visit and never would. He also knew that Dolly had no wish to see him there.

Sometimes as he worked alone at his carpenter's bench, he stopped, bent his head and closed his eyes as something— was it a prayer or a yearning for light?—filled his heart. He subscribed for a city newspaper and sometimes he had read of great actresses or of a beautiful singer at whose feet whole nations seemed to bow. What happened to them when they no longer received the applause of the public, when their talents were useless, when they grew old, lonely and neglected?

Now, he slowly came from the shed, his deep-set penetrating eyes fastened on the figure resting by the well. In his mind was a clear picture of her whole life, in his heart was a deep understanding but all he found to say was, "You are tired?"

She raised her eyes and anger flashed in them. "I am never tired." She picked up the bucket but stopped on the path and turned to him. "You drive to the town tomorrow? There are some few things I wish."

"You will write them down? I sometimes forget or perhaps you will come."

"I will make a list."

"While I am busy you might visit some friends."

She looked off toward the roadway. "The old friends of our age are mostly gone. If I visited some of them it would be in the cemetery. The younger men and women and boys and girls have no need for an old woman."

"Except your own and Silvia's boys and girls."

"To them I am not a useless old woman." She smiled almost tenderly.

Suddenly the muscles about her mouth twitched and tears stood in her eyes. "Hayes, you are content with nothing more than work. Is that not true?"

He frowned. "A man might well thank God for work to do and strength to do it."

Again she looked off toward the highway. "I sat here thinking of the days when you came here, living alone first in your leanto, then in your cabin. Alone. How many times I have thought that alone you seem strong. You have neither fear nor want. For me, loneliness is worse than death."

She turned and walked rapidly into the house before he could collect his thoughts or find words for an answer.

She was setting the bucket down on the kitchen floor when she saw the postman turning into their enclosure. She walked to the parlor door, opened, held a few minutes of pleasant chat with him then turned with the letter in her hand.

From Jerry. She sat in her low rocker as she read, then read again. Slowly she folded it and sat a long time without moving. The old clock in the corner ticked steadily, the only sound that broke the silence in the room. There was a strained look in her face then, as if her thoughts had clarified, her lips set in a hard straight line and an expression of determination changed her entire countenance. She pressed her shoulders against the back of the rocker and awaited Hayes' coming.

He entered with arms filled with logs which he emptied into the wood box. Long afterwards, pondering over the events of the weeks that followed, he would remember being conscious at that moment of a strange atmosphere in the room. He noted the expression on Dolly's face, the jerky motion of her hand as she pointed to the letter the sharpness in her voice as she said, "Read."

He read slowly and when he finished, he smiled, "It is a nice thought."

Surely there was nothing here that could cause that baffling light in her eyes. Jerry had written that, if he had calculated right in the following November would occur the fiftieth anniversary of the wedding of Hayes and Dolly. Would it not be fitting to gather together the family for such an occasion? He had learned the whereabouts of Nat and had written him. Also Daniel, who had replied that he and Lizzie would journey from Ohio for such an event although they felt it best not to bring the children for the snow might be deep and the weather cold and it would break into their schooling. About Silvia, there was doubt. Jerry was puzzled because she did not seem to be sick yet thought it best not to plan for the trip. However, she would be sure to send presents and love and be there in spirit as she never had ceased to be.

It was a long letter, a tender, loving, appreciative letter and when Hayes laid it down there was moisture in his eyes. He said simply, "It is a nice thought. We will welcome them."

Dolly sat gazing straight into space. Suddenly she rose. "I'll prepare everything. There are not too many days to count before they come."

She walked to the fire and held out her hands toward the heat. She spoke in so low a tone that Hayes hardly heard her words. "It may be that I'll give them a surprise." She repeated, "A great surprise."

He wondered a little why the letter seemed to effect her so strangely. Why did she not express happiness? He looked toward her but the back of her head told him nothing. Perplexed he asked, "Will you write at once to Silvia? She would be sorely missed."

For some time she was silent. He waited then repeated his question. "You will write to Silvia and urge her to be here?"

Her voice was low but every word was spoken with decision. "I don't want her to come. The joggling of her back would make her ill." While he stared at her back in amazement she added, "I would not have her here."

He frowned and spoke sharply. "You always go to her.

Could she not come to you for this one occasion?"

Now she turned and lifting her head looked into his face. There was sudden shrillness in her voice. "I do not wish her here for this occasion."

He stared at her. Curiously, at that moment, many vaguely felt misgivings, suggestions that had always been angrily dismissed from his mind now seemed to clarify into definite meaning, even into certainty. Did this mother actually foster this supposed weakness in her daughter so that her own strength should always be needed? Did she want Silvia to be dependent on her?

He could not express such thoughts in words but he repeated, "You will surely write to her? This once, she should come to you."

"I will decide that." Her voice was again low in tone but there was that in her manner of speaking, in her face that told him the decision was made.

For a moment a great anger surged up in his breast, even into his throat like some living thing that would choke him. He walked out of the room, busied himself for some time in the shed then, as slowly the anger gave way to a sorrow that filled his heart he laid down his tools. He must not let this pass without trying to come to an understanding.

He returned to the room where she was again sitting in the rocker, her shoulder again pressed against the back, her hands lying idle in her lap. He stopped beside her. "It is not easy for me to find words to express my meaning as you know; but there is something I feel and would try to say. Is it not fitting for a woman, as for a man, when she grows old to accept life as it comes to her? Thankful for her strength and for a good home and means for comfort?"

She bent her head and looked at her hands as he stumbled on. "There is a kind of woman who always wishes to have a babe suckling at her breast or cradled in her arms. You are such a woman. You might always wish to see your house filled with many people dependent on you, drawing from your great strength. You might always wish to hear praise of your food, your fine dinners, your great hospitality." He stood rigidly beside her as though he were using every ounce of his strength to find and use the exact words he needed. "Your sorrow when Silvia left you was deep and any mother with but one sweet daughter could understand; but," he now spoke very slowly as though weighing every word, "but, it was when Daniel did not return that—" he floundered, stood silent for some time before adding— "you became a different person. You turned to Silvia and in her life and in her home and with her children sought the life denied you here."

With startling suddenness she raised her head. Tears streamed from her eyes as she cried out, "And did not God send me my daughter and her children? Does He give me health and great strength to use sitting idle by the fire? Lying in bed? Stupidly waiting through the long months of winter merely for the end of snow and storm?" She brushed away the tears and now he marveled at the glow in her eyes. "It is nothing to you. You work through all the days. You are strong, and alone you become stronger. You do not need me. You cannot understand. Your talk is idle."

Need her? He turned away. Yes, his talk was idle. He fetched his gun and some traps and went off into the forest. Not need her? He scarcely saw the path as he climbed. Why could he not say the right words?

"Not to cook my food or mend my clothes. *That* is not a man's need after fifty years."

He returned with game and they ate their supper in silence.

Lying in his bed, he thought, how dull he was never to have thought of the anniversary. Fifty years! How like eternity it seemed in length! How like a moment or the shortness of a day it also seemed!

When he thought her asleep she suddenly spoke. "I harbor no ill will toward you, Hayes. I will do what I purpose to do and there will be no wrong."

Vaguely he wondered what was in her mind but knowing

questioning to be futile he did not speak.

The days passed quickly until heavy November snows covered the ground. She filled the hours with activity. One morning she polished every piece of silver. A little later, passing through the room, his eyes opened and stared in astonishment as he saw her placing the tea set, each piece carefully wrapped, in a box which was already padded with straw. To his questions, she tossed her head and spoke lightly, "My grandmother passed these on to my mother, my mother to me and now I shall pass them on to Silvia."

"Of course. That we expect; but why do you pack them now before your party?"

"The china will do well enough for the party. My mother gave them to me when I came here to make my home. Silvia should have had them long ago."

From cellar to attic there was cleaning, putting in order, polishing, preparing of food from her choicest recipes. Yet there was always time for her writing. Letters to Silvia seemed to go back and forth almost daily.

There was something else. He heard her opening boxes and trunks and though he knew her to be orderly and scrupulously clean yet he wondered why even so good a housekeeper should be watching in such things for damage or dust when the days were growing fewer before her family would arrive.

As they finished their dinner one day, she spoke of their money. Would he bring the pouch and, with her, carefully calculate the wealth in the house and that in the town bank? That was easily accomplished although he saw no reason for figuring up the exact sum. He spoke to reassure her if any future lack could be worrying her. "It is a good amount and each harvest adds to it." She did not raise her eyes to meet his but kept them turned toward the figures as she said, "Then half that amount rightly belongs to me?"

He frowned. "Why waste time in such talk? We share together."

A full week before the party, a man alighted from the stage, walked rapidly down their drive and Nat, without knocking, stepped into the parlor. It was a moment of rejoicing. The lad, who was now a middle-aged man, was splendid to look at. Ravenously, he devoured and praised the good dinner and Hayes, watching the clear eyes, the ruddy complexion, was happy as he told himself, "A rover, yes, but no brawler."

Hardly was the meal completed when Nat asked for a gun and hatchet. Would Hayes want to go with him to the forest?

He turned to Dolly, "Wouldn't some venison be welcome?"

Together father and son hunted for days until there was all that could be used even for so many.

In the early morning Nat was up, brushing them aside. "I shall do the milking and feed the cattle."

Already there was a festive air as his hearty voice and infectious laugh filled the rooms.

Two days before the event, Nat drove to the station to meet Daniel and Lizzie. In her pleasant voice and with her usual fluency, Lizzie exclaimed as she named the familiar peaks and praised the beauty of the forest road. Nat cordially agreed and kept the conversation light and merry even while he was conscious of Daniel's silence, of the tense expression in his brother's face and even of the curious knitting of his eyebrows so like that of their father.

When the sleigh turned into the driveway, Hayes opened the door. With some nervousness, he glanced at Dolly who was walking slowly across the room. She wore a fine wool dress, her gold beads and pin, while at her neck and wrists one instantly noticed the beautifully embroidered collar and cuffs. With poise and dignity she stood waiting but some slight quivering about her lips and an added intensity in her eyes told Hayes how difficult the moment was. However, he never questioned her endurance.

She received Lizzie's demonstrative hugs and kisses pleasantly but it was she who laid her hands on Daniel's shoulders and for a moment bit hard on her lips to hold back tears. It had been seven years since her eyes had rested on that loved face.

The weather held fair. Although the snow deepened, the sun shone and there were no storms. On the evening before the great day, Dolly warmed and cleaned her deep ovens and into them went the whole wild turkey, the jars of pork and beans, the Indian puddings and all the delicious dishes she knew so well how to plan and cook.

About the great blazing logs they sat on that last evening, happy in looking into each other's faces, listening to the well known and loved voices, laughing, telling of their children, and their education, of schools, plans, dreams, health, reverses and prosperity.

They slept. In that night a great peace seemed to descend on the white world without. The moon rose clear and across the clearing, over the old farmhouse and throughout the Glen, its silver light turned all to cold, bright beauty.

Then what a bustle there was in the morning! Jerry and Nat at home in barn and shed, the wives clearing dishes, offering every help to Dolly in the kitchen.

Once, while helping prepare vegetables, Jerry's wife, Susan, laughed, "Why, Mother Copp, you seem to be as strong and active as on the day I first saw you when Jerry brought me here. I never shall forget how frightened I was. Imagine how scared any young girl would be in trying to cook for a man who had sat all his life at your table." They all laughed and she went on, "Are you really as well and strong as you appear to be?"

Had she blundered? Asked the wrong question? There was an awkward silence as Dolly's face changed. There was bitterness in her expression as her lips twisted, an angry mocking light in her eyes when she jerked up her head and answered tartly, "I have nothing to complain of—except" as her sharp eyes looked from face to face— "except when I have no use for my strength—no need for filling my ovens—no reason for rising in the morning—no way of passing the long day."

It was that ever-clever Lizzie who had lived with her longest and knew her most intimately who spoke sympathetically, "It must be very lonely when the eaglets all leave the nest, all grown to large to crowd in, and all wanting nests and eaglets of their own." She continued, "Perhaps Nature planned better for the eagles than for the humans. When we are old and finished with one brood we can't start another."

Dolly's eyes were sharp and bright and a light flashed in them as she replied, "I am not old and I am not finished. I shall not sit like an old pot in the shed to rust in idleness until it is thrown out."

They all might be middle-aged people, living their own lives with dignity and efficiency, but they could be made to feel infantile, commonplace and even weak when they found themselves pitted against the restless spirit and inflexible force in this woman. They would watch their tongues and speak pleasantly of impersonal matters but in each mind there was some foreboding, mixed with uneasiness.

Dutifully they helped in preparations for the dinner. When Lizzie went to the drawer to fetch the table cloth, she noted, not without some wondering, that the drawer seemed to contain few pieces of linen though it had always before been well filled. Dolly stood by her side selecting the handsomest cloth, spreading it out and smoothing the beautiful fringe. When the younger woman asked for the silver set, Dolly answered crisply, "We'll use the china." Quietly to herself, Lizzie thought, "There is something wrong."

That there was nothing wrong with the odors emanating from those ovens they were all agreed as they took their places about the board. Napkins were tied about the necks of Jerry's younger children, the turkey was set before Hayes and then there was a pause.

There was that which touched every heart as they turned toward their father. His face was lighted with the happiness of looking into the eyes of his three fine sons. He had not picked up the carving knife and now with a tremulous smile, he spoke. "I believe God knows of our thankfulness without our speaking and yet I think it would be fitting—" he bent his head— "to thank him for his mercies."

The prayer was not eloquent but he asked blessings on each absent one. When he spoke thanks that Death had never taken one from their midst, there was an uneasy moving. Each one would have insisted that there could be found no ignorant remnant of superstition in any mind—yet an evil should not be mentioned. However, when they raised their heads there were only smiles and happiness in their faces and they ate as only hearty, healthy, hungry men and women could.

It was when Nat who had refilled the mugs of cider, raised his and with his hearty laugh suggested, "We will drink to the sixtieth wedding anniversary," that the merriment reached its height. Was it only Lizzie who noticed that Dolly did not lift her glass? No. Nat noticed. "Come, Mother, we are drinking to you as well as to Father."

She rose quickly. Would the girls clear the dishes while she brought the pudding and pie? As she walked away she spoke clearly, "Don't drink to any such anniversary."

Only for a moment, a dark, sober, forboding expression was visible in Hayes' face as his eyes followed Dolly who moved quickly toward her oven.

When the delicious desserts had been eaten and duly praised, the dishes washed and returned to the closets, they sat about the fire smoking or cracking nuts.

As the brilliant light of sun on snow diminished, the flames from the crackling fire grew brighter. That Dolly did not join them for any length of time, that she seemed busy about affairs of her own, going upstairs, then seemingly occupied here and there, they hardly noticed.

They spoke often of Silvia. If she were with them, it would be all heart could wish.

It was Susan who said, "I didn't hear the reason. She's not really ill? Are the children all well?"

Where was Dolly? They looked to her for answers but she was not among them.

Again, later, they asked, where was Dolly?

A child answered, "She's gone upstairs."

It was Lizzie called her.

There were footsteps descending much more slowly than was Dolly's habit. She entered the door and stood looking from one face to another.

When proffered a chair she shook her head and remained standing. Her expression troubled them. She smiled but it was a smile without joy.

She spoke with a brevity strange to her. She noted that they were all together and that it was a suitable time for her to say that which she had to say.

The words dropped heavily. "Hayes is well enough but fifty years is long enough to live with any man."

There was a hush in the room There was no movement but from Hayes. His elbows dropped to his knees. He bent his head and gazed at the floor. Evenly, she told them that she had listed, with Hayes' checking, all their money. She had listed all their possessions and such could be divided to the least value honestly and fairly, half for him and half for herself. She would leave in the morning to go to Silvia who had long needed her and waited for her. There was naught but love in her heart for them all and she rejoiced that they had made for themselves happy and useful lives far beyond any need of her. She would spend the remaining days of her life with the daughter who did have need of her.

Fifty years ago had the bright blue eyes of a pretty girl lighted with the same eagerness? She had loved her family and had been a faithful, devoted daughter but there had been that within her which could not be denied: Had the lips pressed together with the same firmness when she had stood before them and stated her determination to leave them all for love of a young man and for a share in his great adventure in the wilderness?

Only the youngest children stared up into her face. The others sat with bowed heads as they slowly and painfully tried to adjust their minds to the full import of her words. Then harshly, with fearful jarring to all their nerves, Nat laughed loudly and boisterously as he sprang up from his chair, rushed out of the room, grabbed his coat and cap and went off into the night darkness.

Now Jerry rose, speaking gently and quietly as he emptied his pipe at the fire, "No one of us has the right to question your decisions, Mother. It seems to me this is a question to be settled between you and Father." Then to Susan, he spoke in a matter-of-fact voice, "It is time the children were in bed. Will you take them up?"

Lizzie whose ready wit and ease in conversation seemed to desert her, found herself very tired and she too would retire early. But not to rest. Was there something of guilt in her heart that caused her to toss restlessly? Through the long hours of the night when she spoke softly she always found Daniel awake and staring into the darkness.

Surely it had been a natural and expected event when Jerry had married and sought possession of a farm and home of his own. And no one could have expected Silvia to refuse to marry and join her young husband in his own home. One could not expect Nat to change his roving habits but had not she, Lizzie, enticed and argued and finally persuaded Daniel to do that which he had never dreamed of doing—desert his father and mother and leave this home he had loved?

There was the low murmur of voices from the room where Jerry and Susan slept. The old clock, in its deep metallic voice had called out the hour of twelve when Nat returned and crept up the creaking stairs.

There was a brave attempt at cheerfulness and naturalness when they gathered at the breakfast table. The usual chores and tasks about the house were quickly accomplished and soon Jerry bundled his wife and children into their sled. He kissed his mother with great tenderness and there was entreaty in his voice. "I'm sure we will all meet here again, Mother." His father was standing in the snow on the drive, the youngest girl flinging her arms about him and merrily bidding him goodbye. Jerry grasped his hand but found no words.

Nat was to drive Lizzie and Daniel to the station. Daniel's wife looked small and pale and utterly miserable as she shrank down under the heavy blanket that he pulled about her. When he went back to the door to speak again to his parents, Nat called impatiently that the train would be missed if he lingered. It was with brows gathered into a hard frown and an expression almost as stern as his father's that Dan at last took his place in the sleigh.

When Nat returned, Dolly was standing at the kitchen door. She spoke pleasantly enough. "You need not unharness." He tied the horse to a post.

The day was mild and beautiful. In those hours since breakfast she had packed the remaining treasures which were hers—china, and all that which should go to Silvia.

She wore her heavy wool dress, her good coat with the sable collar of Hayes' trapping. When she came for the last time down the stairs her warm hood was tied beneath her chin.

Nat stood as silent as the old man sitting in front of the fire. He saw his father turn his head and look long at Dolly's feet. She was wearing her fine kid shoes, such shoes as for fifty years he had ordered in Portland and paid for willingly and happily.

The little feet. The vanity that had so endeared them to him; as weakness can. He watched the feet move quickly across the room toward him, knowing that his eyes would never follow them again.

He did not raise his eyes, except when the small feet passed through the door. Hayes and Dolly Copp were never to meet again.

Without, Nat arranged the trunk and packages, he, too, hardly glancing at his mother's face. She kissed him goodbye and picked up the reins. When the sleigh turned from the clearing into the road he watched until it was lost in the forest, then he swore and as anger consumed him, wished he knew more oaths to hurl into the air.

He returned to the parlor where his father sat. Once he

came near and placed his hand hard on the shoulder but he had no words here.

At the noon hour he tried laughing. "I guess we'd better tackle some of this food. There's enough here for a week."

It was at the table that he nervously remarked that he wished he could stay but he was to meet his wife in Boston and their tickets were already bought for the train that would take them back to the West.

His father looked up. The deep eyes looked into his son's face. He smiled. "Don't worry, Nat. I will make out. You must go to your wife and family."

Still, on the next morning when he was to leave, Nat's nerves betrayed him. Twice he started and turned back. The second time his face was drawn with misery. "Father, I can't bear to leave. I should come home."

Hayes shook his head. "No, Nat. You will live your own life as I have lived mine. Have no worry. I will make out."

"You'll stay here?"

"No. I shall go away. Someday, if it is ever your wish, you may come here and do what you will with the place."

Nat fairly gasped the words, "Why—she—my mother will come back. She'll change her mind. It's her love for Silvia. You remember it was always like that but—she will come back."

The muscles about the younger man's mouth quivered and his eyes stared incredulously into the stern countenance turned to him as Hayes spoke. "She will not come back. Her need was great." He repeated slowly as though trying to impart his larger understanding into the simple words. "Her need was great—too great for her endurance." Then there was almost entreaty in his voice. "Never did three boys have a better mother; never did man have a better wife."

He stopped and smiled but with such pathos that his son could not speak.

That the story of that fiftieth wedding anniversary should spread through the Glen and amazingly soon to the towns, might have been expected. Men came to buy the cattle and in a few weeks the stables and stalls were empty. Through all the hours of daylight there was the sound of hammering as Hayes fitted boards and nailed them to window after window until the light was shut out. Were the blows of the hammer on wood or on his heart? They were young, strong hands that had driven the nails into this house, and now the gnarled wrinkled hands struck just as swiftly and surely.

Once, going through the attic his feet hit an obstacle in the semidarkness. He looked down and moved the crude red-painted cradle. He had cut the wood, shaped and fashioned it for Jerry. It had been repainted for Nat and for Silvia and Daniel, but it was Dolly's small foot he saw most clearly, her knitting needles flying as her toe reached out to keep the cradle rocking.

On one winter day, he placed his trunk in the back of the old sled that he had kept for this purpose. His good horse was harnessed. Into a sack, he placed the last of the food, then he went for his great coat and fur cap. He locked the door and, when outside, he put in place the frame he had measured, then he hammered in the last nails.

He stood a moment looking about. The river was covered with ice but beneath it was still brawling. The eagle had gone from his mountain home seeking food in a warmer climate. The great peaks were white.

He climbed into the sled, pulled the bear robe about him and picked up the reins. He drove out of the clearing, into the forest road.

He did not look back. Every detail of the picture made by house and sheds and barns, river and forest was etched so deeply into his mind and heart that there would be no moment of the day or night, through any number of years, when he would be able to free himself from the vision.

Fifty years. His work was done. He would stop overnight at any inn and drive on to Stow, Maine, the town from which he had come and there he would find some way of passing his days.

Only once he glanced up at the Cliff where he had stood, fifty-five years before, a blond, curly-haired lad wishing he could, like the eagle above him, fly over the great forest and see the silver river and the wooded Glen where he purposed to make a home.

Old and bent and sad, his deep set eyes looked straight ahead up the long road through the forest.

The End

Historical Epilogue

Dolly Emery Copp

Hayes Dodifer Copp

"Thus it was that because of Silvia's urging, a fine picture of both Hayes Copp and Dolly was to be made, pictures that posterity would treasure beyond their imaginings."

Today the Dolly Copp Campground is the lasting memorial to this pioneering woman in the White Mountains. The Hayes Copp Ski Trail traverses the hills that he knew so well and dedicated his life to clearing and farming. Dolly's neighbors, the Barnes Family, whose infant daughter she cared for, are remembered at the Barnes Field Campground adjoining the Dolly Copp Campground. Culhane Brook, named after another neighboring farm family, flows through the Dolly Copp Campground. (Note: Mrs. Downes uses the name Culbane in *The Pilgrim Soul*. This spelling is used in *Incidents of White Mountain History* by Benjamin Willey, one of Mrs. Downes' references. Other books have always referred to the Culhane family.)

After dividing their property, Hayes and Dolly Copp separated and left the farm that for half a century had been their home. Hayes Copp moved to Stow, Maine, where he died on

November 6, 1889. Dolly moved to live with her daughter, Sylvia, in Auburn, Maine, and died there on October 4, 1891. Jerry died in Meredith, New Hampshire, on September 5, 1910. Nat, the rover, died in Brunswick, Maine, on February 27, 1912. Daniel always lived in Ohio and died there on March 13, 1922. Sylvia died in Auburn, Maine, on October 29, 1929. The Copp Homestead was purchased by the Federal Government in 1915 and made a part of the White Mountain National Forest. Since 1921, the Dolly Copp Campground has welcomed visitors to the White Mountains just as Dolly did for the half century that she lived there.

The Copp homestead.

About the Author

Anne Miller Downes was born in Utica, New York and educated at the Paltz State Normal School and the Columbia University School of Journalism. Before becoming a writer, she had a career as a concert pianist and taught music in both New York City and Utica. Mrs. Downes published fourteen novels and also contributed articles to various periodicals. Her 1927 article "The Cost of Illness," published in *The Atlantic Monthly*, described problems with the financing of health care and resulted in federal legislation about health insurance. Mrs. Downes' article about the discovery of unpublished letters written in 1871 by the mother of James Whistler and describing how he had painted her famous portrait, "Whistler's Mother," was published in *The New York Times* in 1934. *The New York Herald Tribune* once wrote: "Anne Miller Downes writes fiction with a clear purpose and faith—to remind us of ideals that have shaped our national destiny and to reaffirm the old-fashioned virtues of which those ideals are the symbol. Her novels are frankly built on a theme, and their eloquence is in their exposition of the theme." Mrs. Downes died in 1964.

Books by Anne Miller Downes
No Parade for Mrs. Greenia, The High Hills Calling, The Quality of Mercy, So Stands the Rock, Until the Shearing, The Captive Rider, The Pilgrim Soul, The Eagle's Song, Kate Cavanaugh, Mary Donovan, Angels Fell, Heartwood, Natalia, and *Speak To Me, Brother.*

About the Artist

Gloria J. Laurie is a native of New Hampshire. Her love of nature was nurtured by many childhood camping adventures with her family in the White Mountains and Lakes Region of New Hampshire. She describes herself as a self-taught artist and acknowledges the important role that her faith in her Creator has played in the development of her artistic abilities. Today she lives and works in Lebanon, New Hampshire.